"Elinor, they who suffer little may be proud and independent as they like"

—Marianne Dashwood,
Sense and Sensibility by Jane Austen

TO MY FAMILY
—M.S.

Story and art by Manuela Santoni
Translation by Matteo Benassi

First American edition published in 2018 by Graphic Universe™

Copyright © 2016 by Manuela Santoni
Copyright © 2017 by BeccoGiallo S.r.l. for the Italian edition.

Published in arrangement with AMBook (www.ambook.ch)

Graphic Universe™ is a trademark of Lerner Publishing Group, Inc.

Graphic Universe™
A division of Lerner Publishing Group, Inc.
241 First Avenue North
Minneapolis, MN 55401 USA

For reading levels and more information, look up this title at www.lernerbooks.com.

Additional image © National Portrait Gallery, London, UK/De Agostini Picture Library/ Bridgeman Images, p. 94.

Main body text set in Dinkle Bold 10.5/10.5. Typeface provided by Chank.

Library of Congress Cataloging-in-Publication Data

Names: Santoni, Manuela, 1988– author, illustrator. | Benassi, Matteo, translator.
Title: Jane Austen : her heart did whisper / Manuela Santoni ; translation by Matteo Benassi.
Description: First American edition. | Minneapolis : Graphic Universe, 2018. | Includes bibliographical references.
Identifiers: LCCN 2017047942 (print) | LCCN 2017049264 (ebook) | ISBN 9781541526167 (eb pdf) | ISBN 9781541523661 (lb : alk. paper) | ISBN 9781541526433 (pb : alk. paper)
Subjects: LCSH: Austen, Jane, 1775–1817—Comic books, strips, etc.—Juvenile literature. | Novelists, English—19th century—Biography—Comic books, strips, etc.—Juvenile literature. | Graphic novels.
Classification: LCC PR4037 (ebook) | LCC PR4037 .S2613 2018 (print) | DDC 823/.7 [B] —dc23

LC record available at https://lccn.loc.gov/2017047942

Manufactured in the United States of America
1-44490-34698-3/12/2018

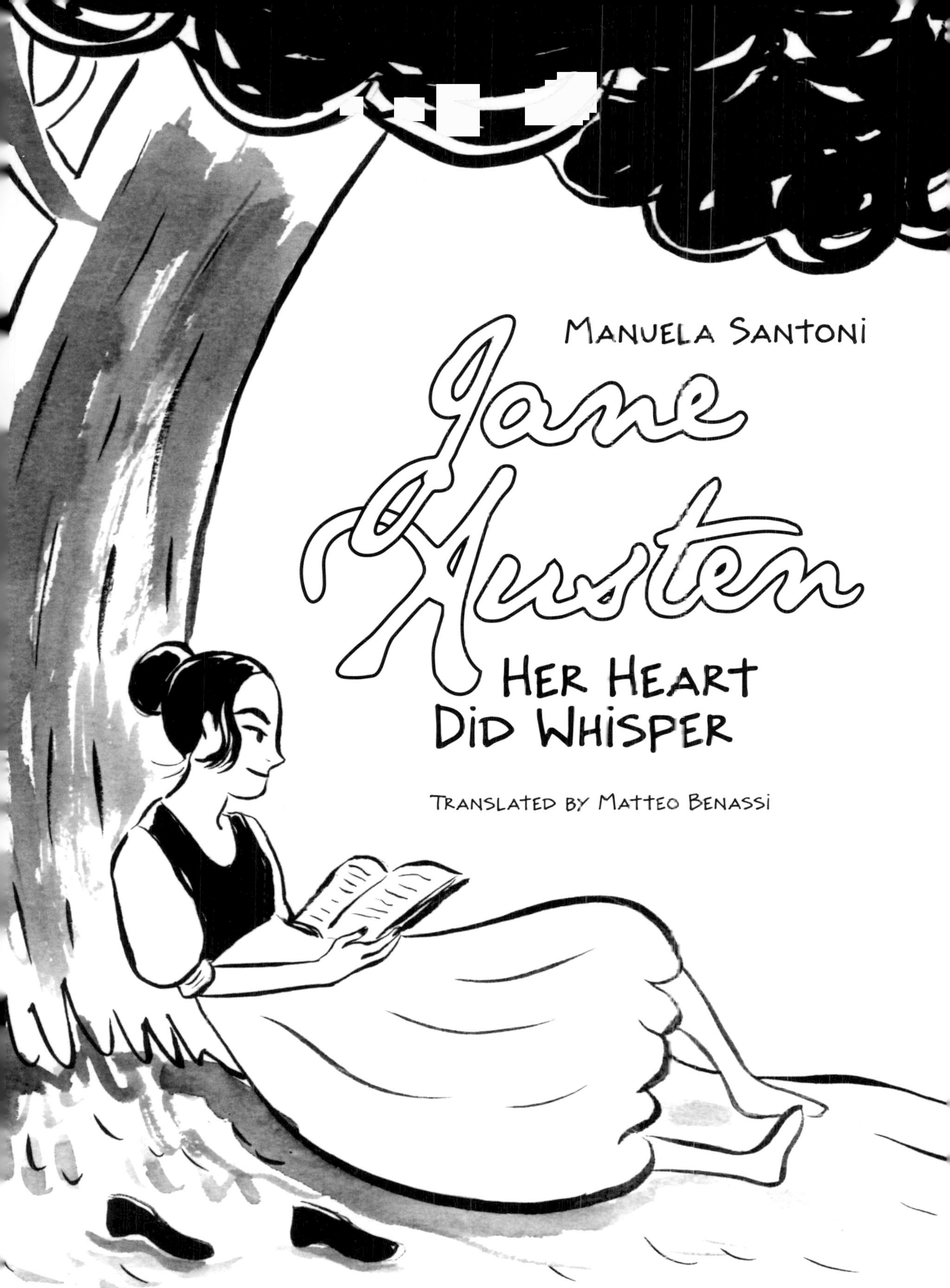

Manuela Santoni

Jane Austen

Her Heart Did Whisper

Translated by Matteo Benassi

Graphic Universe™ • Minneapolis

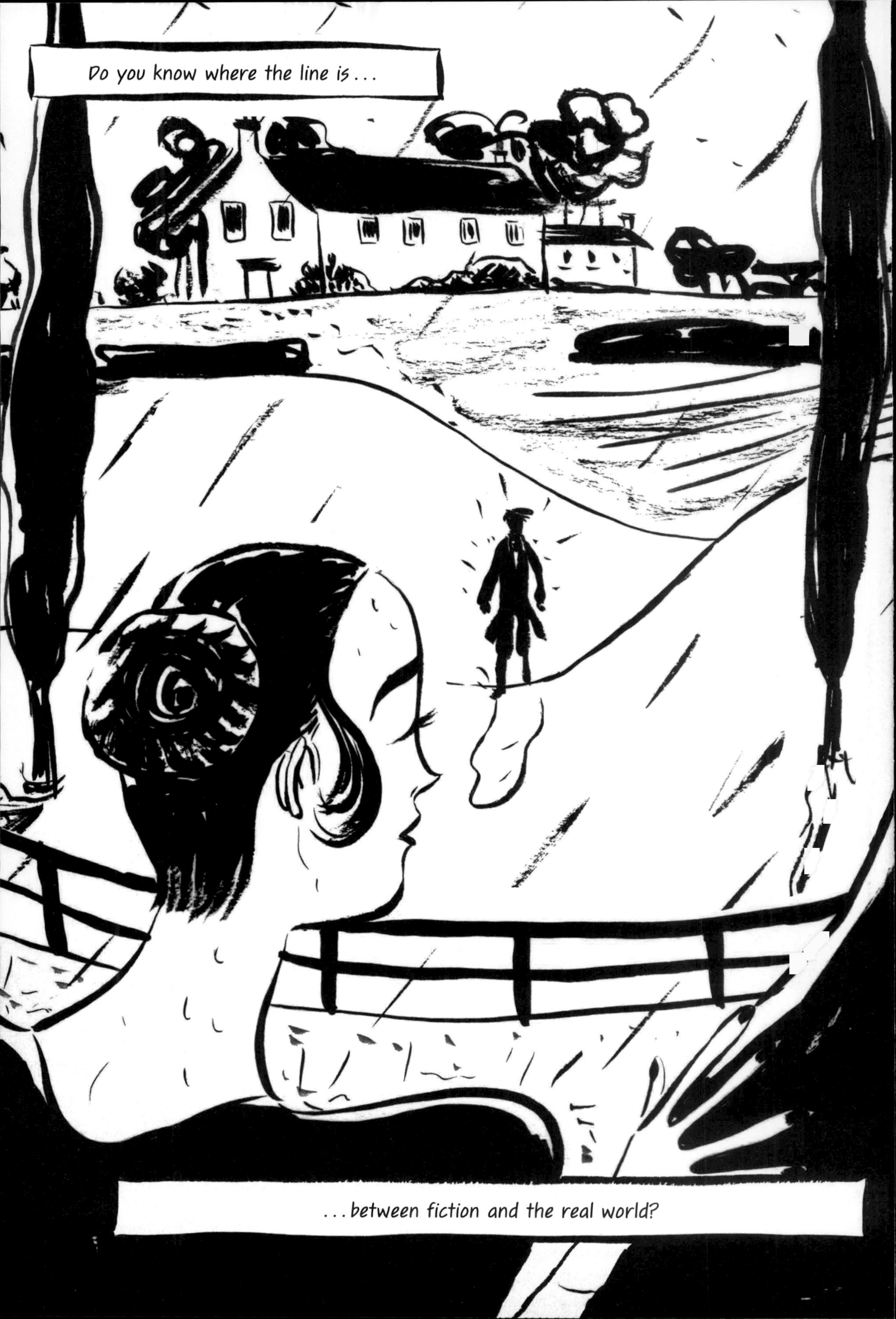
Do you know where the line is . . .
. . . between fiction and the real world?

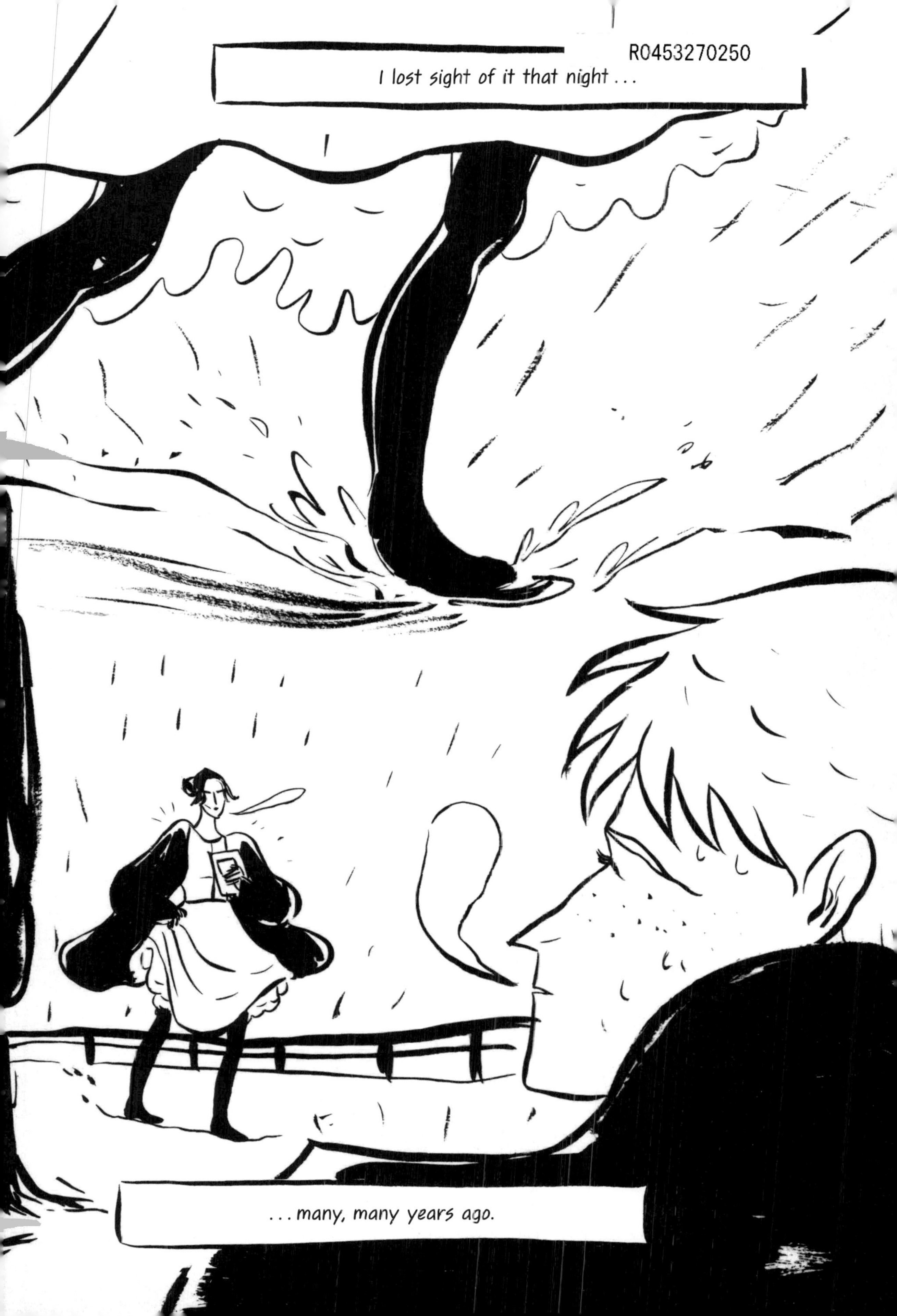
I lost sight of it that night . . .
. . . many, many years ago.

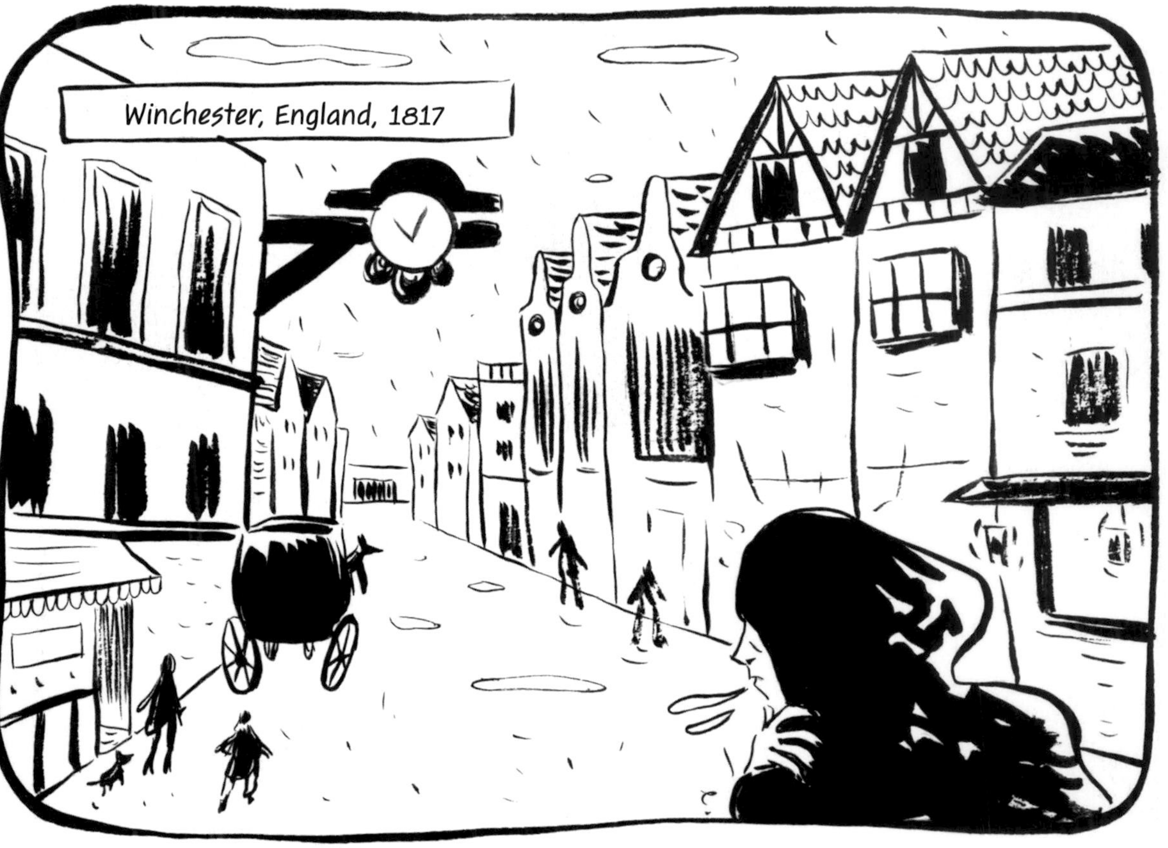
Winchester, England, 1817

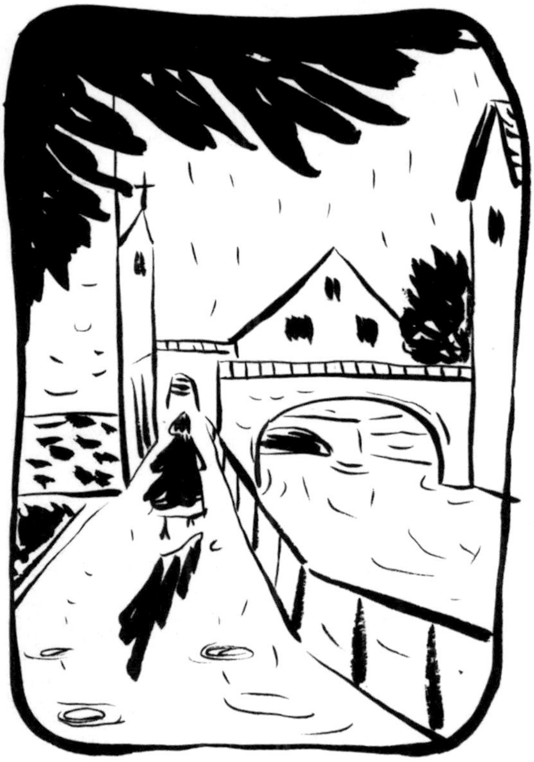

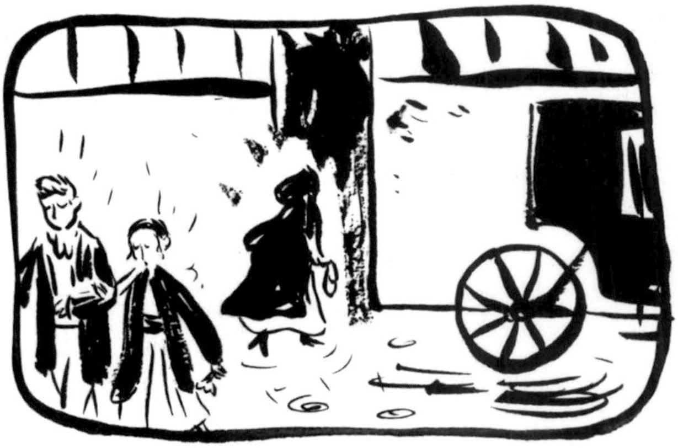

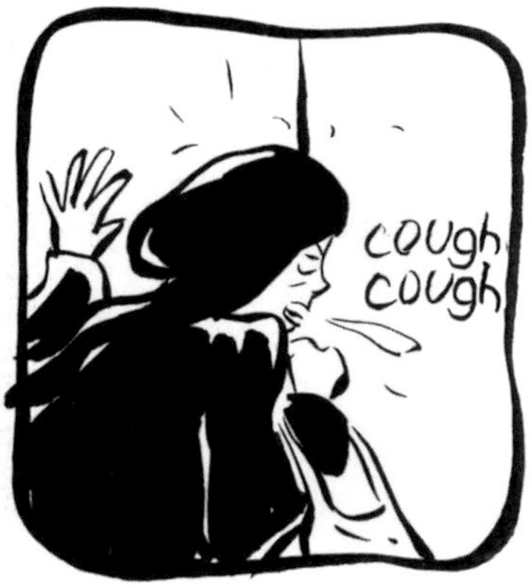
cough
cough

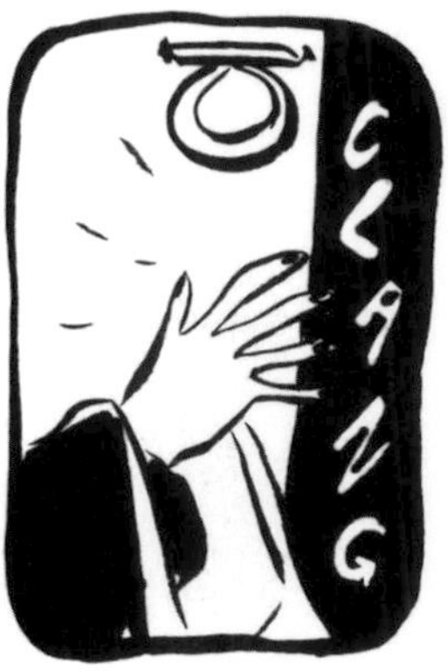
CLANG

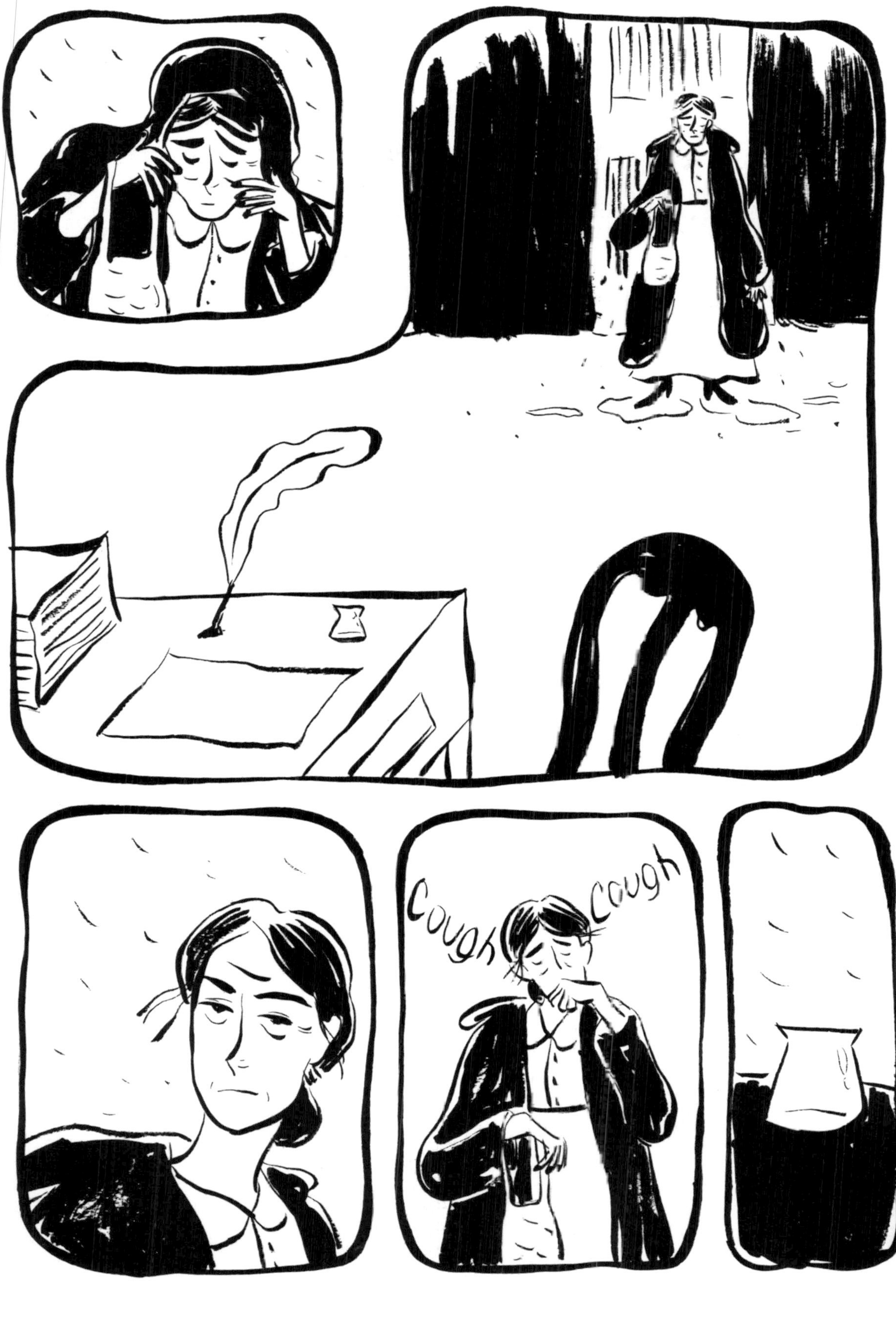
Cough
Cough

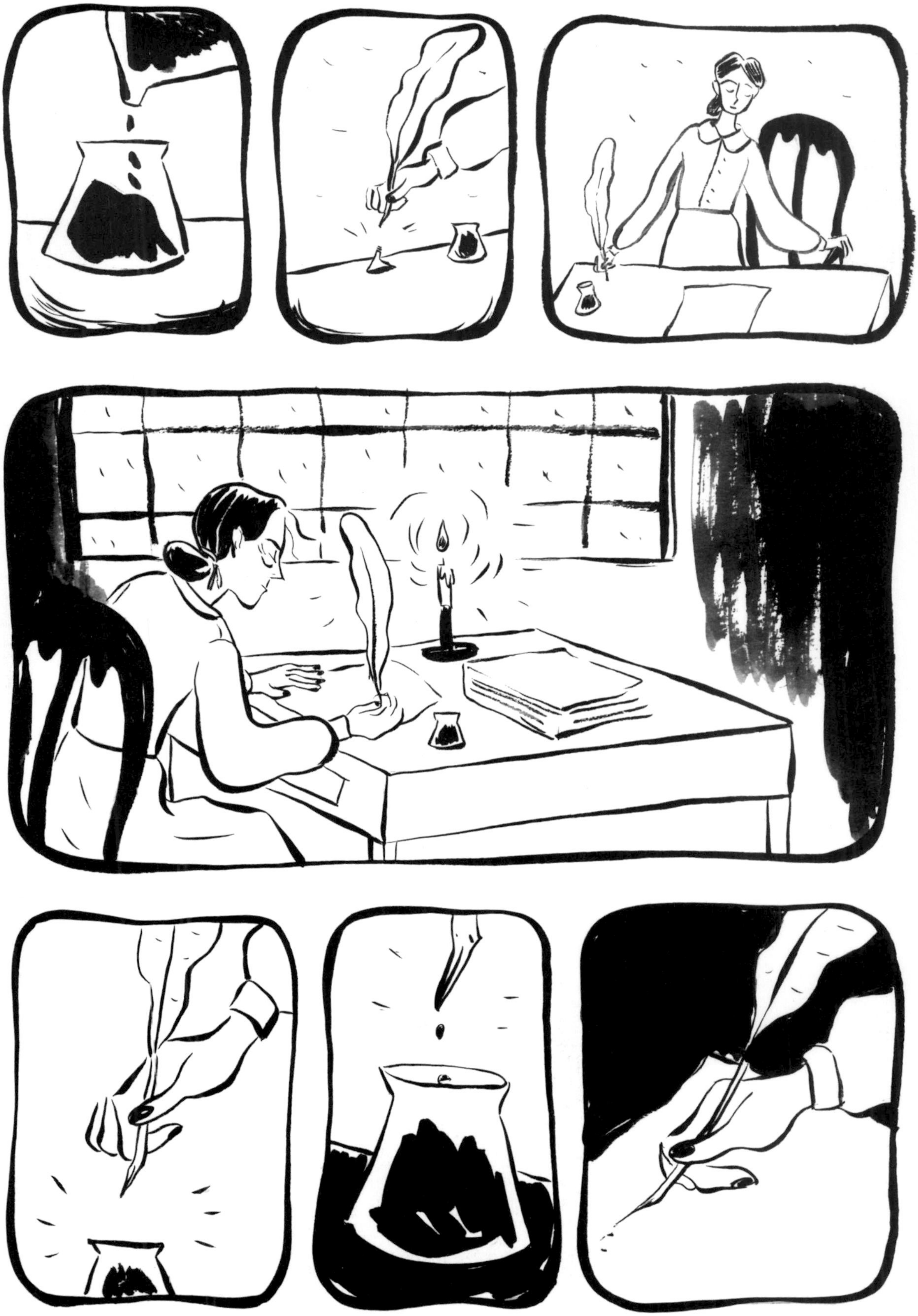

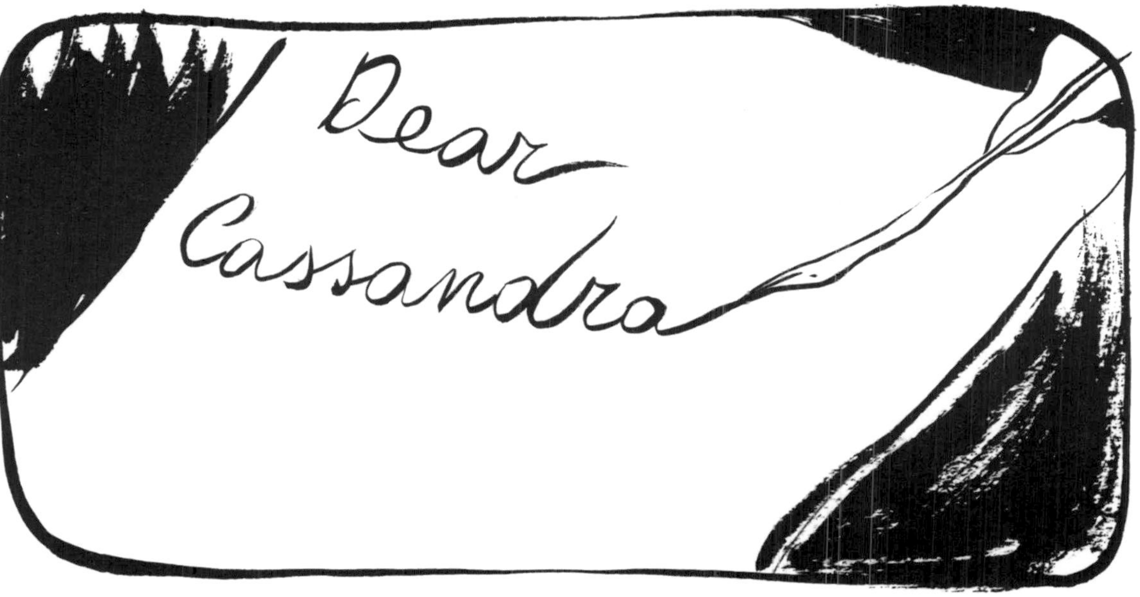
Dear Cassandra

Do you remember when we were little?

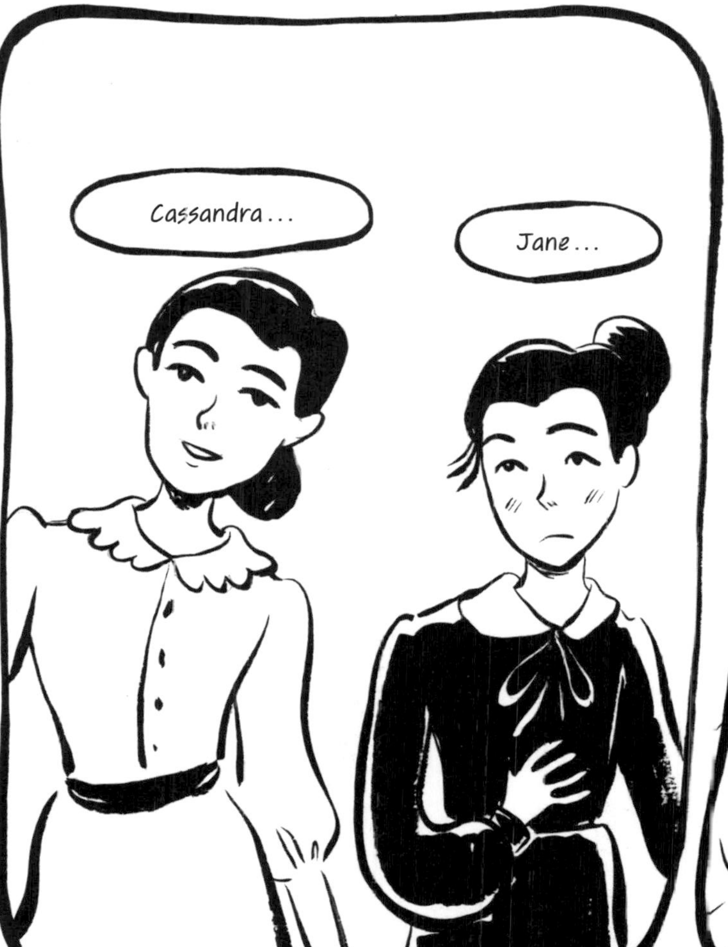
Cassandra...
Jane...

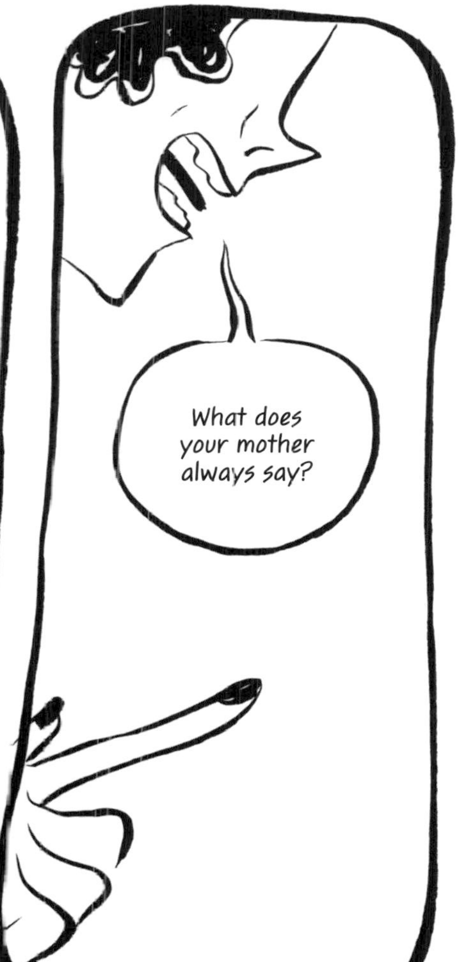
What does your mother always say?

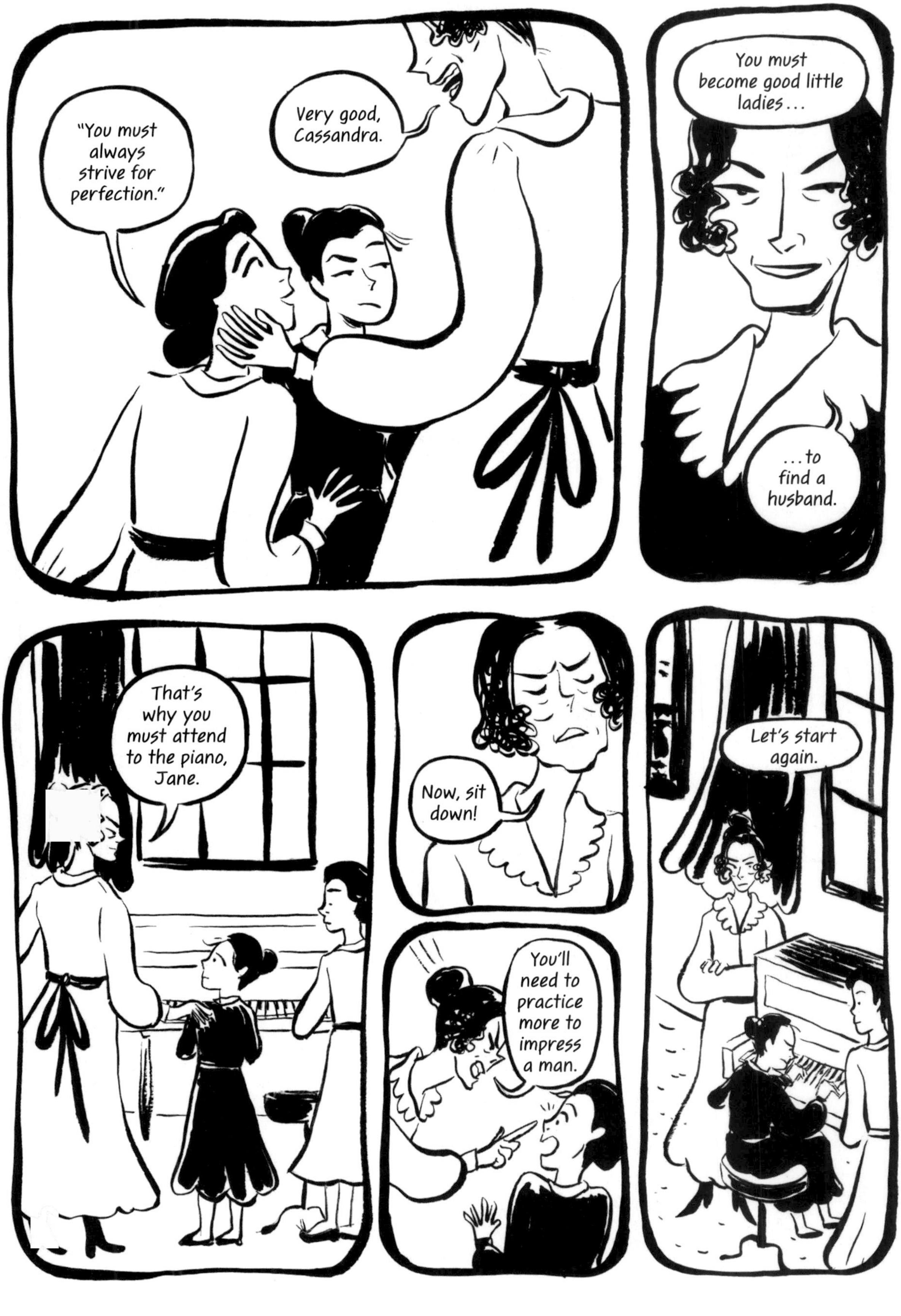

"You must always strive for perfection."
Very good, Cassandra.
You must become good little ladies...
...to find a husband.
That's why you must attend to the piano, Jane.
Now, sit down!
You'll need to practice more to impress a man.
Let's start again.

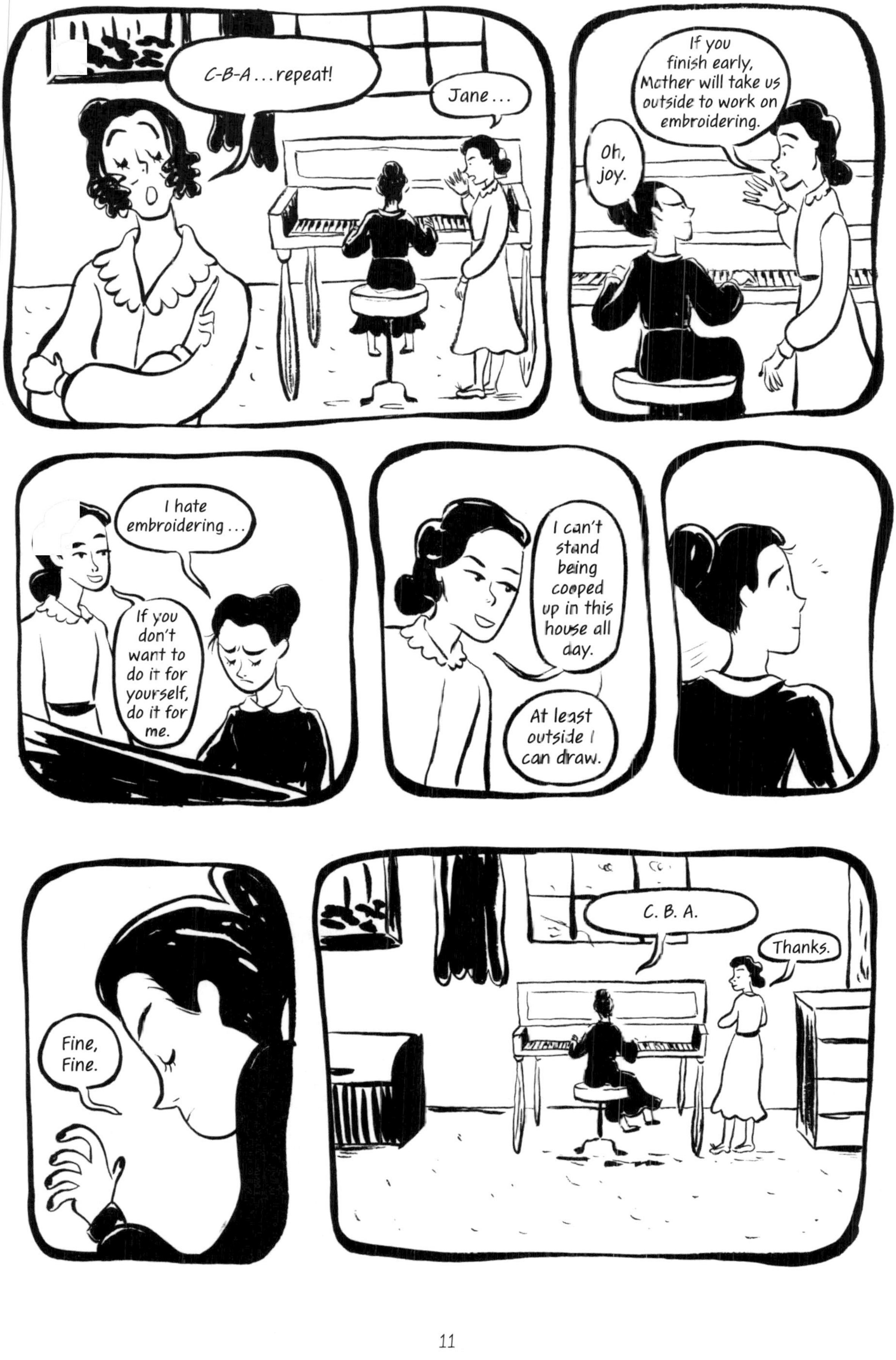
C-B-A . . . repeat!
Jane . . .
If you finish early, Mother will take us outside to work on embroidering.
Oh, joy.
I hate embroidering . . .
If you don't want to do it for yourself, do it for me.
I can't stand being cooped up in this house all day.
At least outside I can draw.
Fine, Fine.
C. B. A.
Thanks.

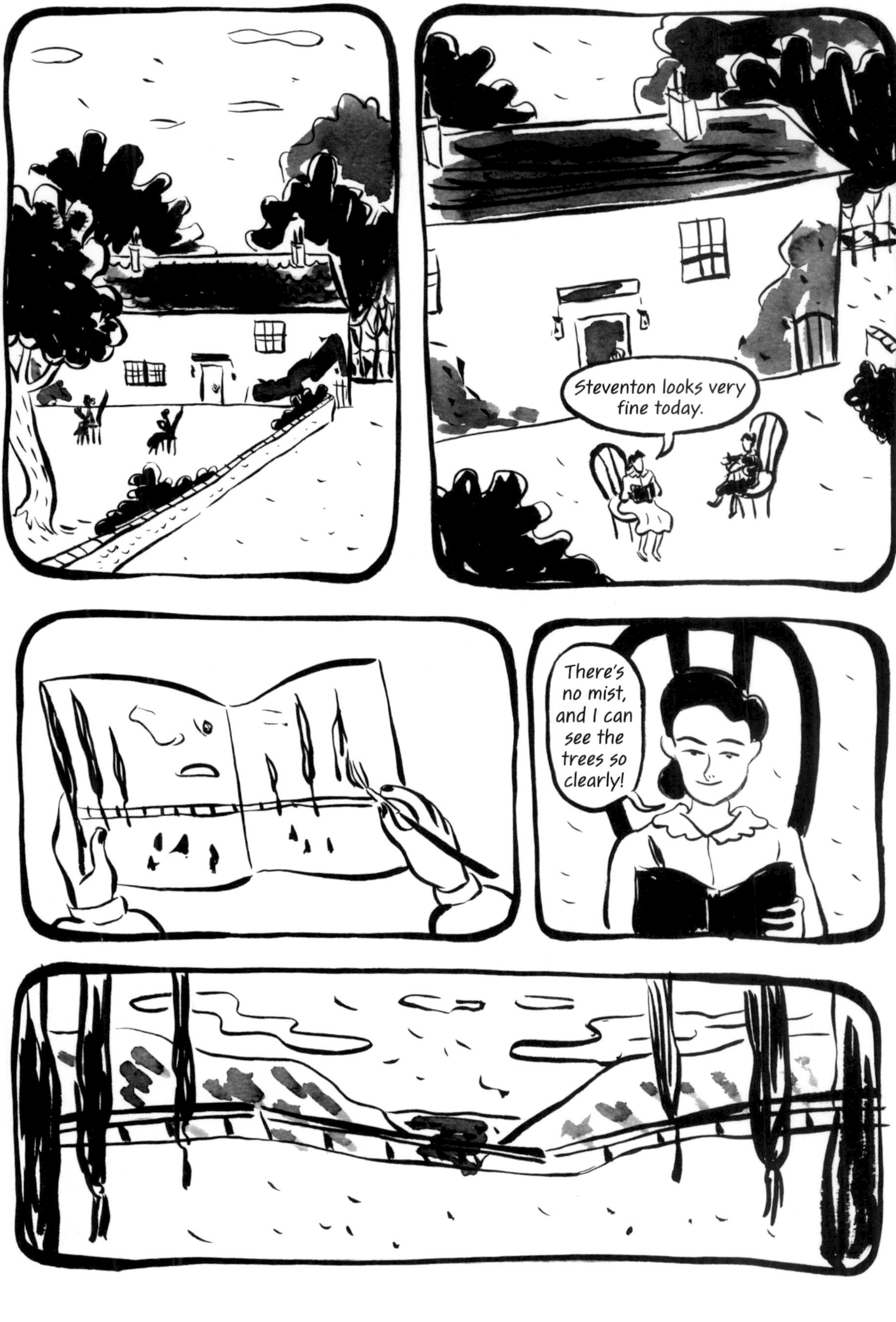
Steventon looks very fine today.
There's no mist, and I can see the trees so clearly!

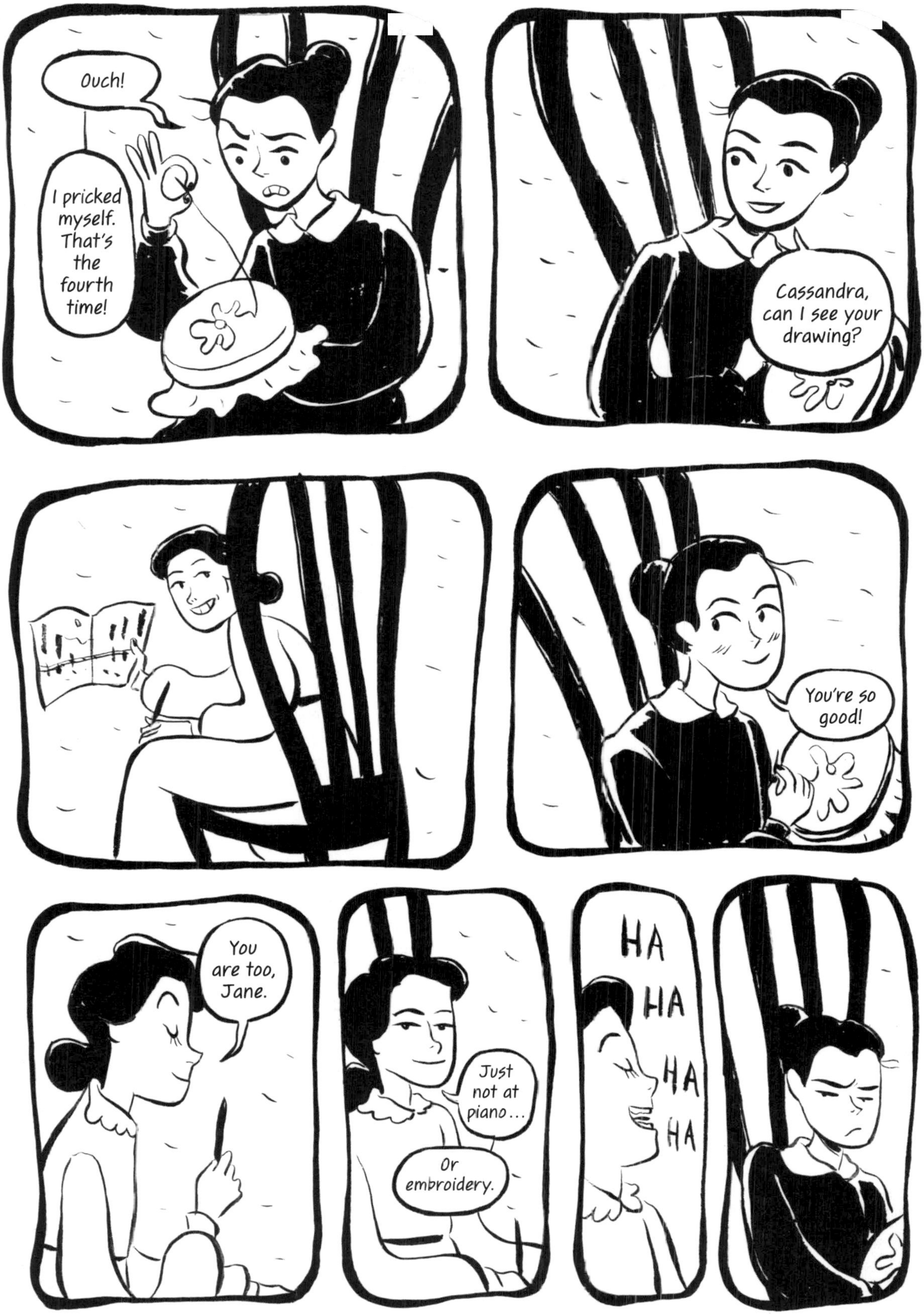
Ouch!
I pricked myself. That's the fourth time!
Cassandra, can I see your drawing?
You're so good!
You are too, Jane.
Just not at piano...
Or embroidery.
HA HA HA HA

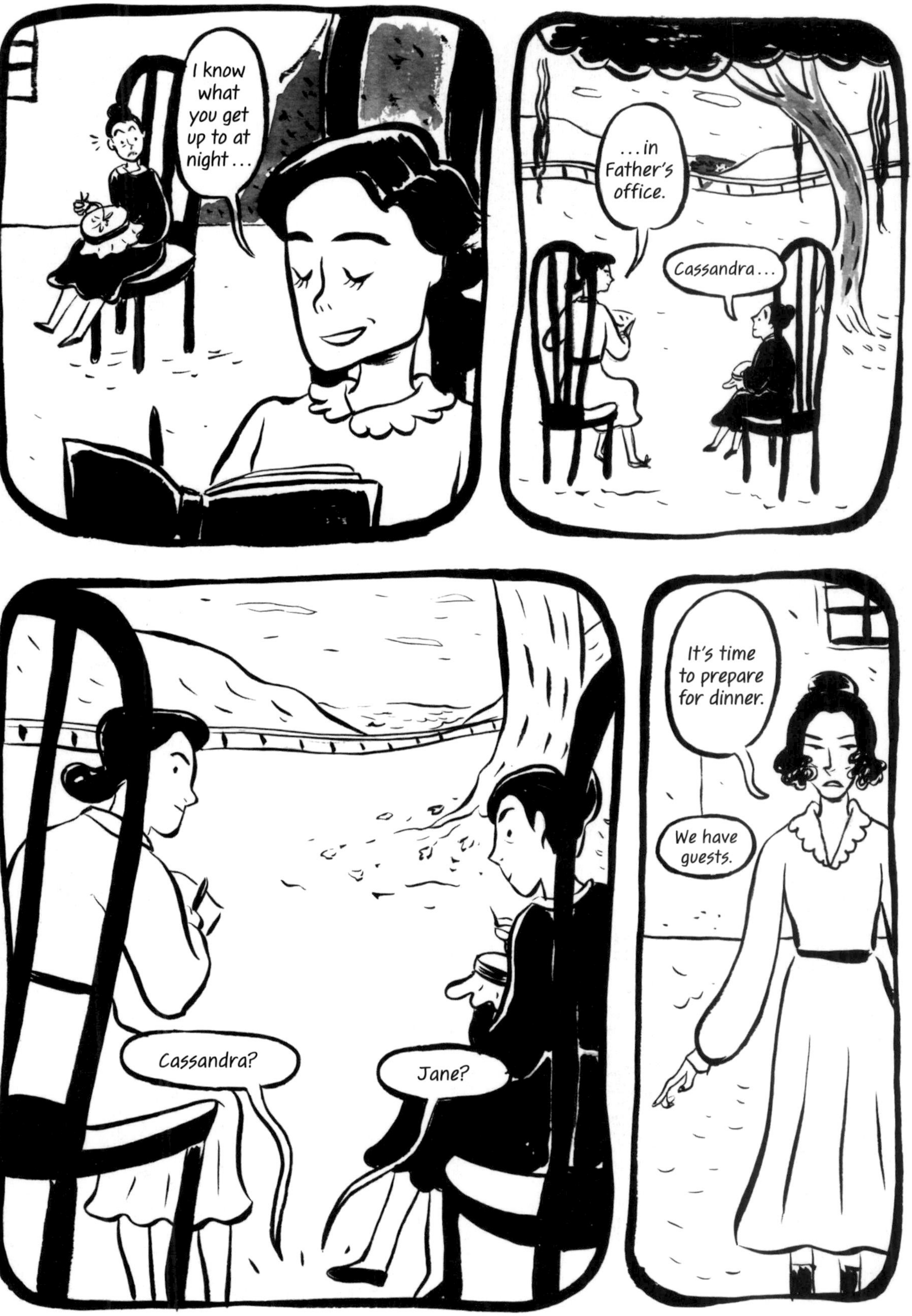
I know what you get up to at night...
...in Father's office.
Cassandra...
Cassandra?
Jane?
It's time to prepare for dinner.
We have guests.

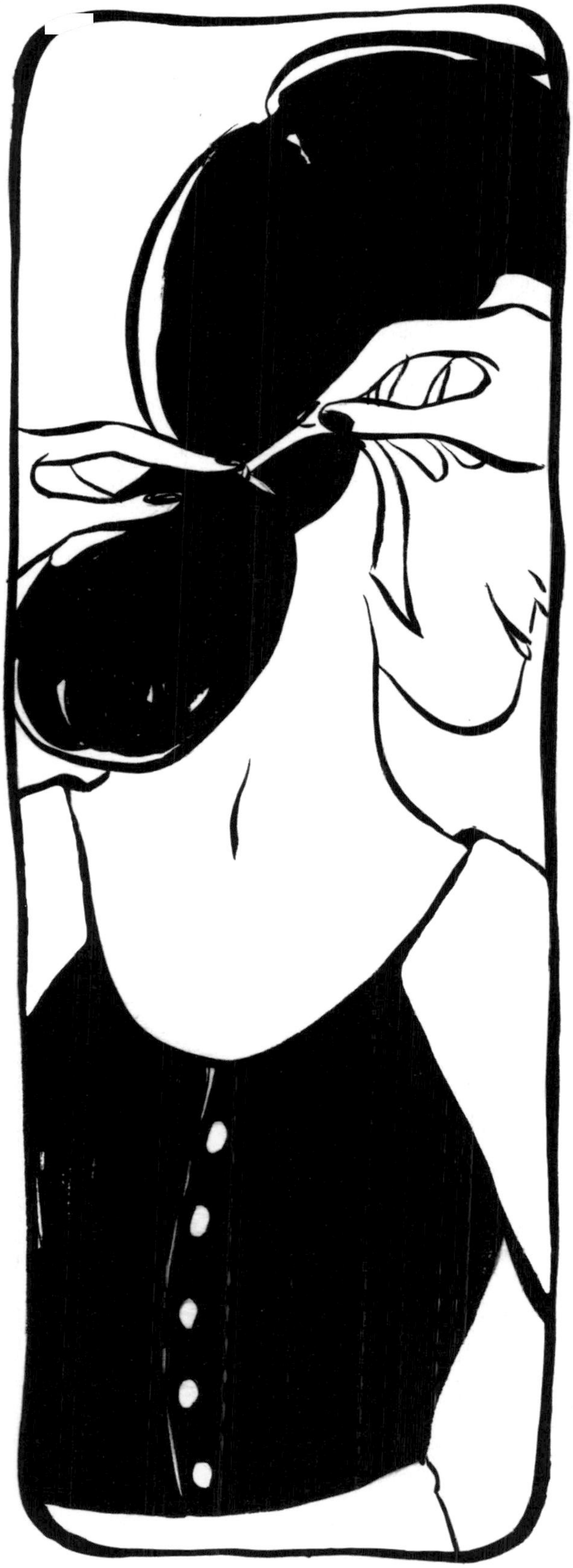

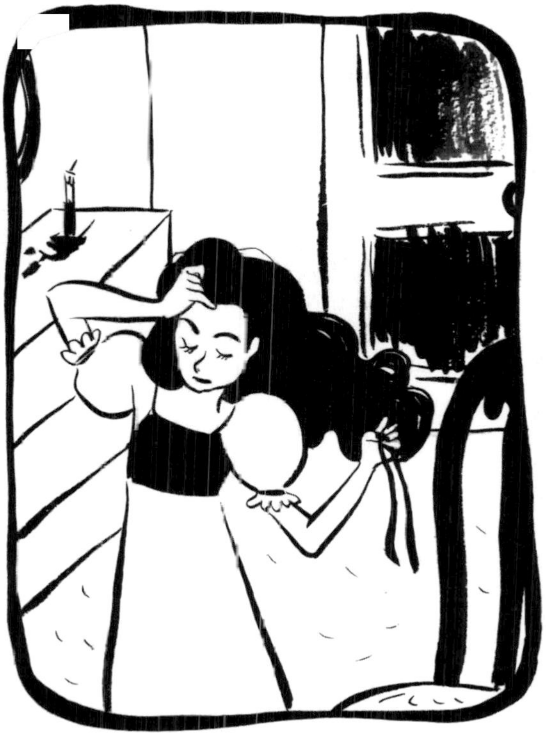

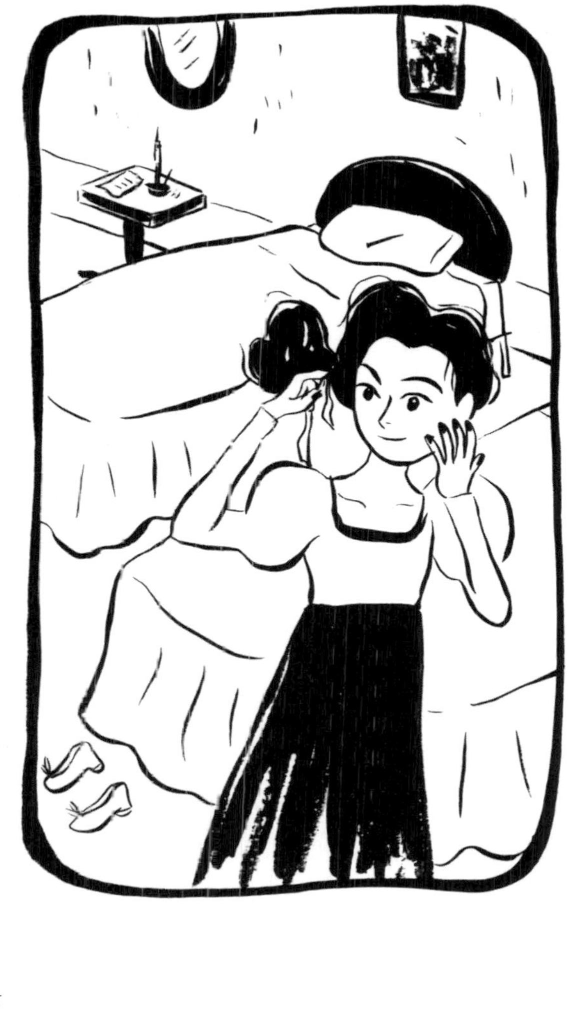

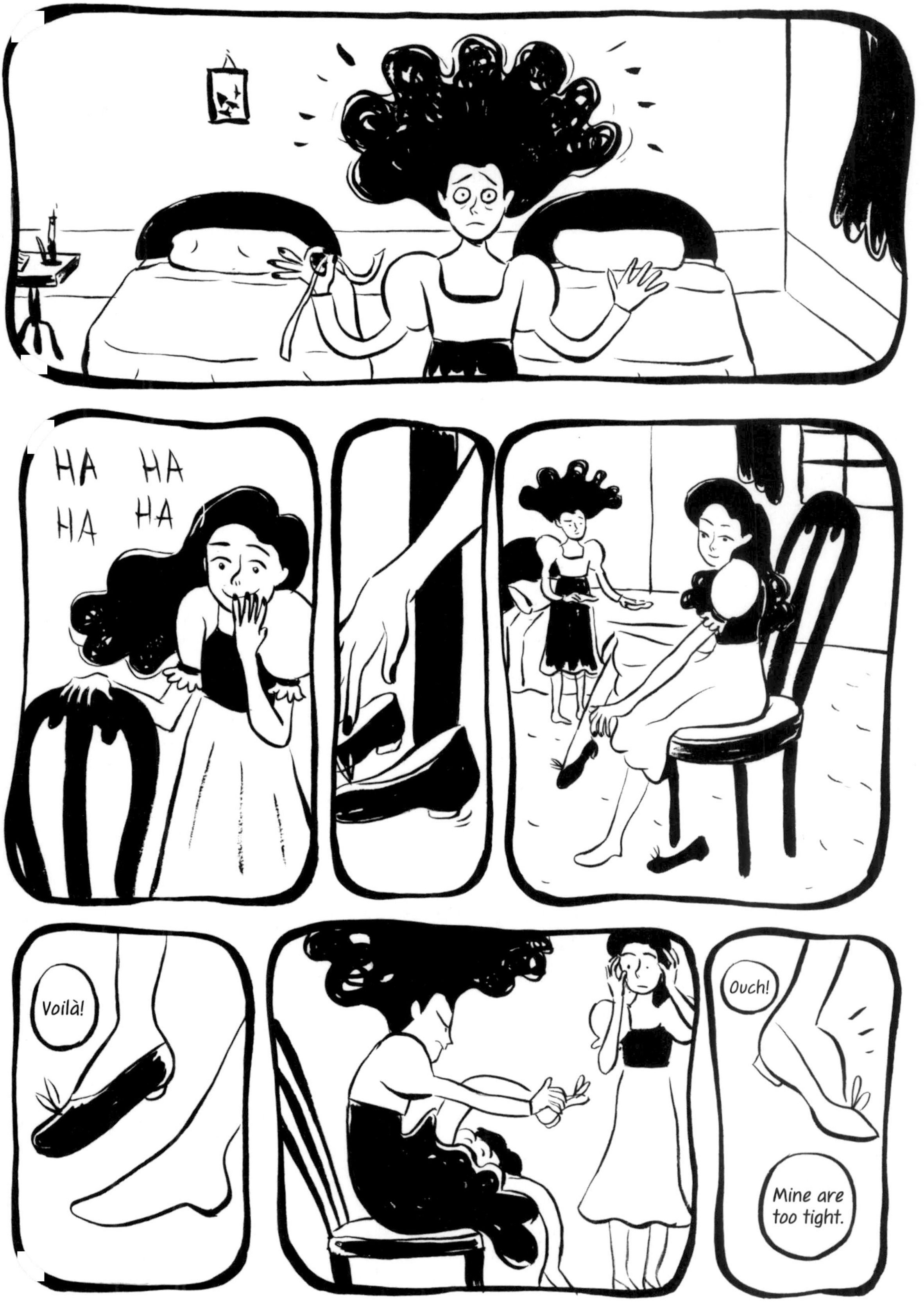
HA HA
HA HA
Voilà!
Ouch!
Mine are too tight.

Every now and then, our father would invite students from his rectory.

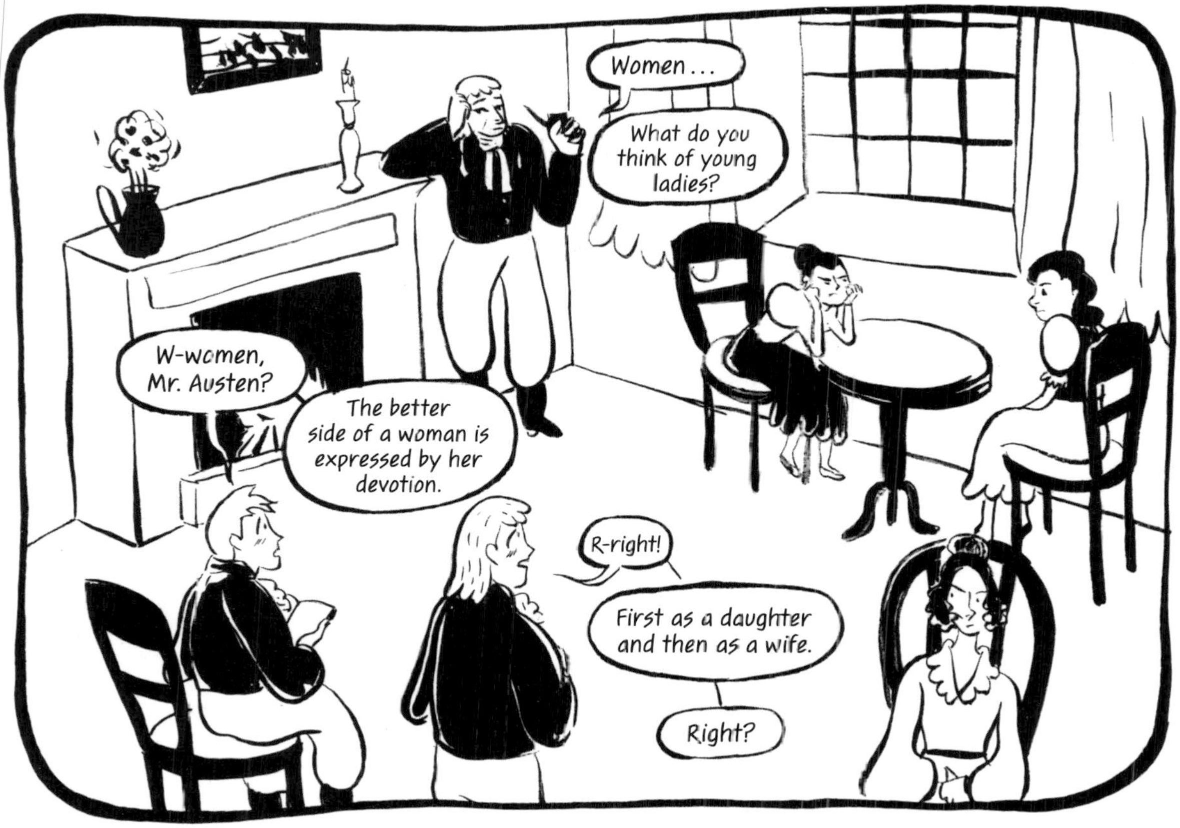
Women . . .
What do you think of young ladies?
W-women, Mr. Austen?
The better side of a woman is expressed by her devotion.
R-right!
First as a daughter and then as a wife.
Right?

On those nights, our house tended to become a private cultural society.

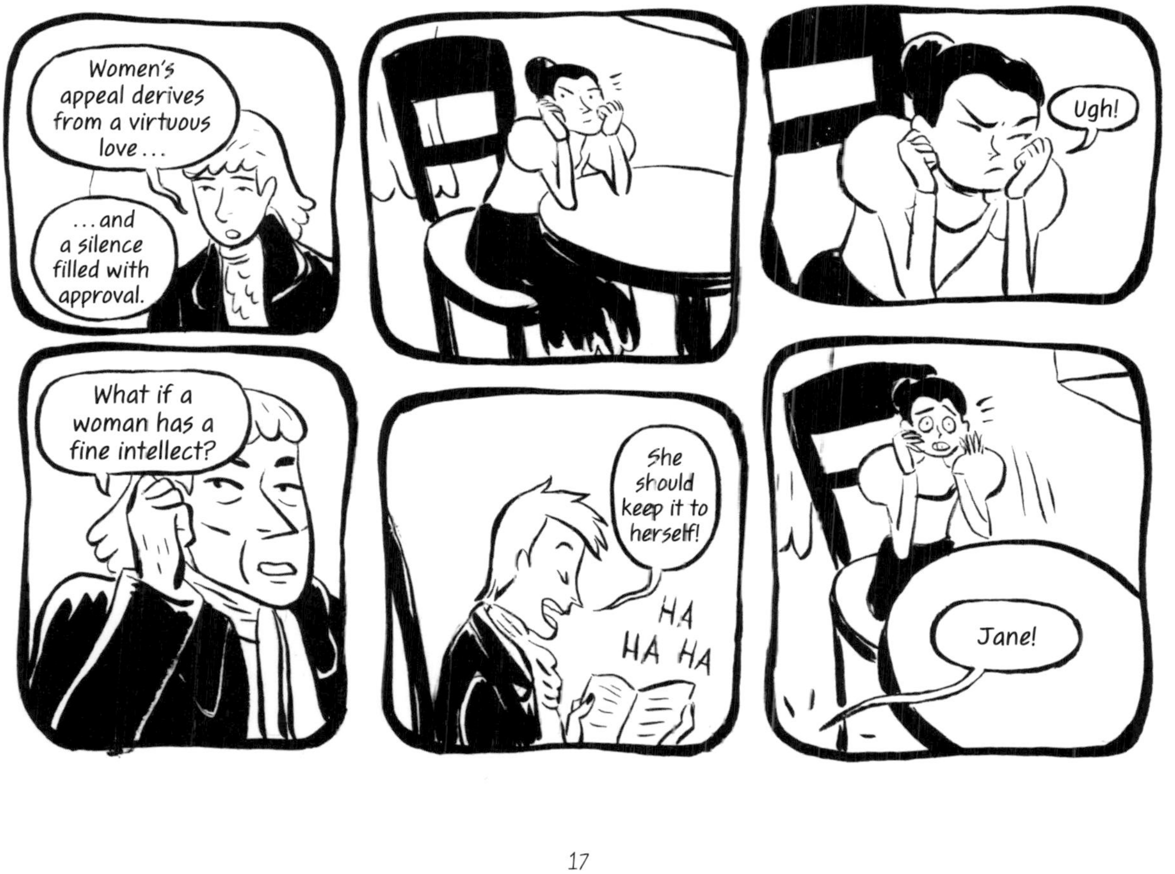
Women's appeal derives from a virtuous love . . .
. . . and a silence filled with approval.
Ugh!
What if a woman has a fine intellect?
She should keep it to herself!
HA HA HA
Jane!

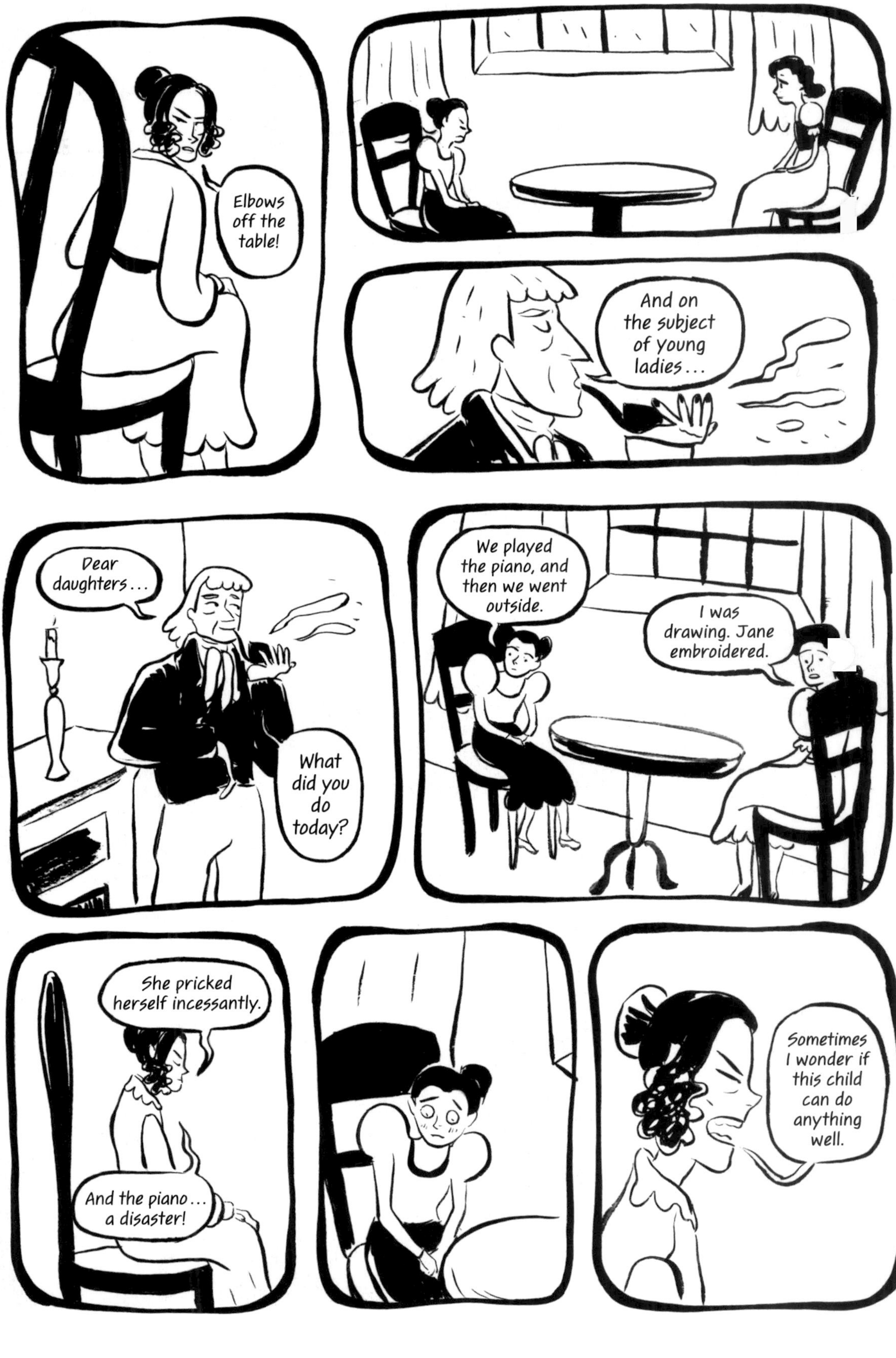
Elbows off the table!
And on the subject of young ladies...
Dear daughters...
What did you do today?
We played the piano, and then we went outside.
I was drawing. Jane embroidered.
She pricked herself incessantly.
And the piano... a disaster!
Sometimes I wonder if this child can do anything well.

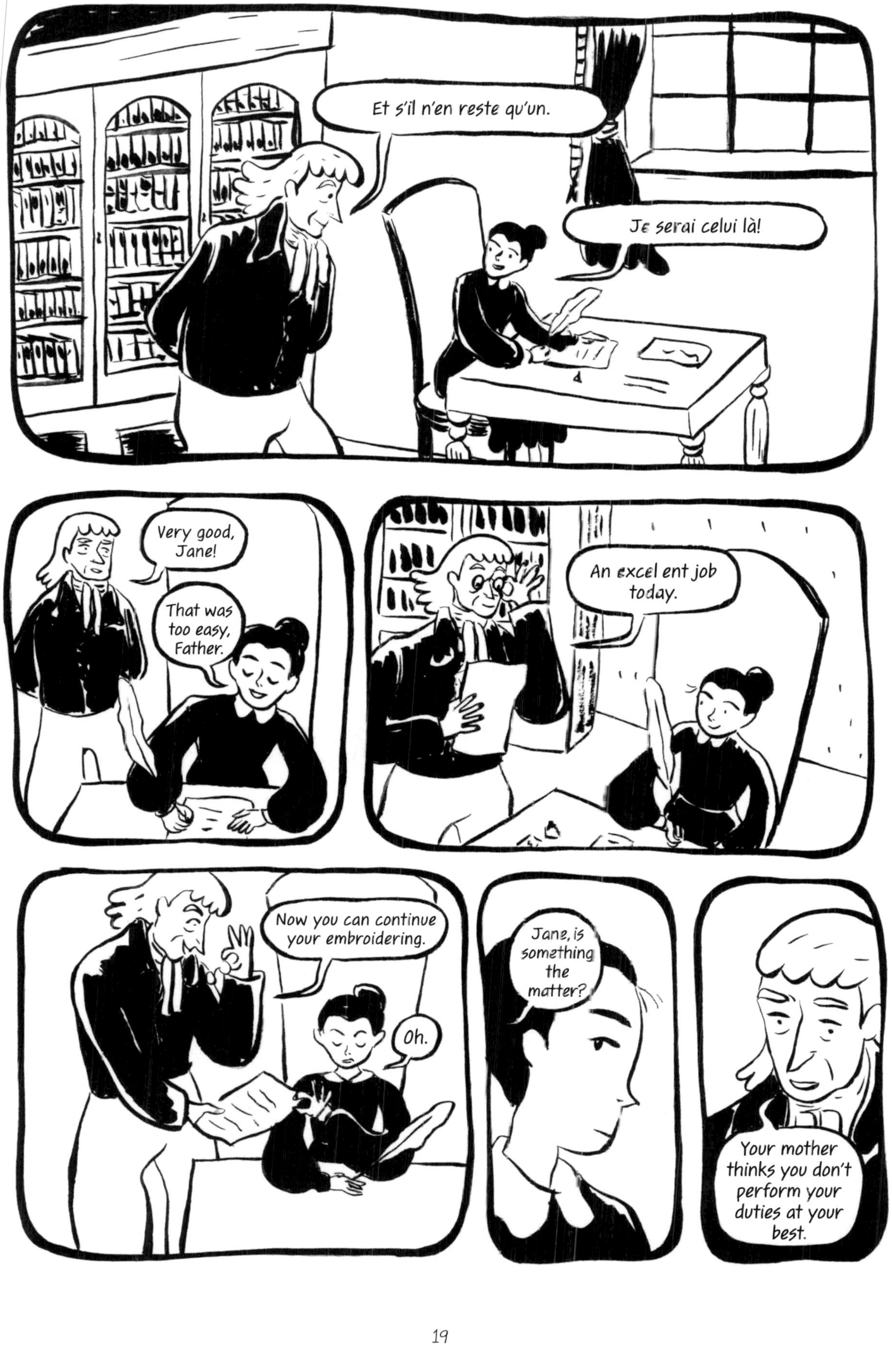
Et s'il n'en reste qu'un.
Je serai celui là!
Very good, Jane!
That was too easy, Father.
An excel ent job today.
Now you can continue your embroidering.
Oh.
Jane, is something the matter?
Your mother thinks you don't perform your duties at your best.

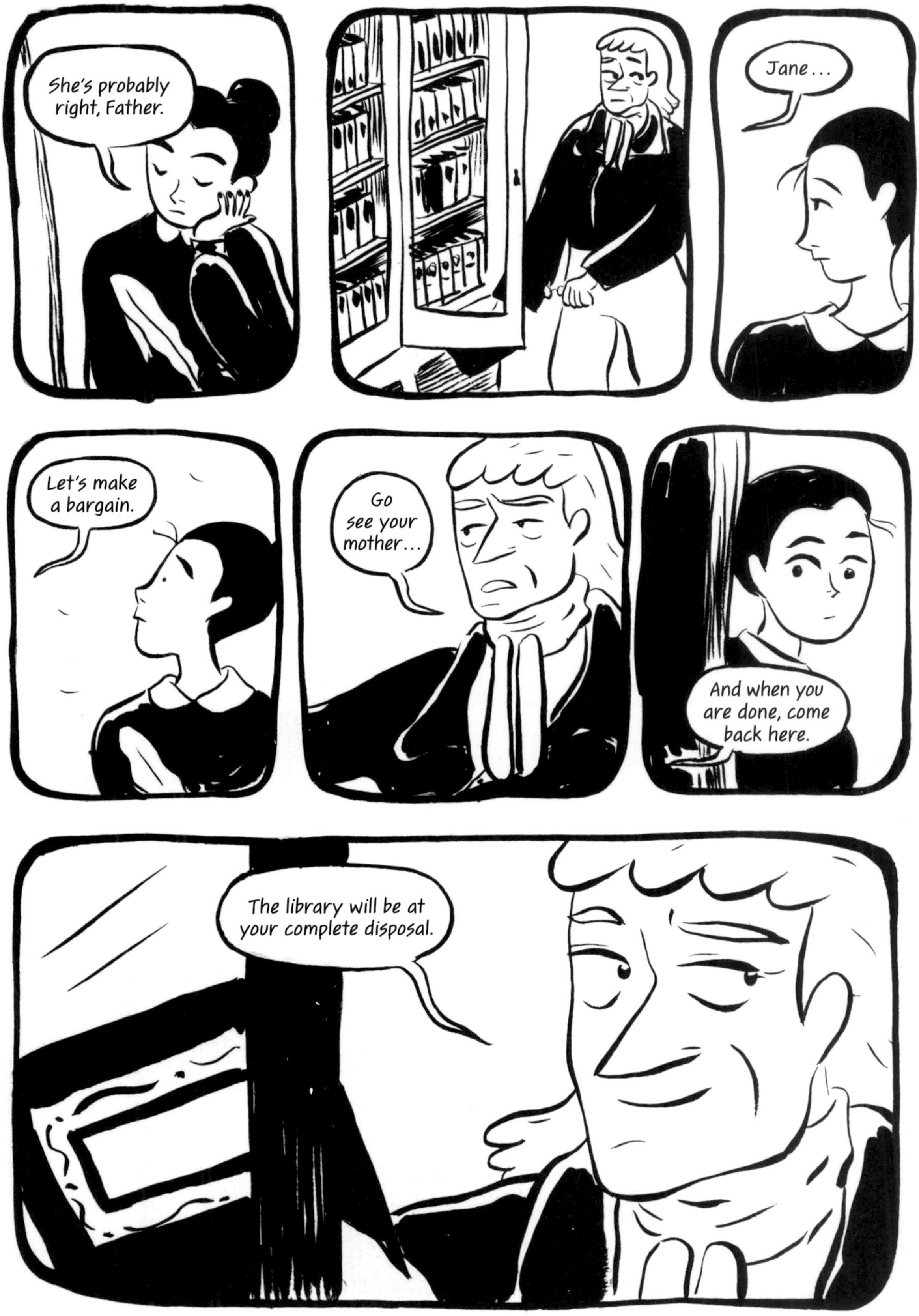
She's probably right, Father.
Jane...
Let's make a bargain.
Go see your mother...
And when you are done, come back here.
The library will be at your complete disposal.

That day, my heart stirred.

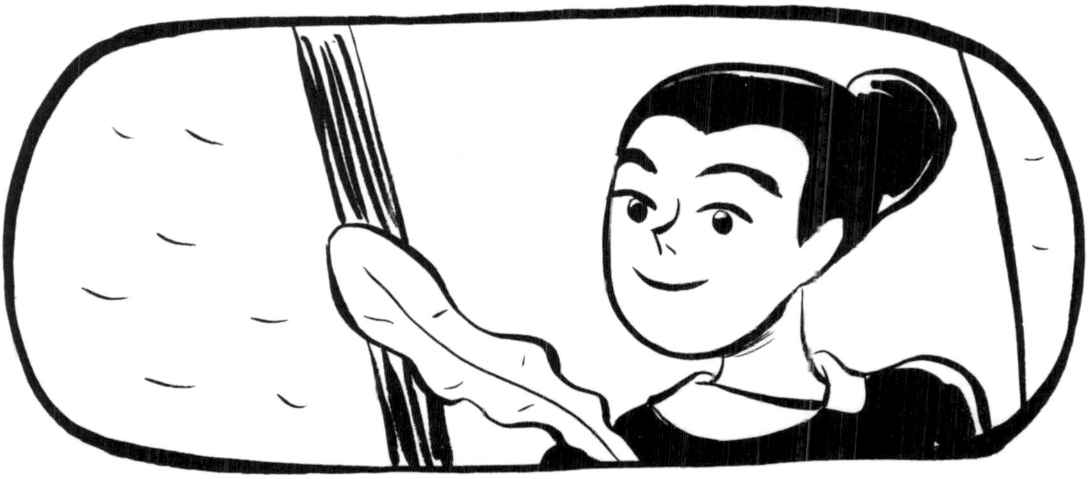

I had free rein of those books. No subterfuge necessary.

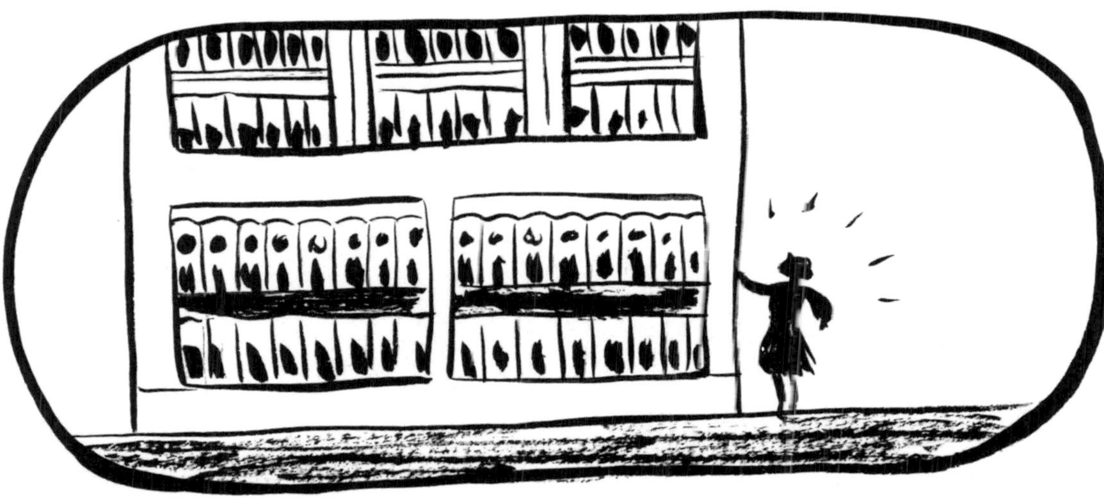

From then on, I worked on my embroidery fervently. I couldn't wait to read them all!

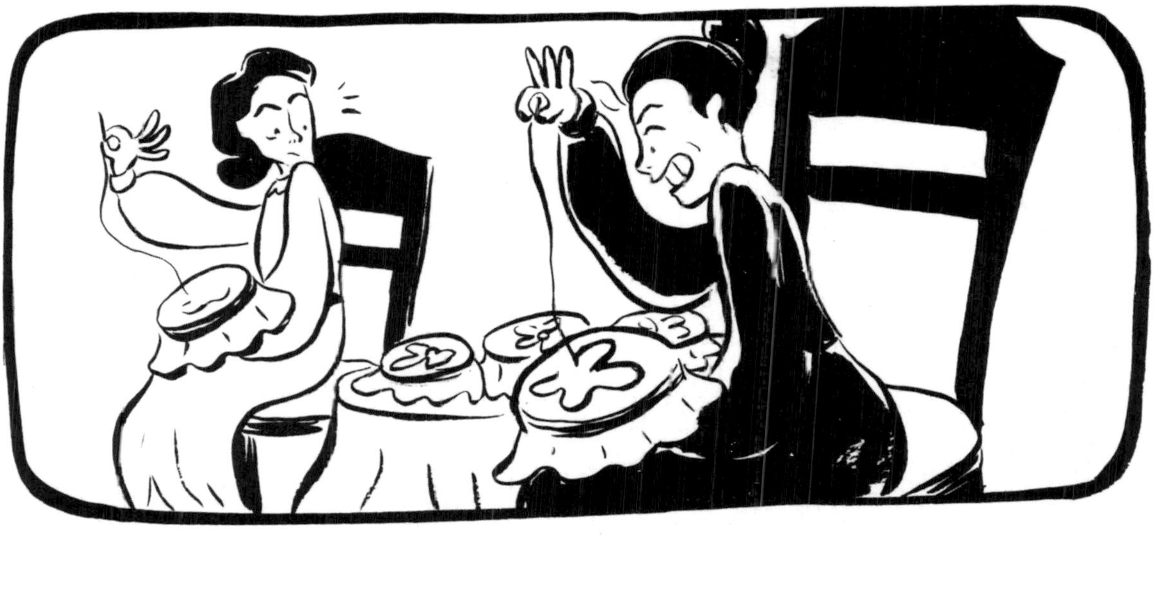

You, sister, had already understood for a long time.

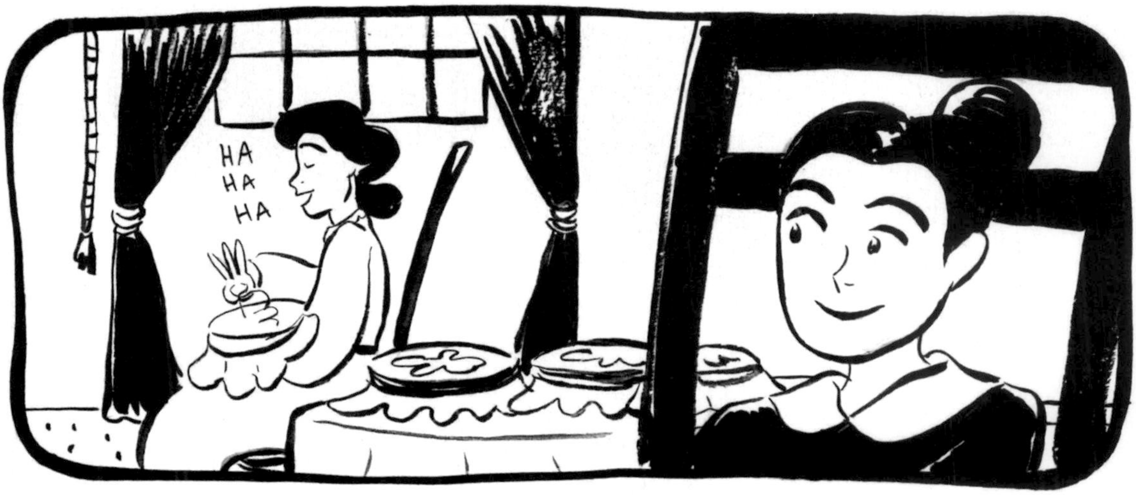
HA
HA
HA

I was always slipping into our father's office at night . . .

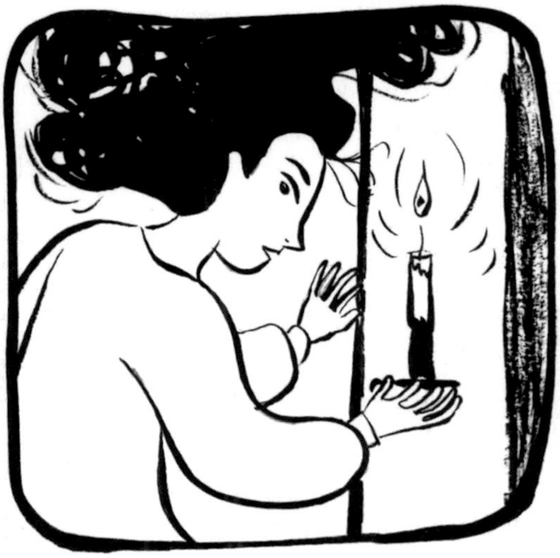

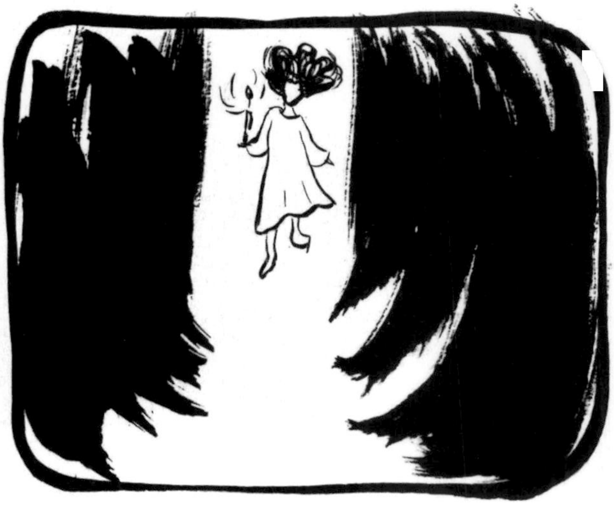

. . . to read in secret.

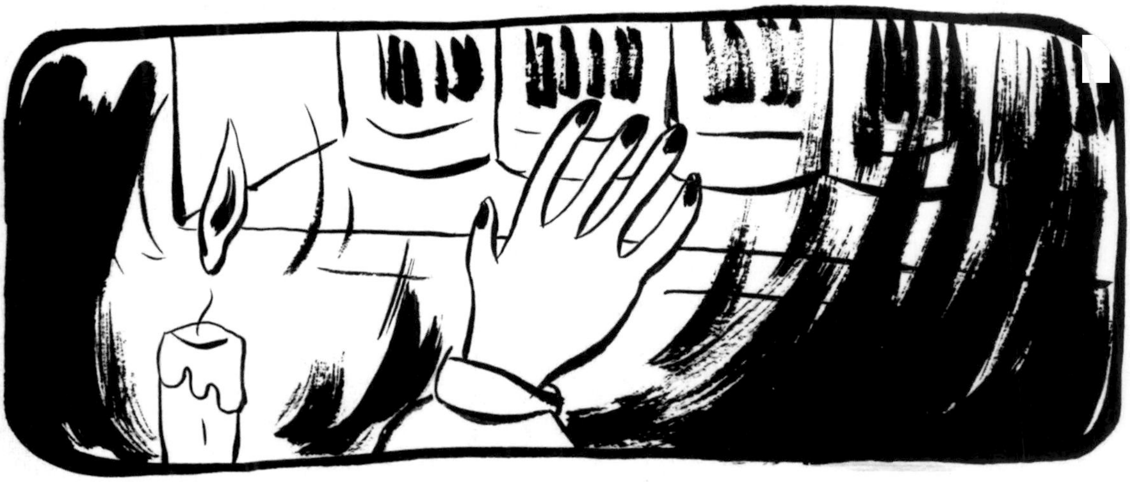

In books, I could find freedom from life's binds.

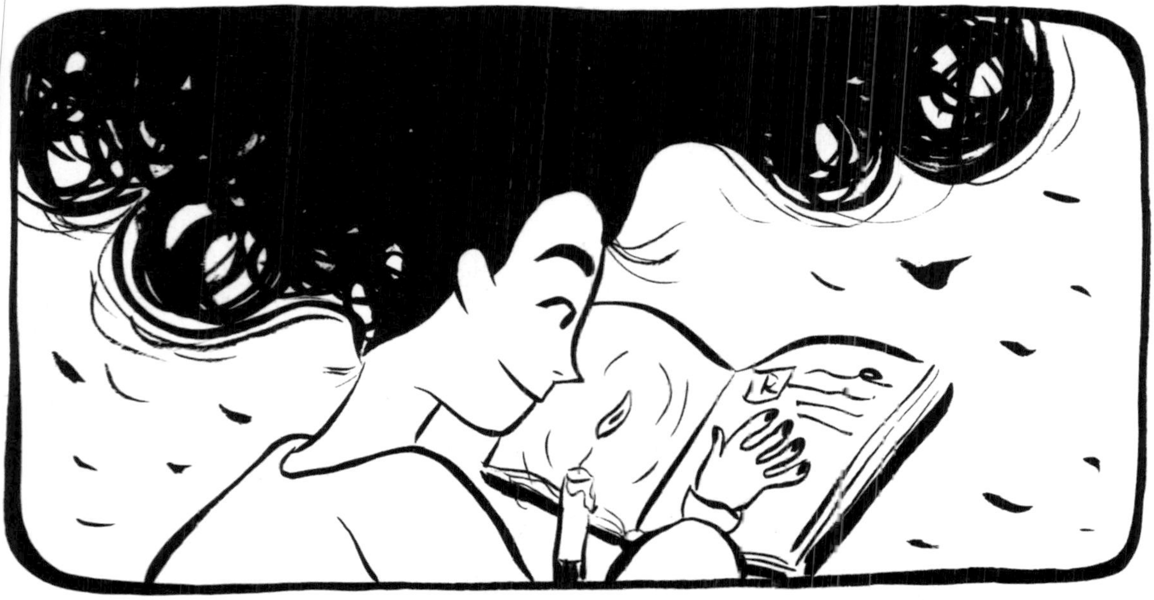

Those were my favorite moments of the day.

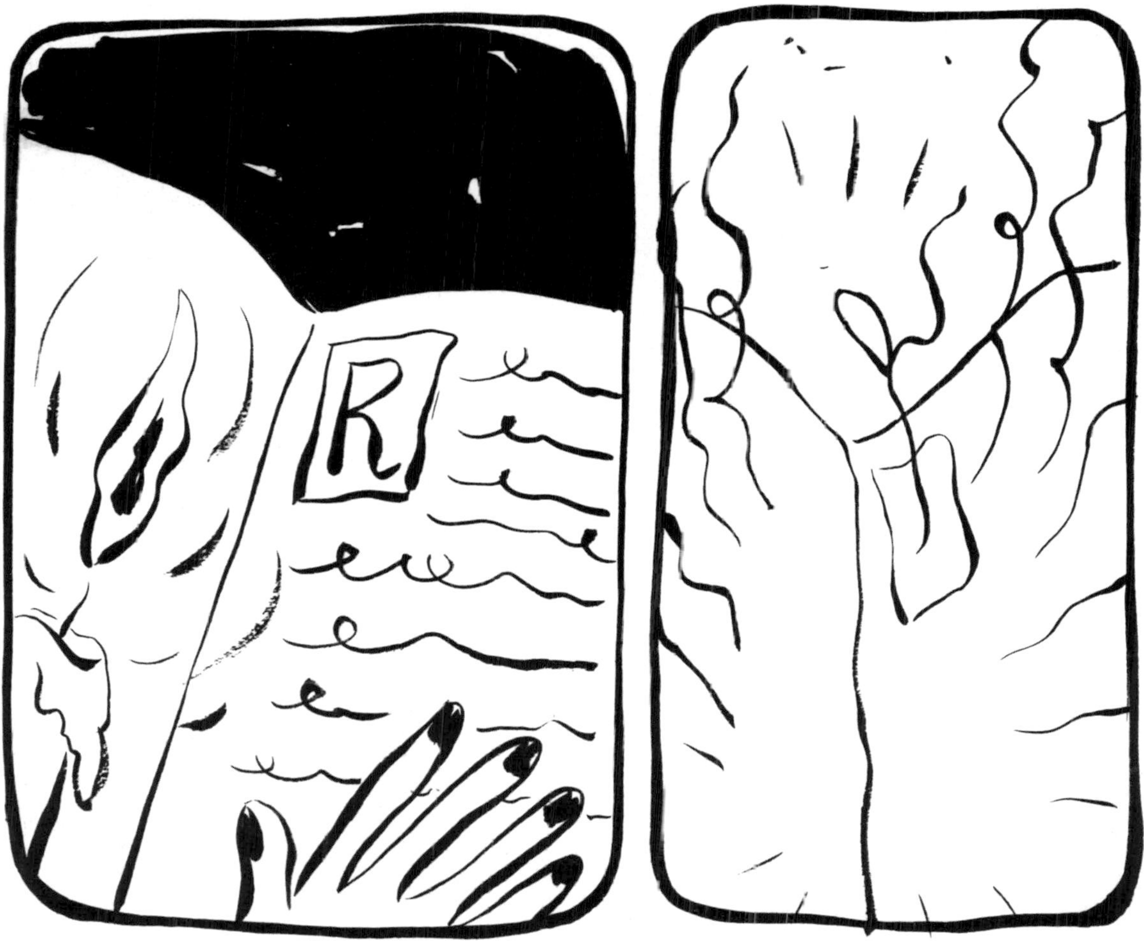

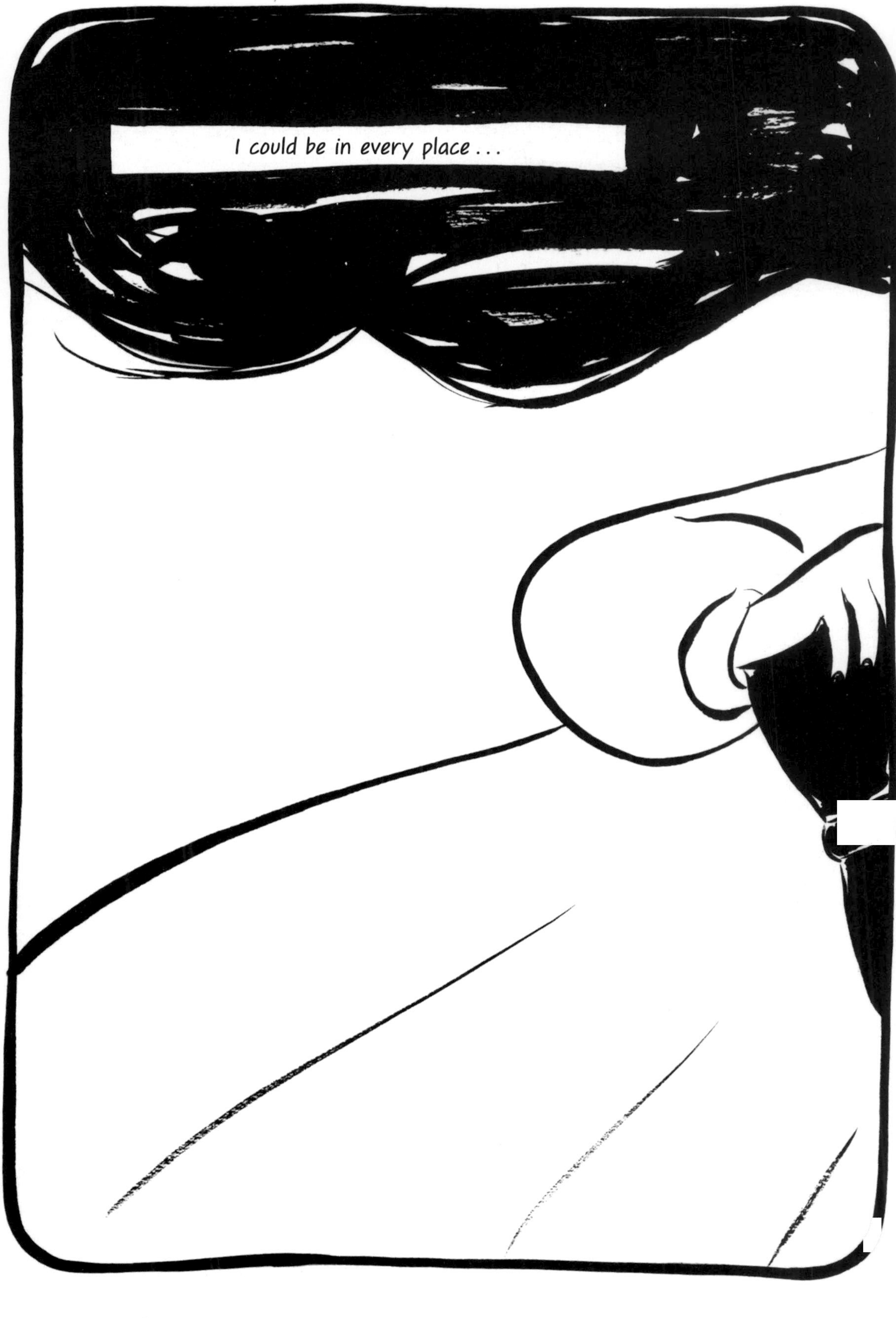
I could be in every place . . .

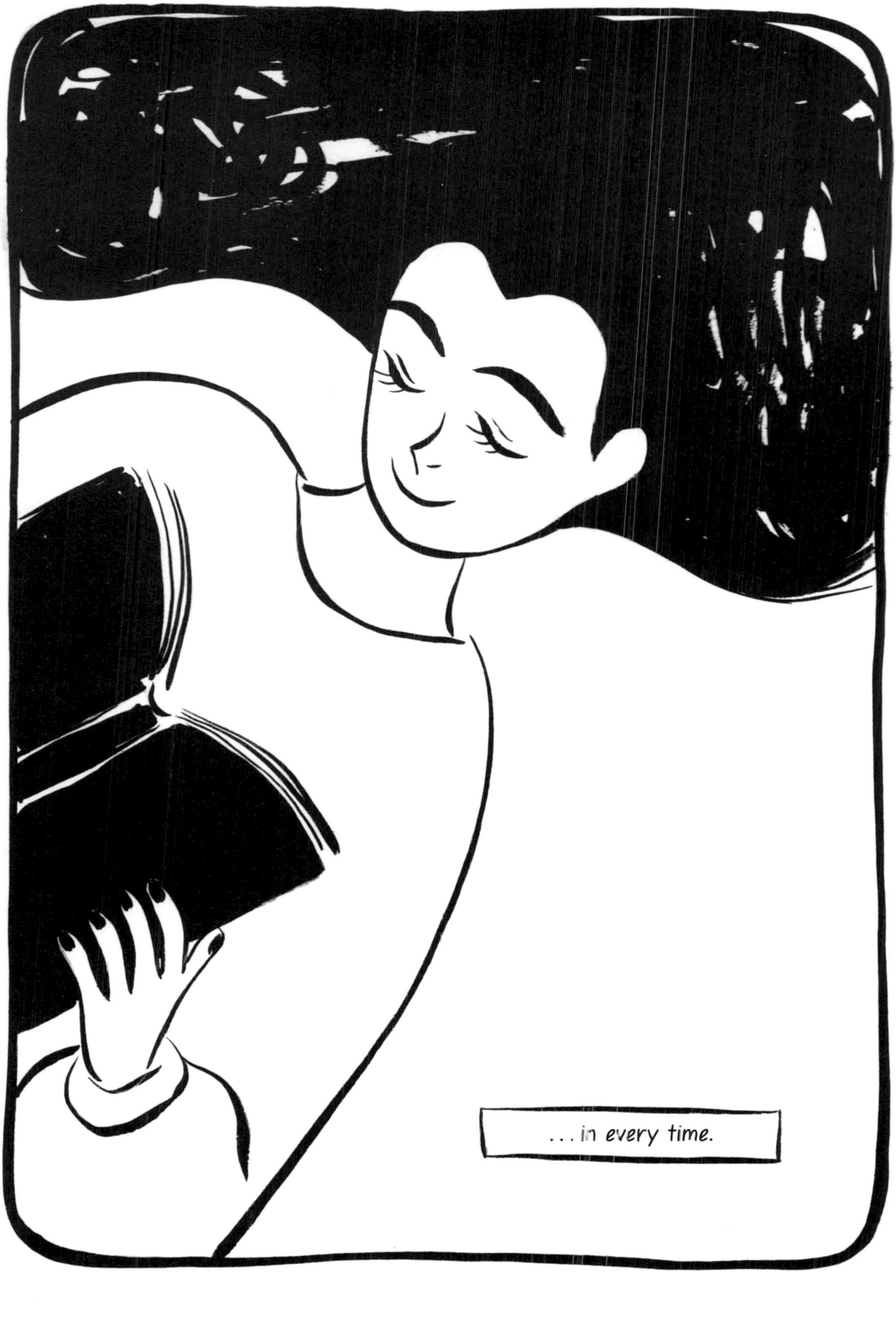
. . . in every time.

Reading became my greatest passion.

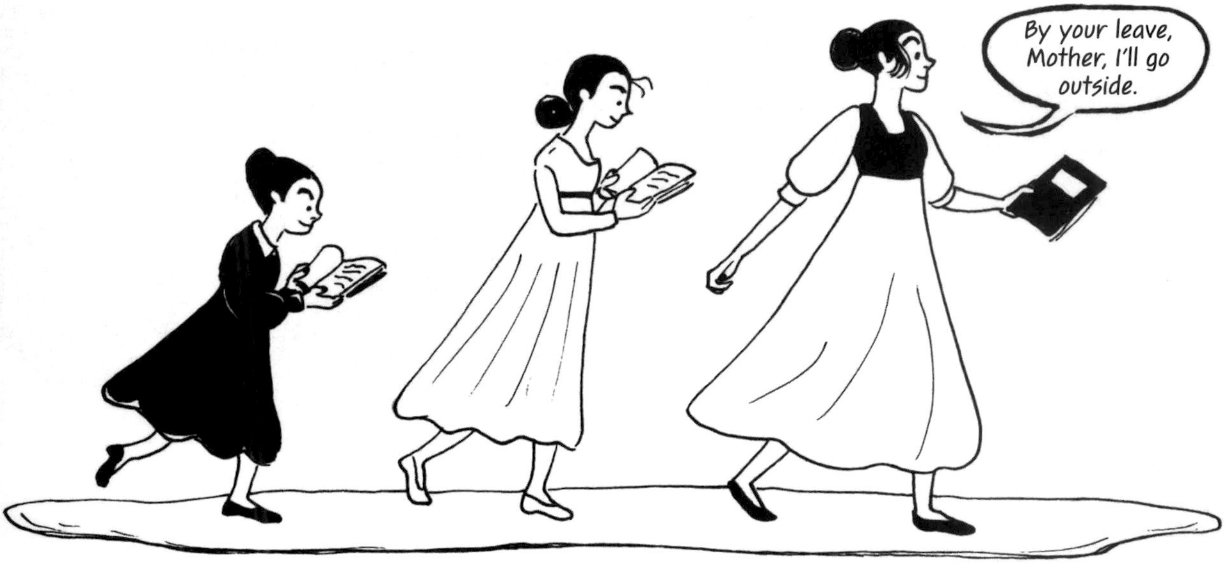
By your leave, Mother, I'll go outside.

My constant companion through adolescence.

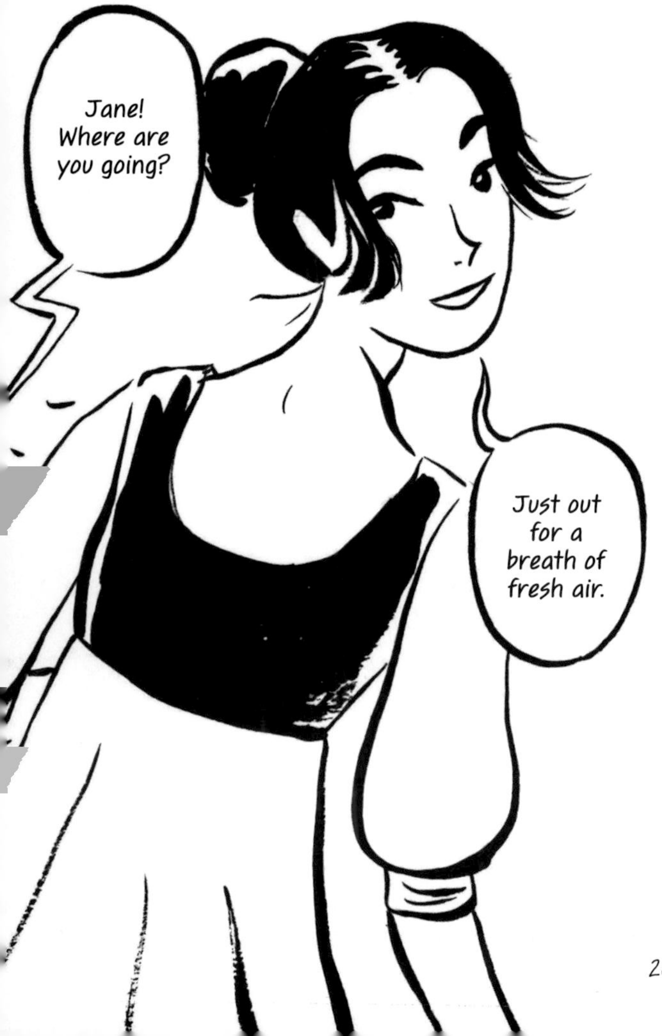
Jane! Where are you going?
Just out for a breath of fresh air.

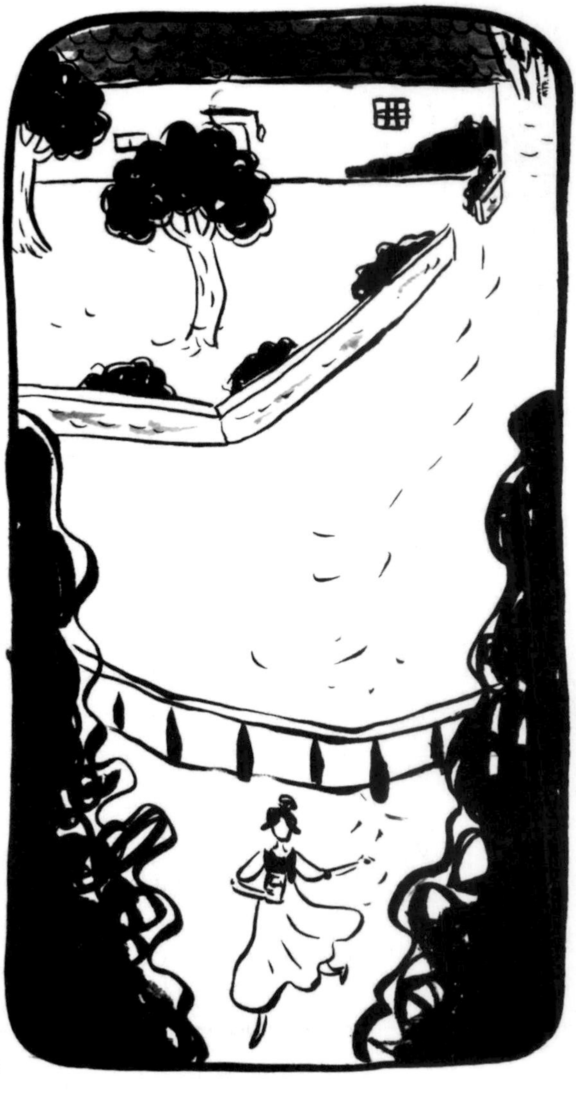

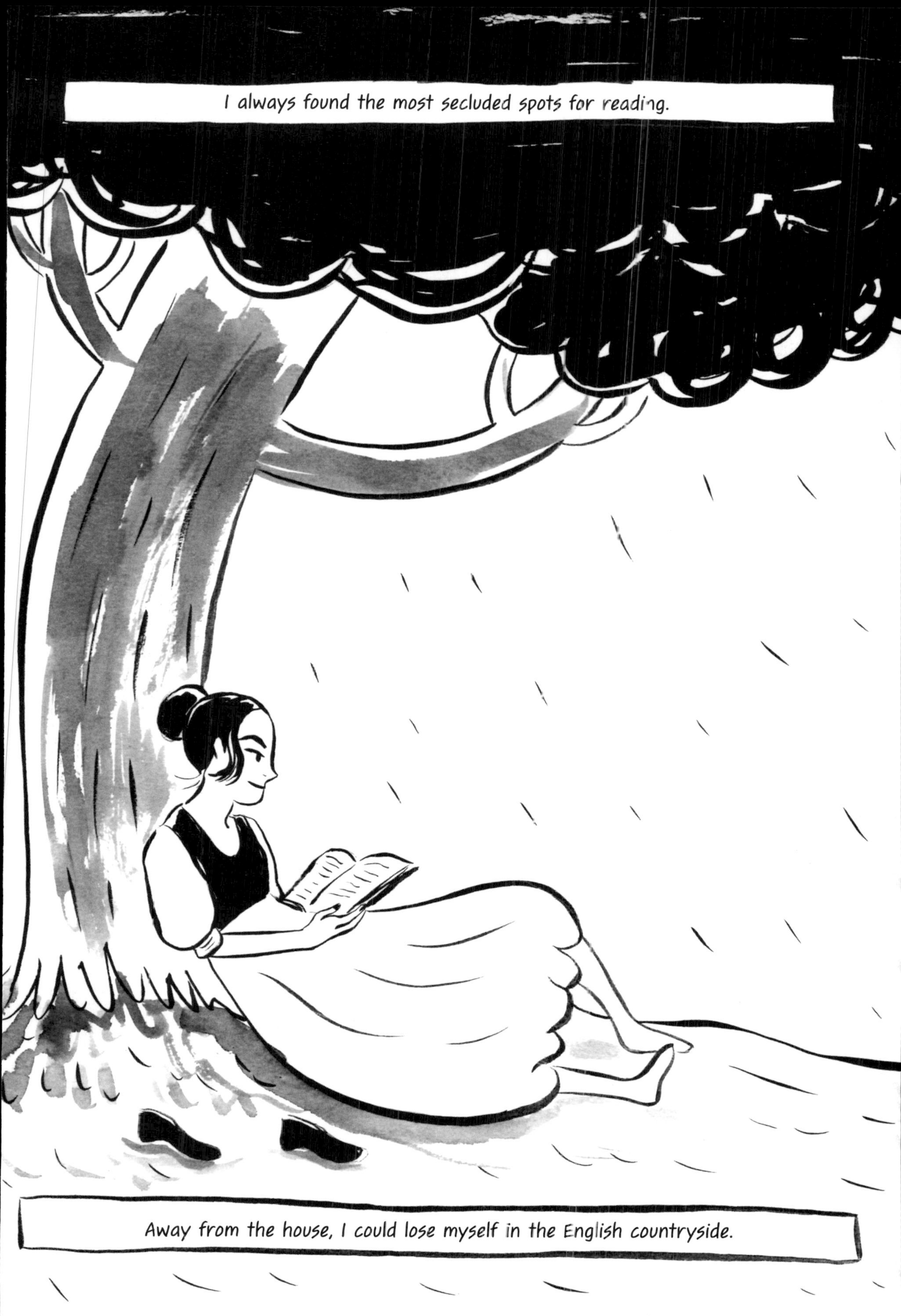
I always found the most secluded spots for reading.
Away from the house, I could lose myself in the English countryside.

Sometimes, while coming back, I'd meet the neighbors.

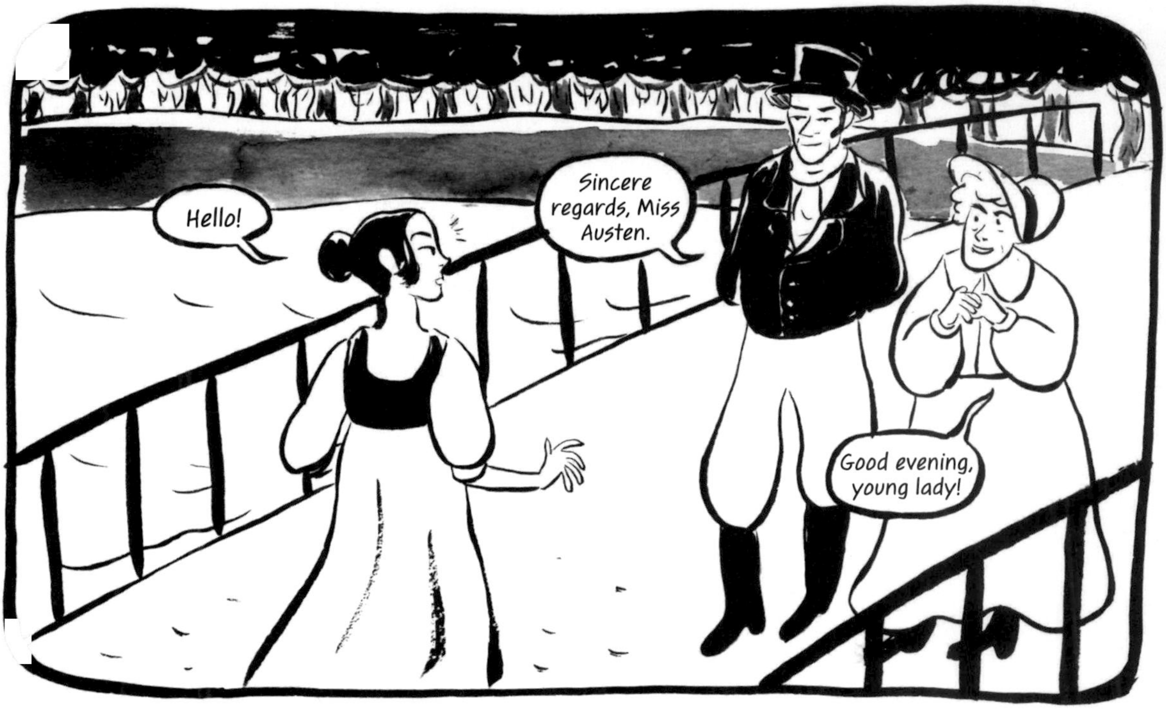
Hello!
Sincere regards, Miss Austen.
Good evening, young lady!

They always told me of their troubles and the latest gossip.

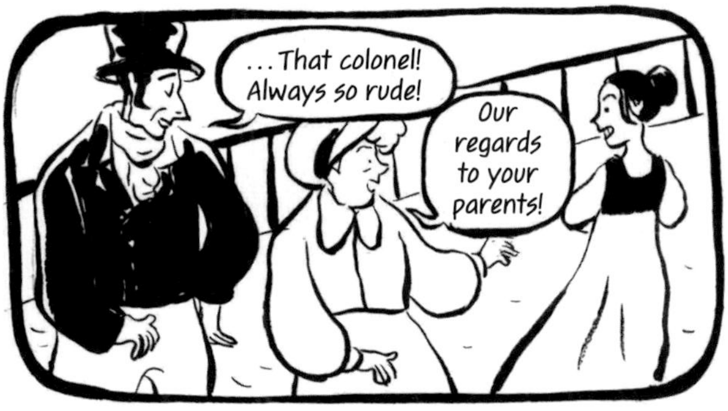
. . . That colonel! Always so rude!
Our regards to your parents!

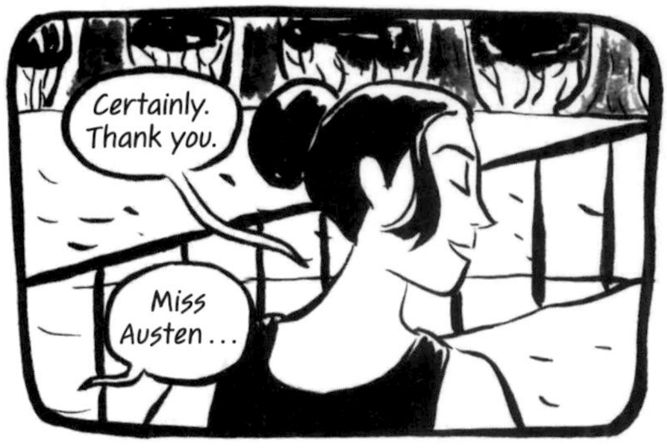
Certainly. Thank you.
Miss Austen . . .

It was during one of these encounters that they invited me to a ball at their house.

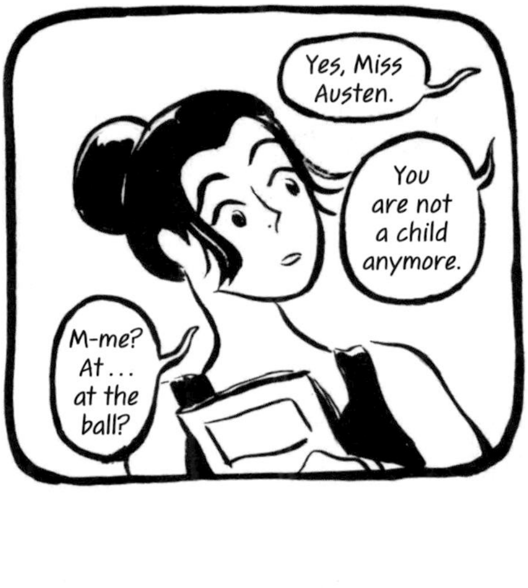
Yes, Miss Austen.
You are not a child anymore.
M-me? At . . . at the ball?

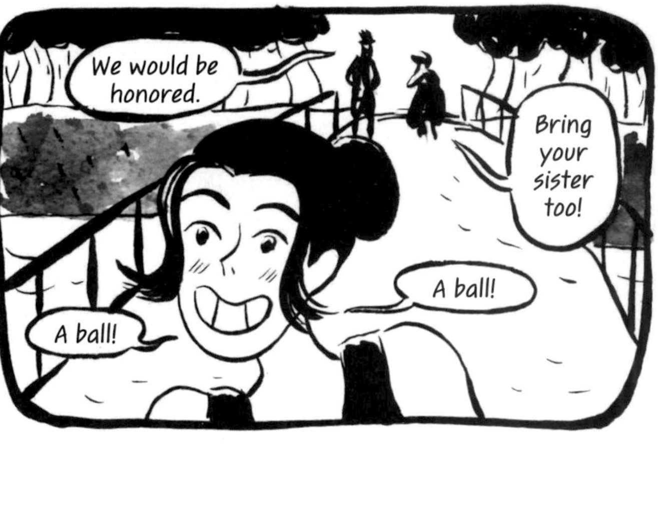
We would be honored.
Bring your sister too!
A ball!
A ball!

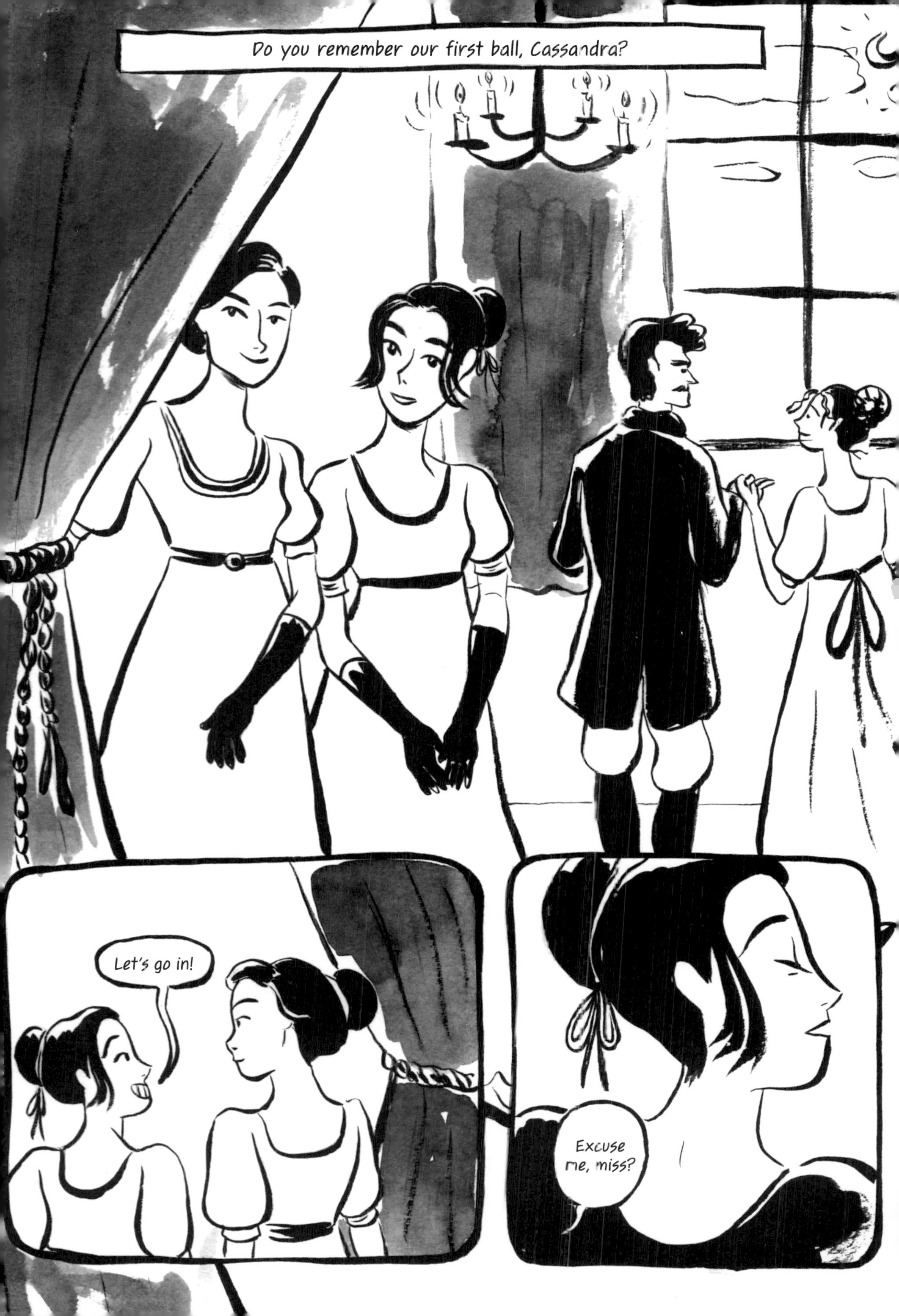
Do you remember our first ball, Cassandra?
Let's go in!
Excuse me, miss?

The balls were a chance to meet new people . . .

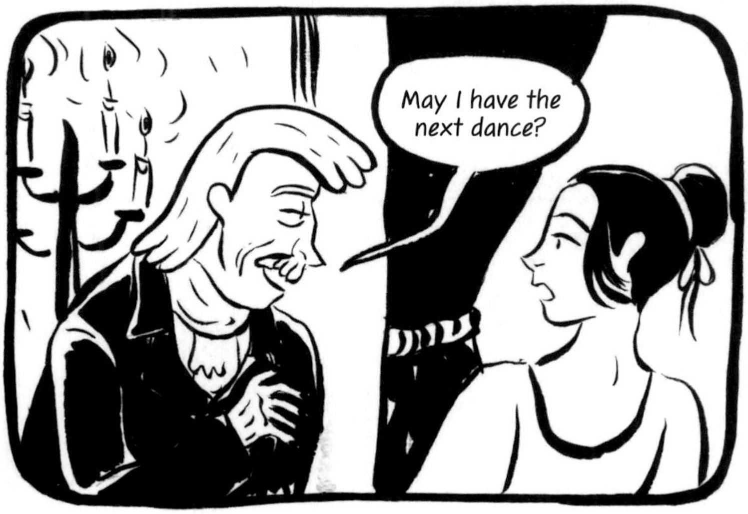
May I have the next dance?

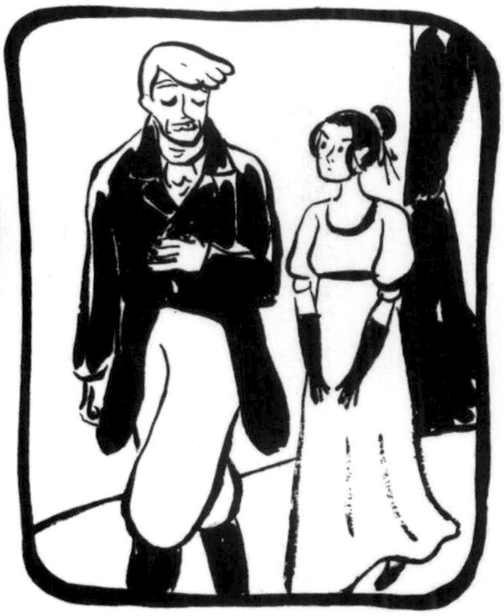

. . . but more than that . . .

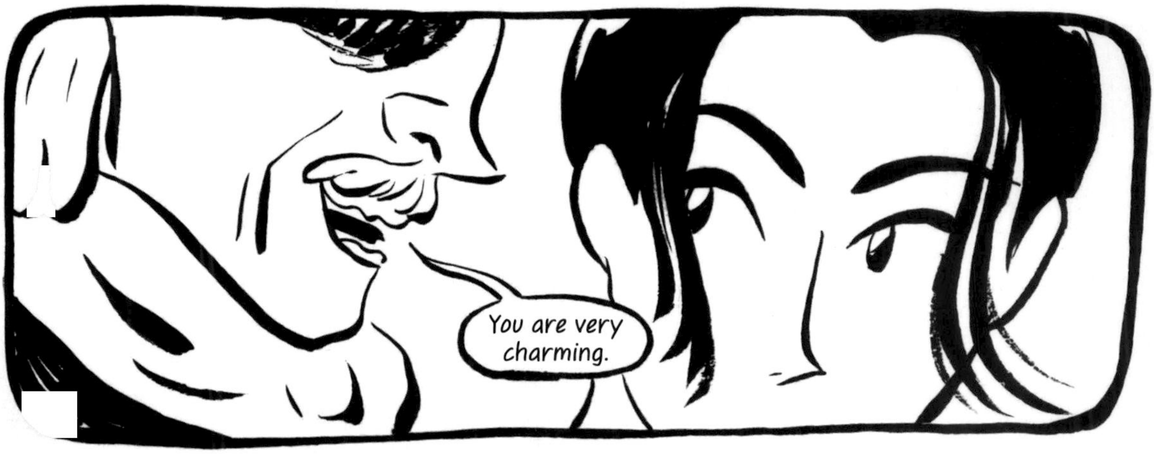
You are very charming.

. . . they were the perfect occasion for arranging a marriage.

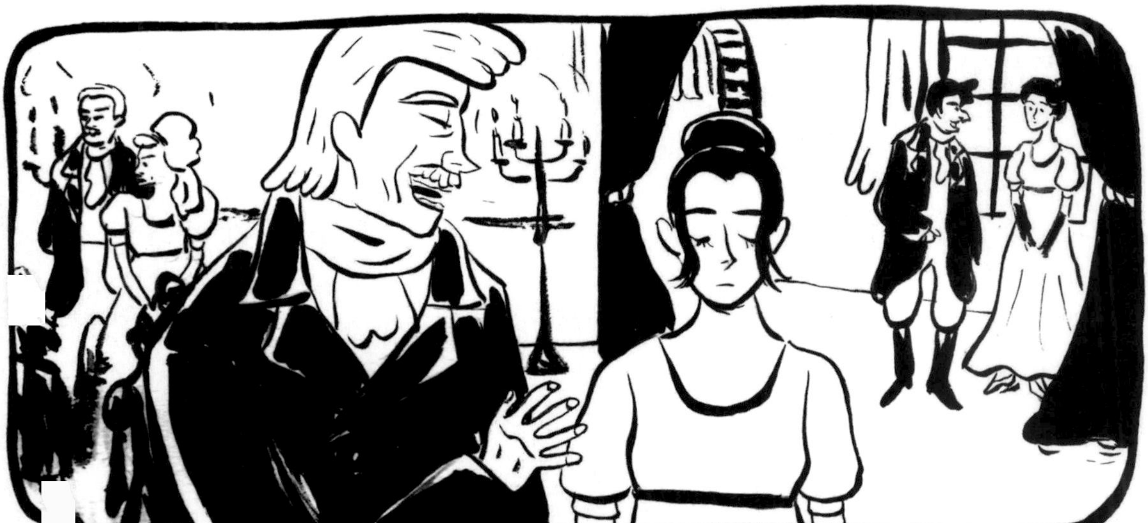

Many of the gentlemen were distinguished but shallow.

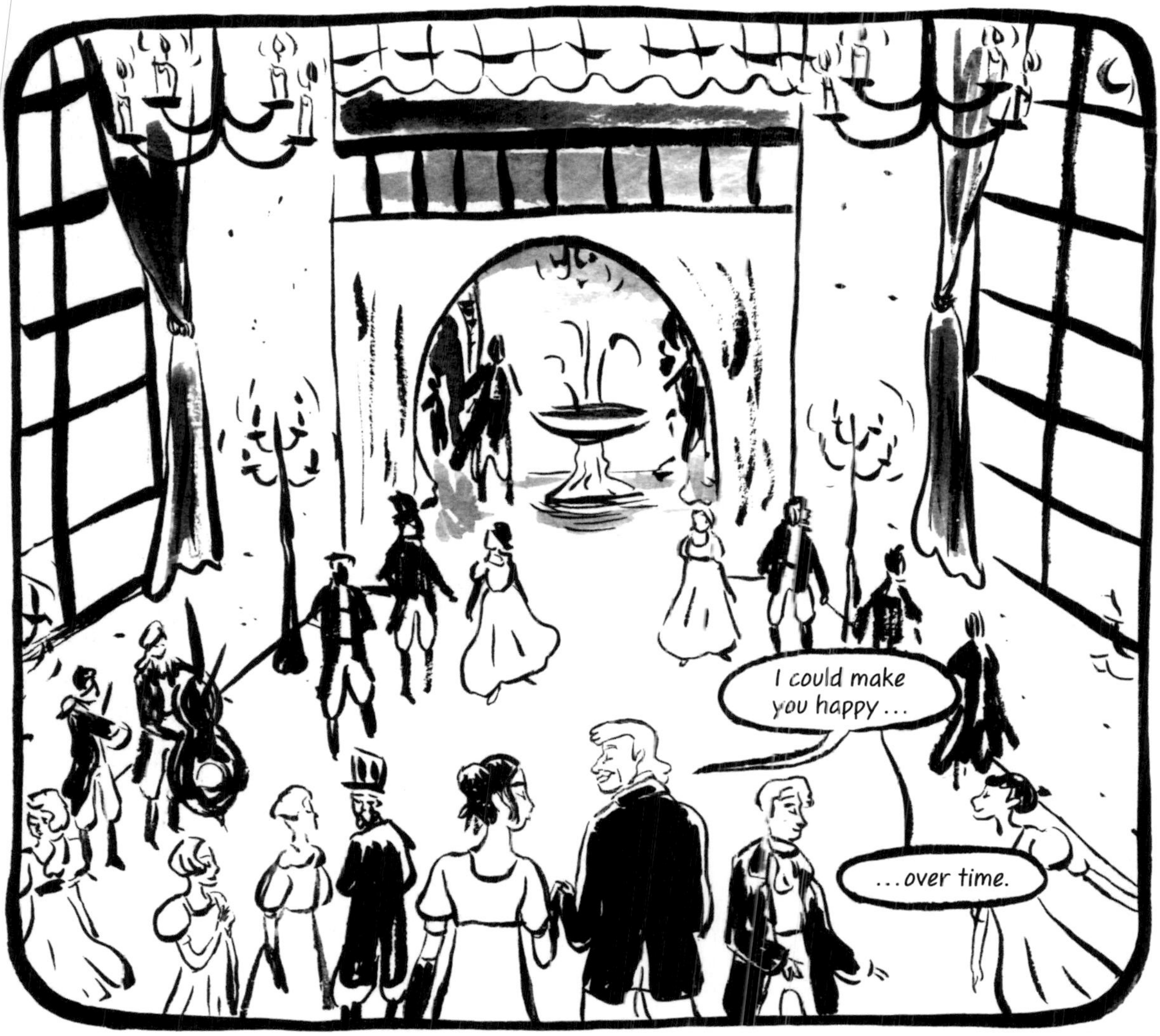

I could make you happy . . .
. . . over time.

Or I simply didn't find them attractive.

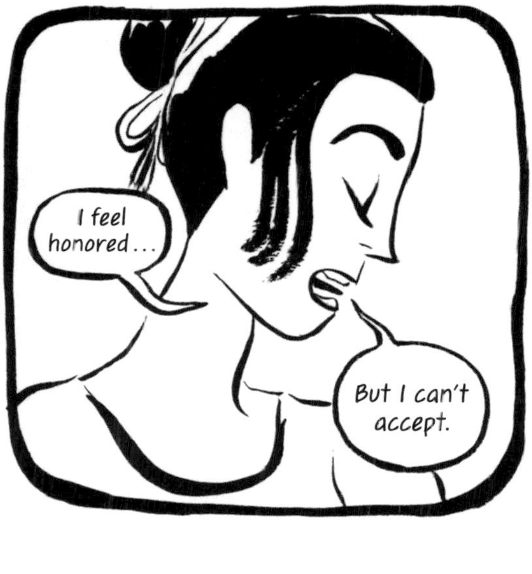

I feel honored . . .
But I can't accept.

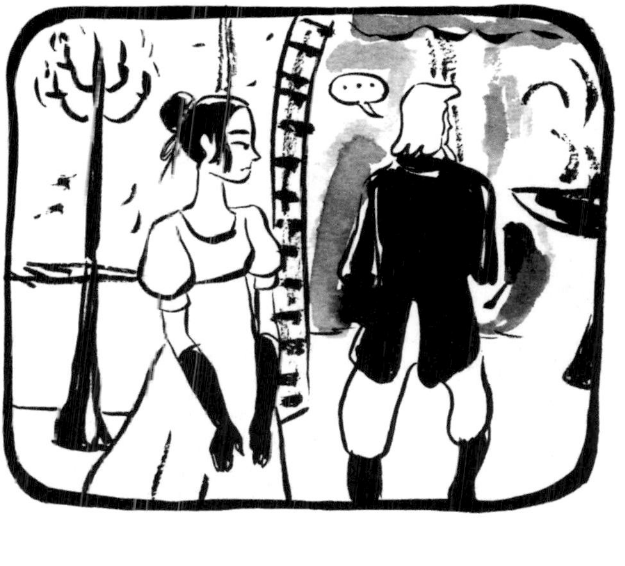

. . .

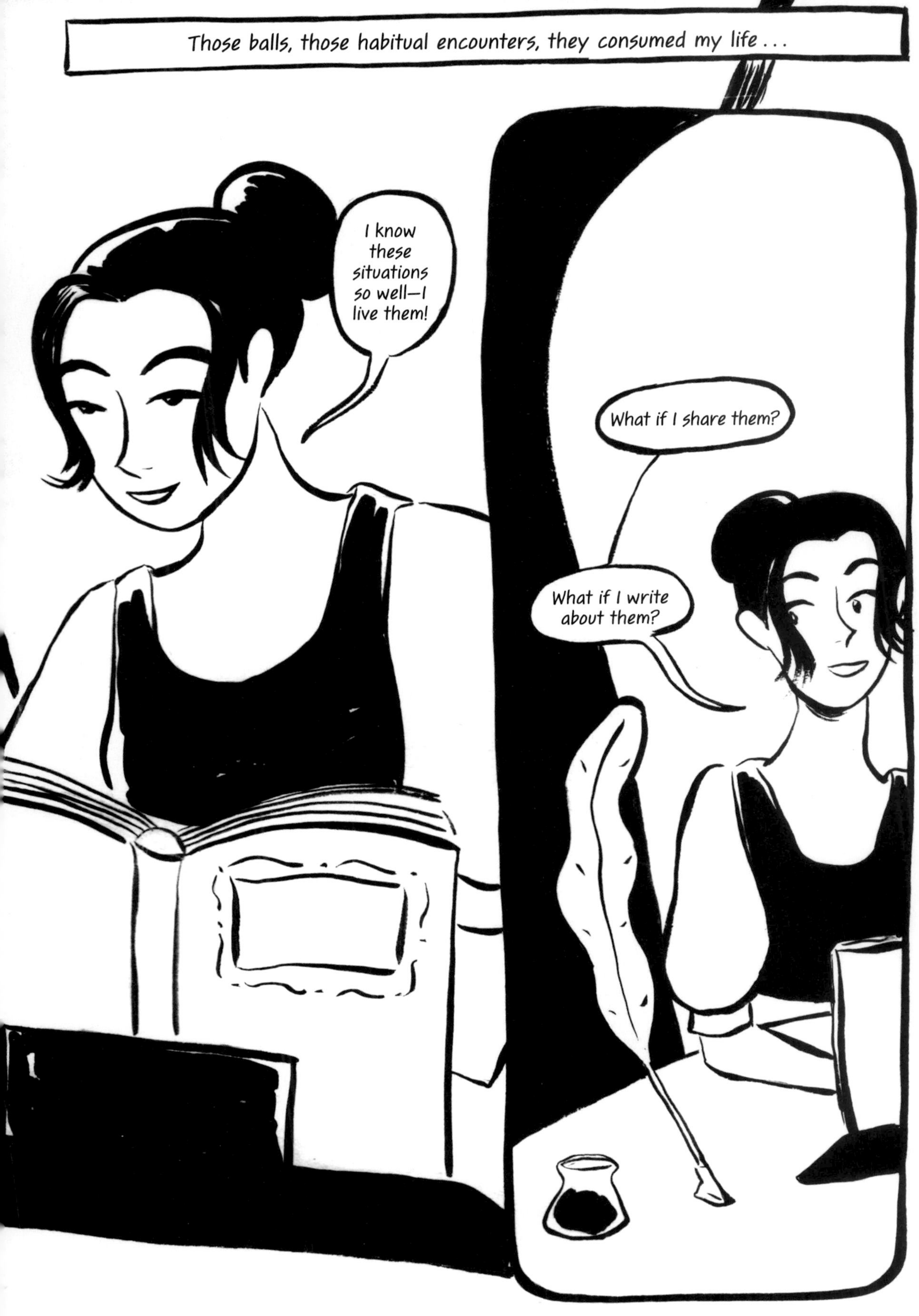
Those balls, those habitual encounters, they consumed my life . . .
I know these situations so well—I live them!
What if I share them?
What if I write about them?

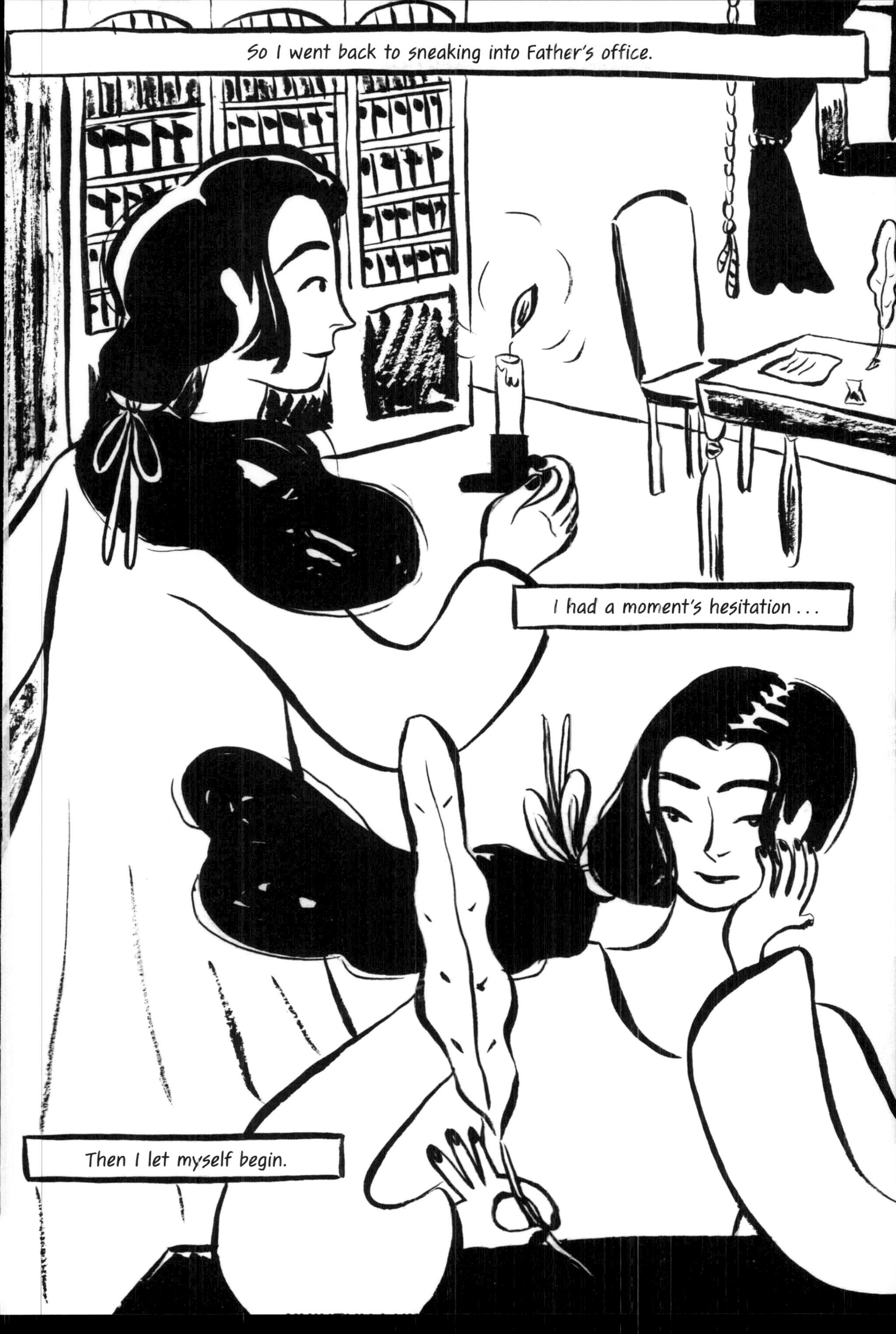
So I went back to sneaking into Father's office.
I had a moment's hesitation . . .
Then I let myself begin.

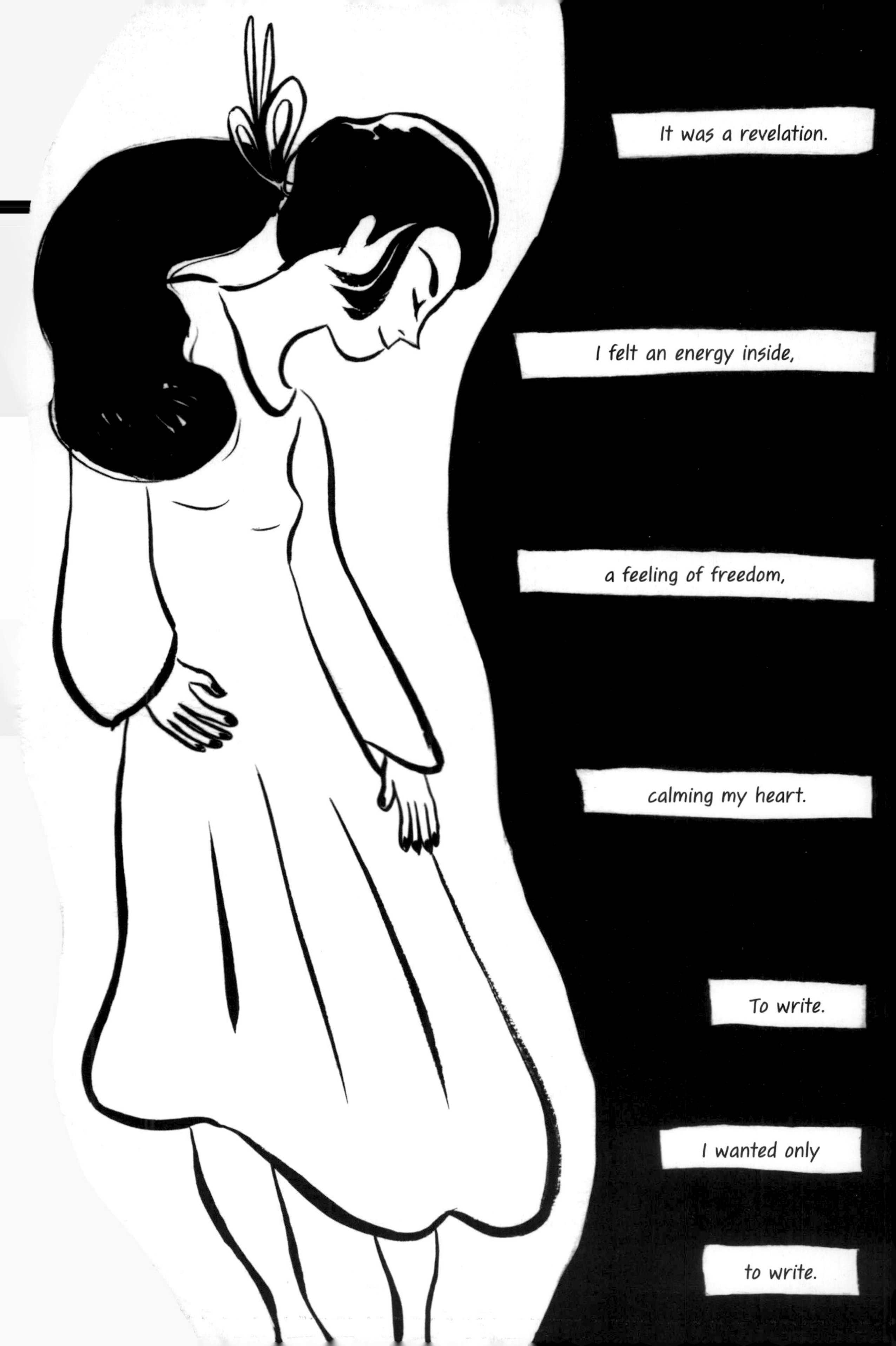
It was a revelation.
I felt an energy inside,
a feeling of freedom,
calming my heart.
To write.
I wanted only
to write.

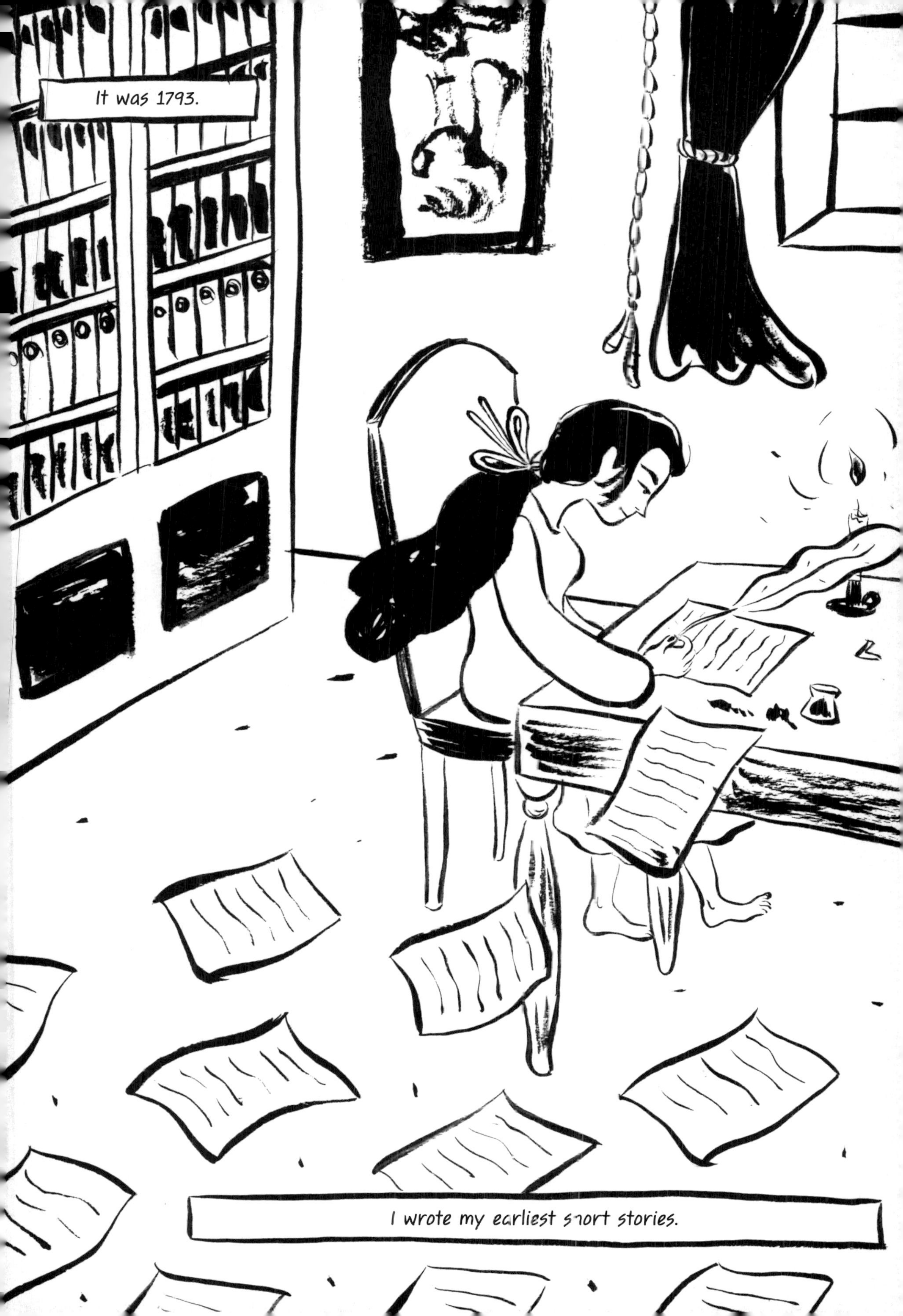
It was 1793.
I wrote my earliest short stories.

The first to appreciate my work was my father.

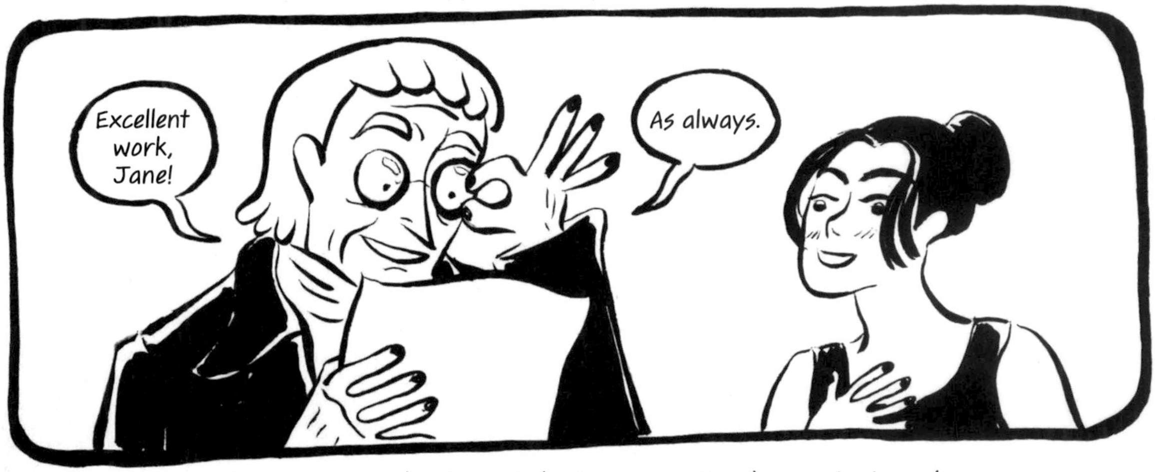
Excellent work, Jane!
As always.

Soon rumors about my talent as a writer began to travel.

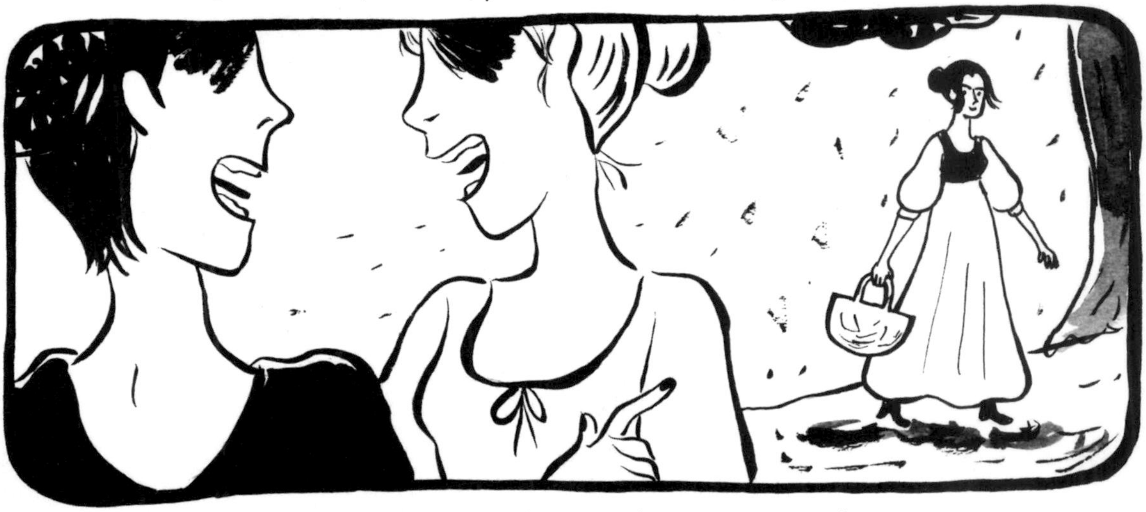

I was invited to read my work in private circles.

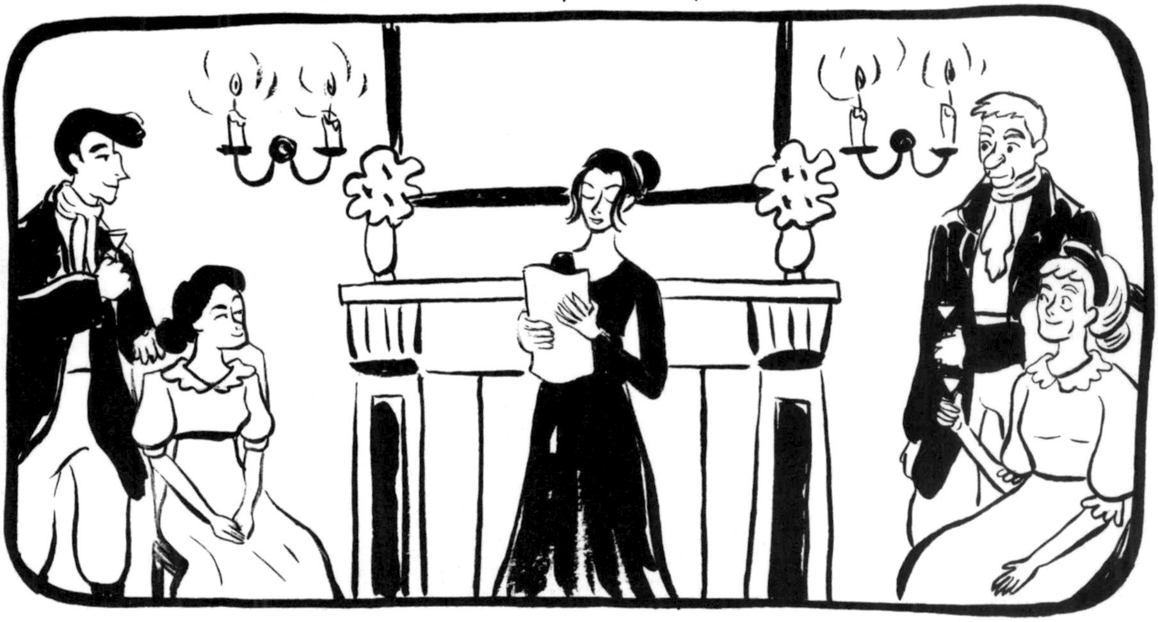

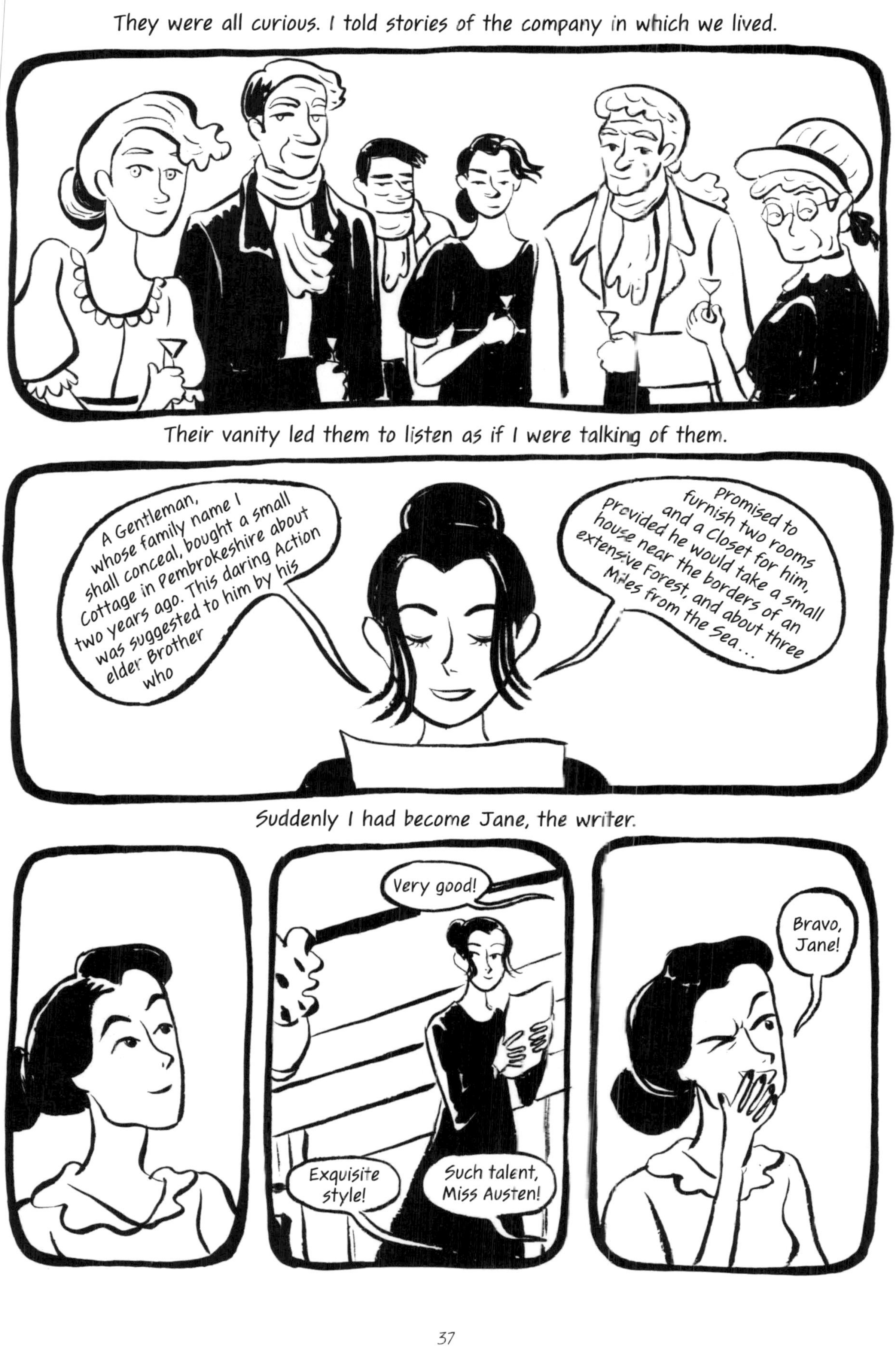
They were all curious. I told stories of the company in which we lived.
Their vanity led them to listen as if I were talking of them.
A Gentleman, whose family name I shall conceal, bought a small Cottage in Pembrokeshire about two years ago. This daring Action was suggested to him by his elder Brother who
Promised to furnish two rooms and a Closet for him, Provided he would take a small house near the borders of an extensive Forest, and about three Miles from the Sea...
Suddenly I had become Jane, the writer.
Very good!
Exquisite style!
Such talent, Miss Austen!
Bravo, Jane!

For the first time

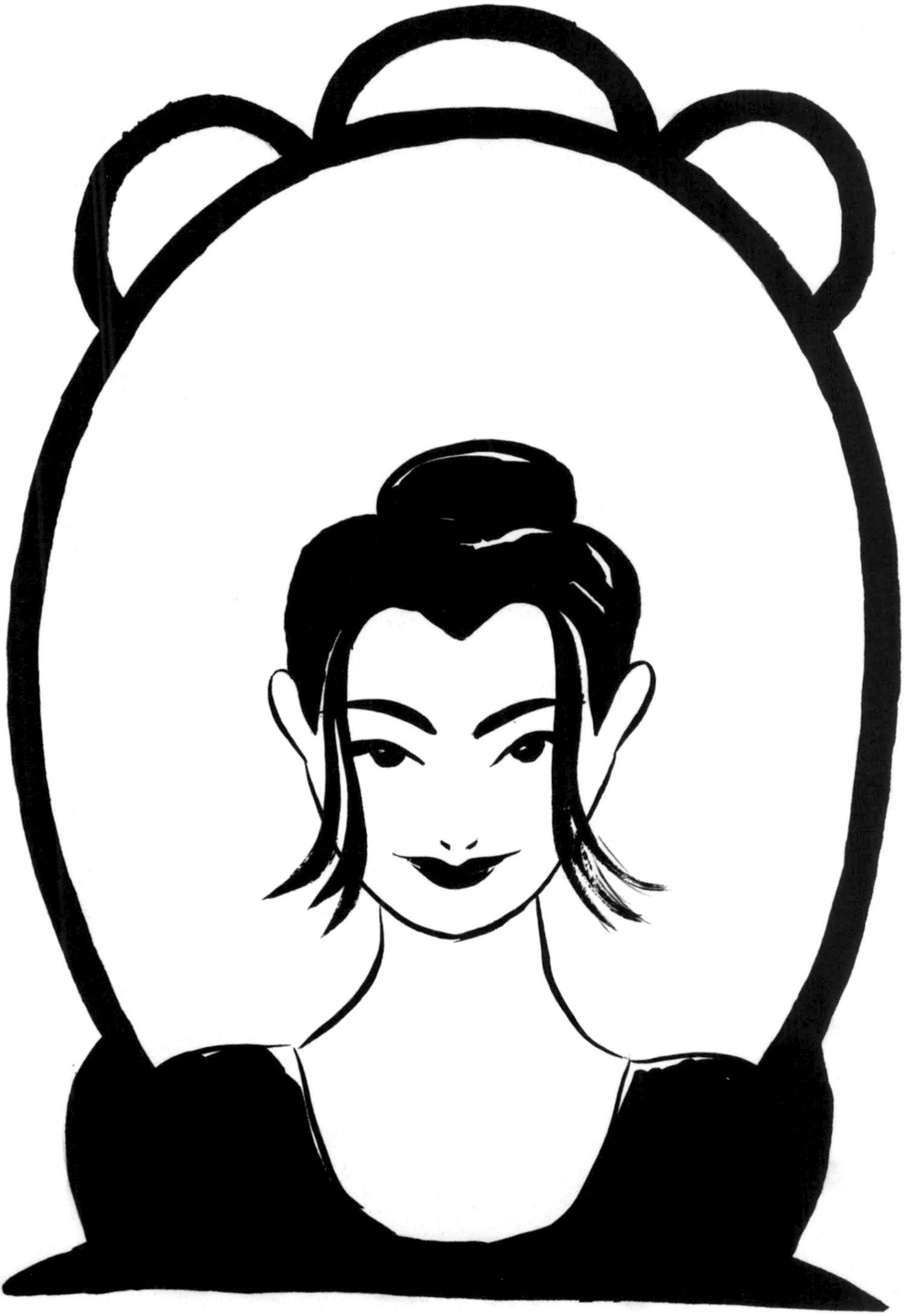

I was happy.

And then

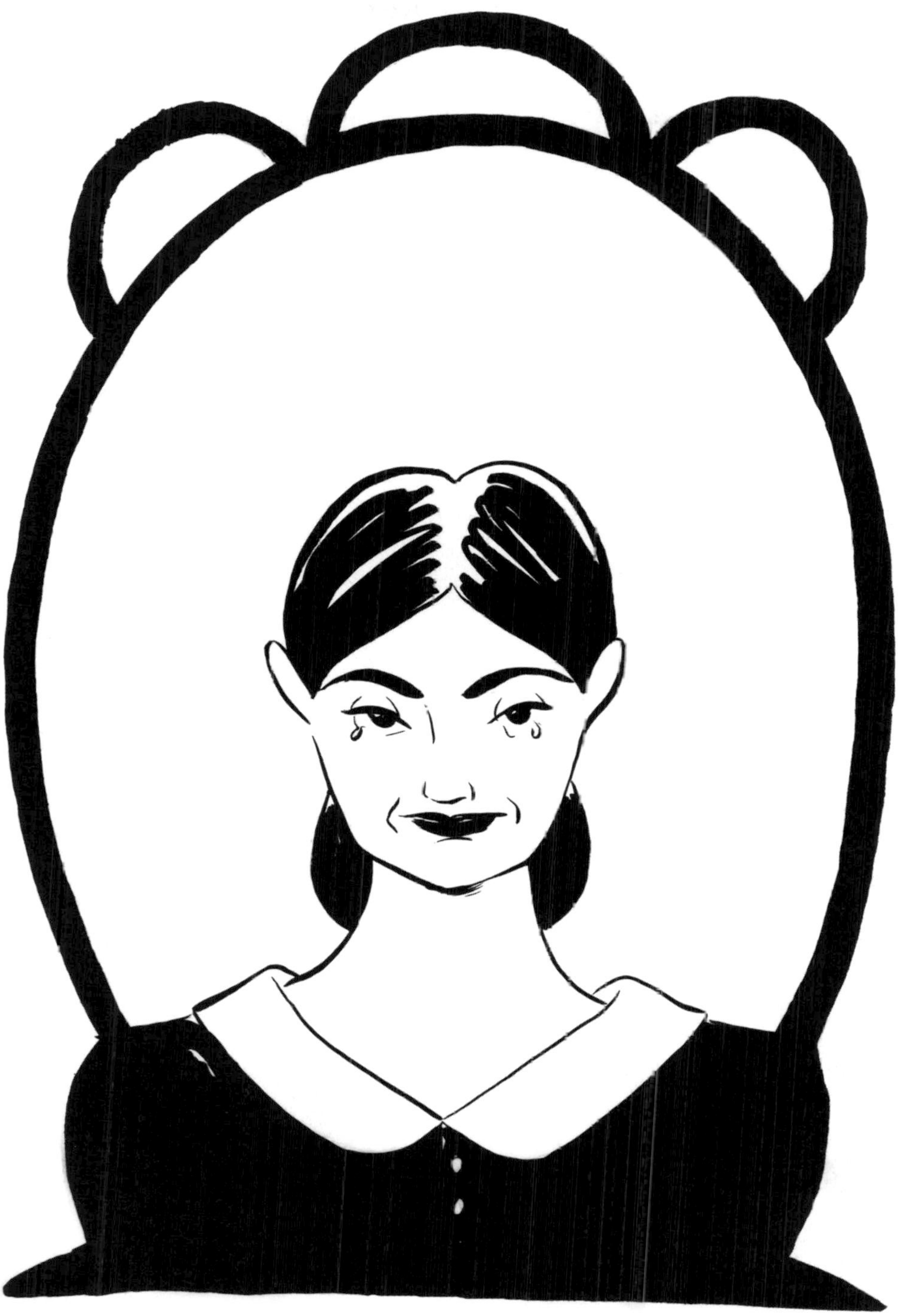

nothing was as before.

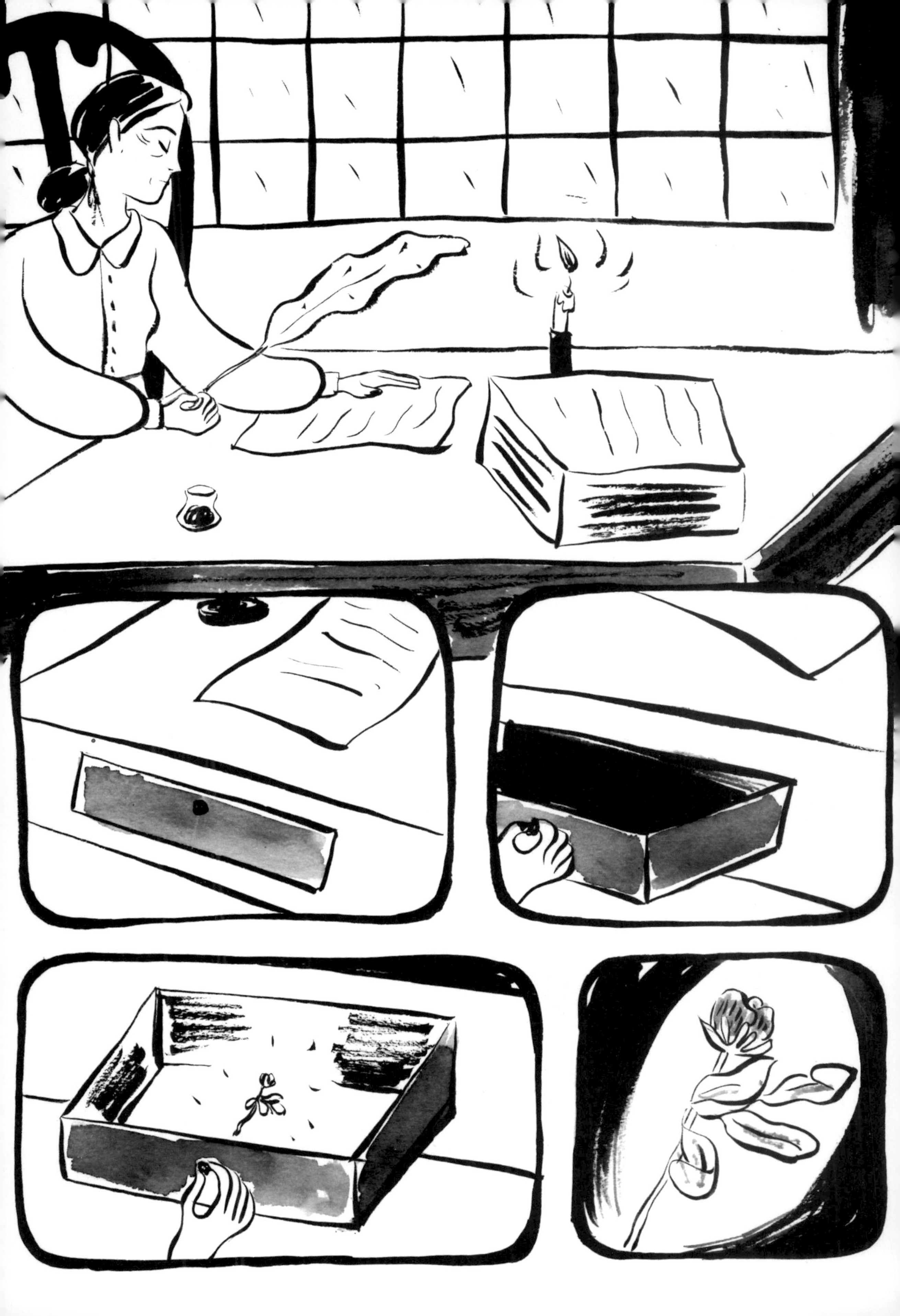

It was during the Christmas season of 1795. I was twenty years old.

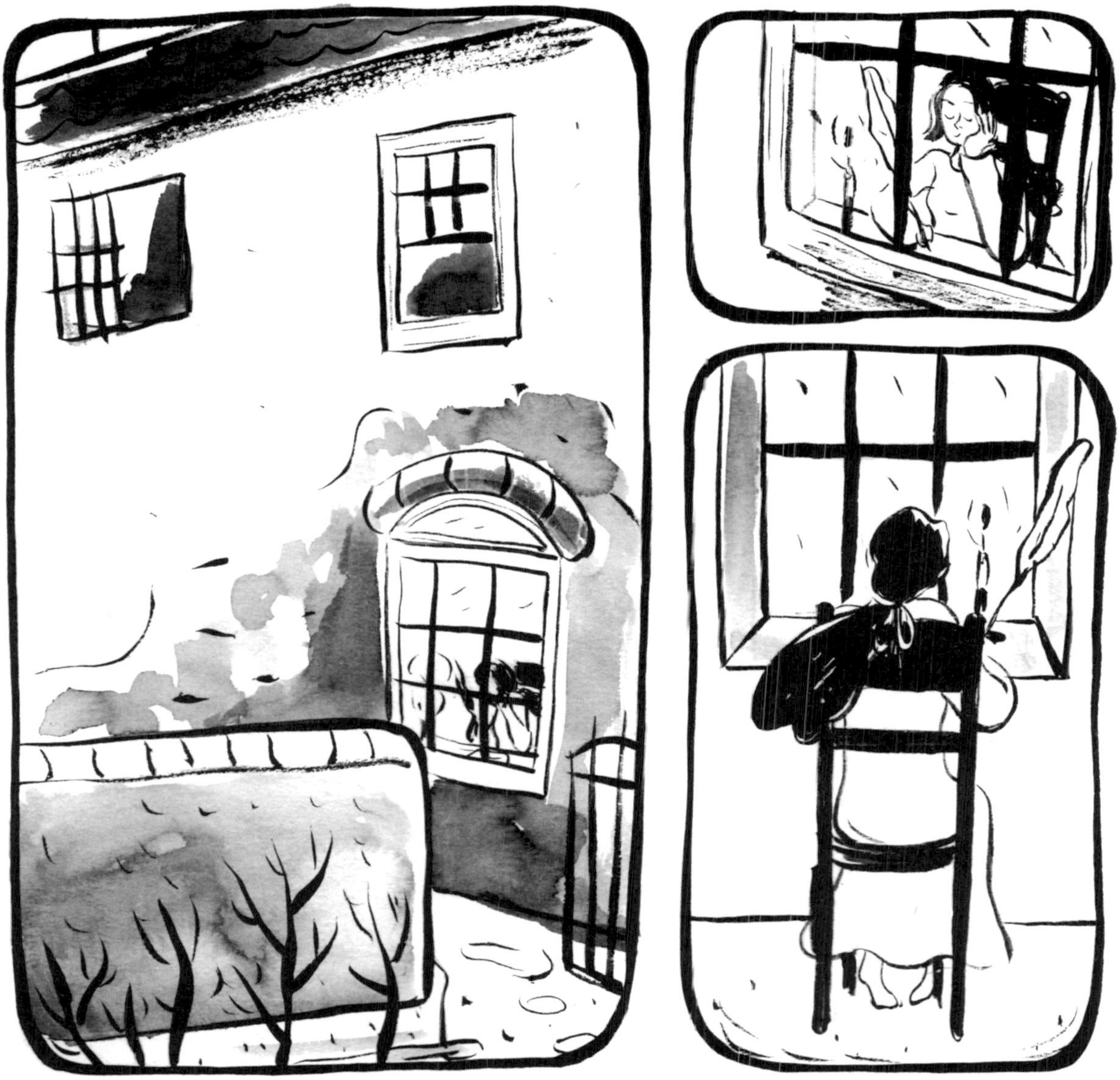

I would write every day and wait for the festivities to begin.

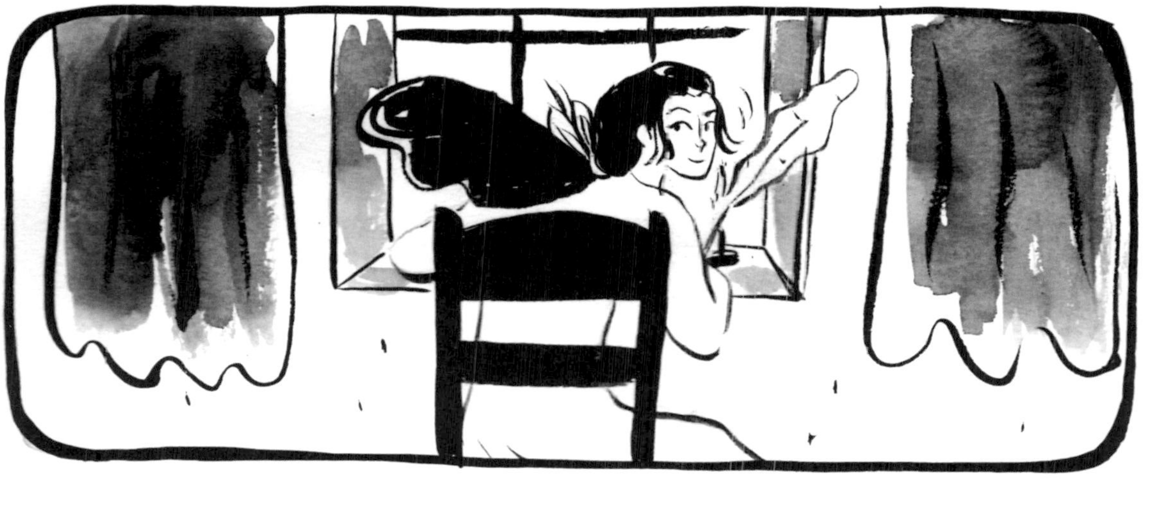

By now, my readings in private circles had become more frequent.

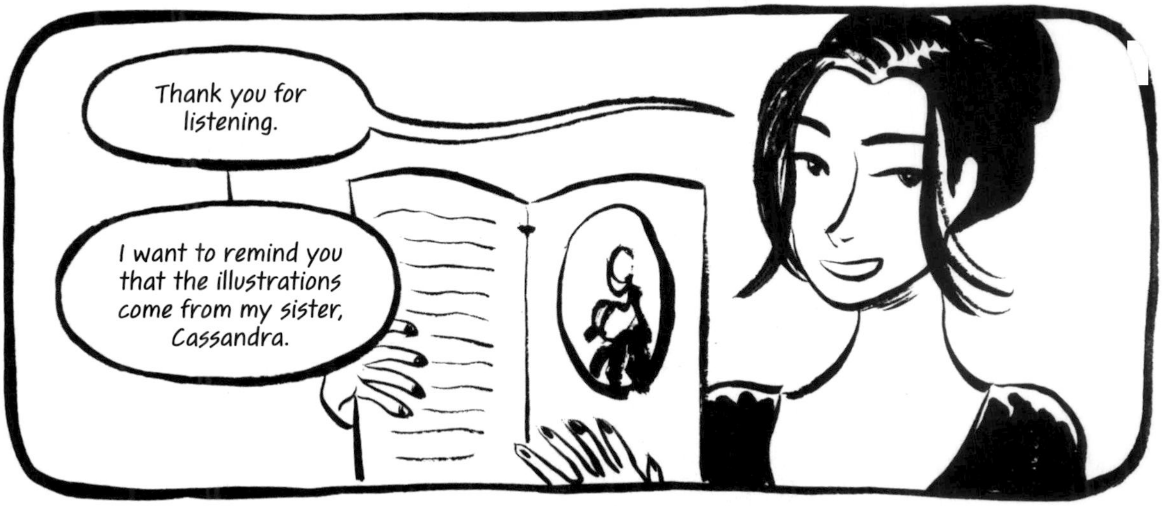
Thank you for listening.
I want to remind you that the illustrations come from my sister, Cassandra.

And so had the invitations to balls.

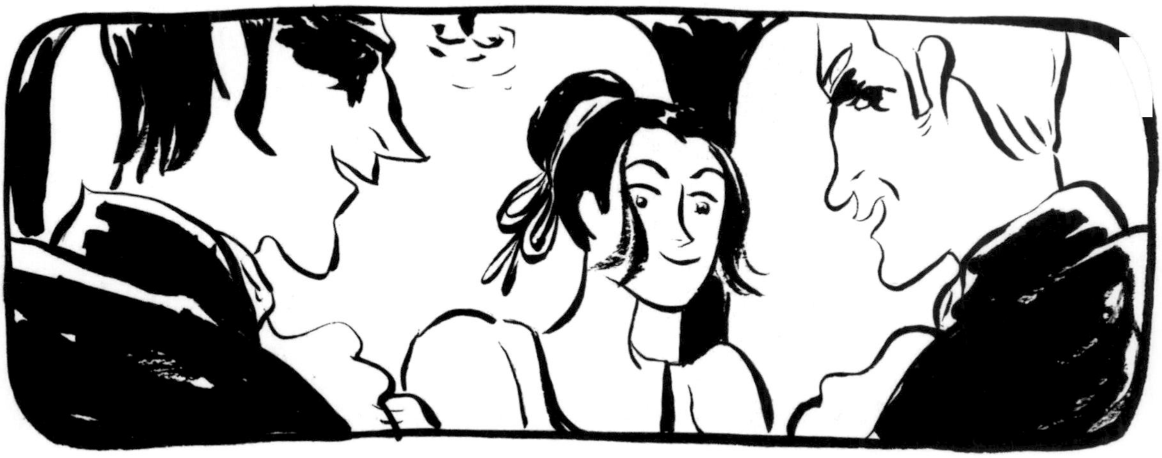

Some pieces, I wrote to entertain friends and relatives.

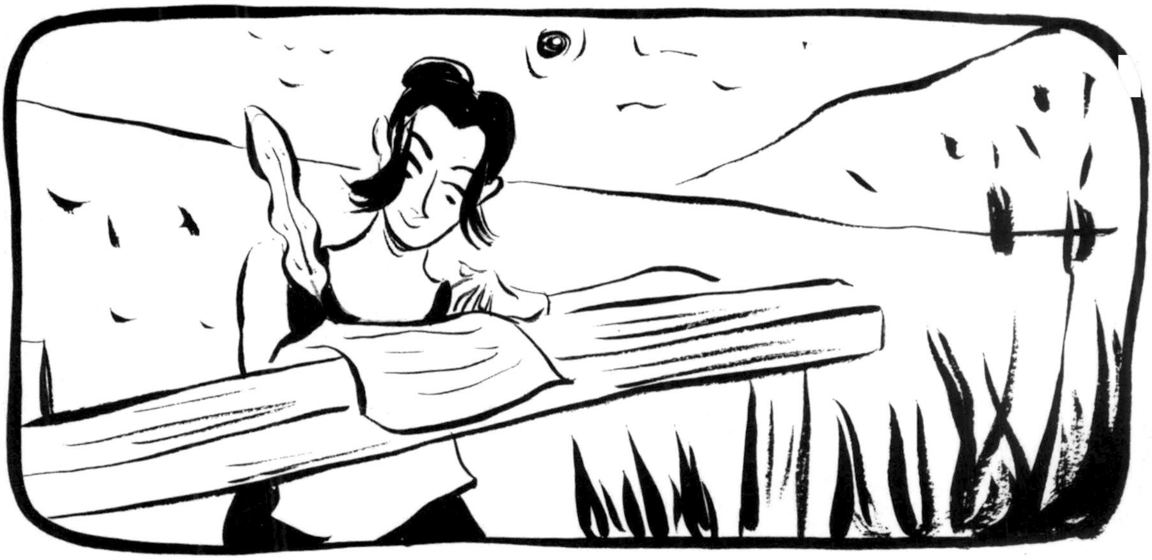

One of them I titled *Elinor and Marianne.*

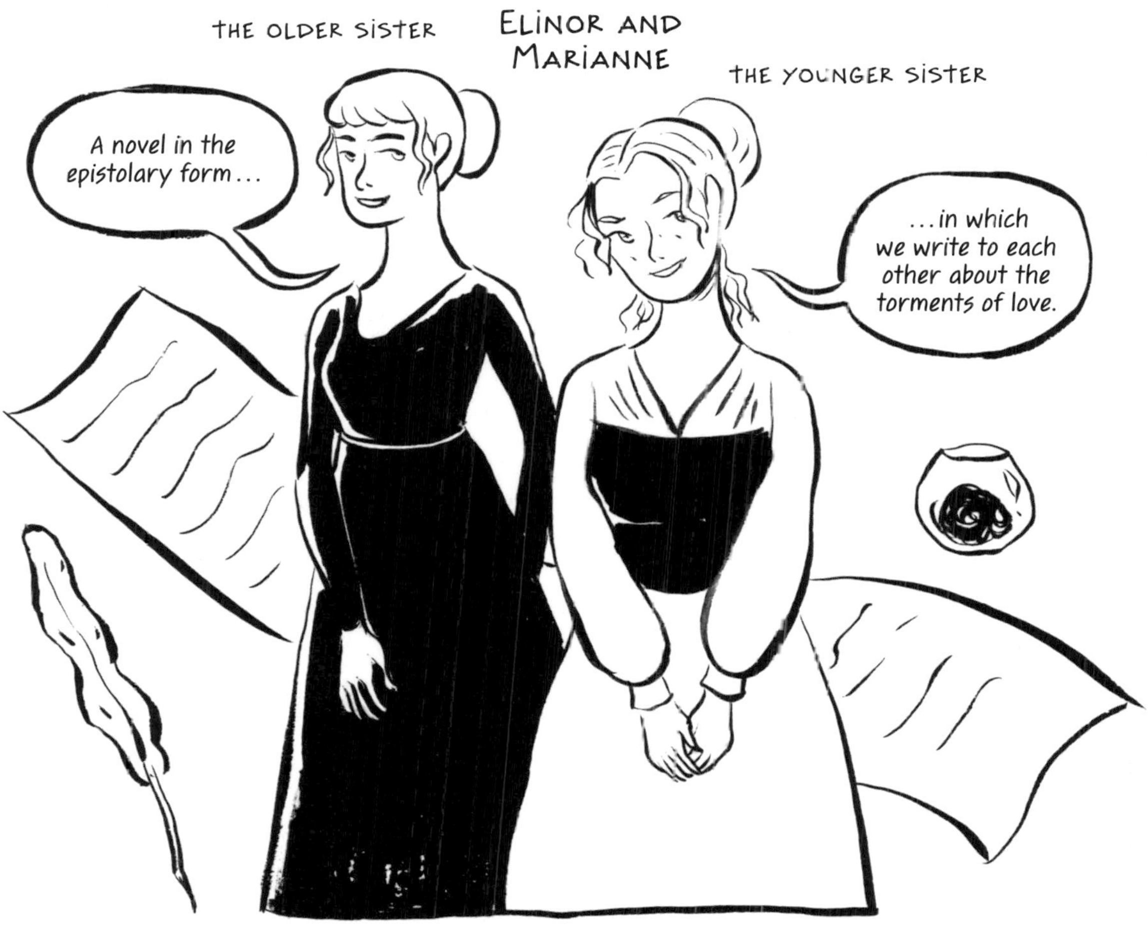
THE OLDER SISTER
ELINOR AND MARIANNE
THE YOUNGER SISTER
A novel in the epistolary form…
…in which we write to each other about the torments of love.

Just as you and I would, Cassandra.

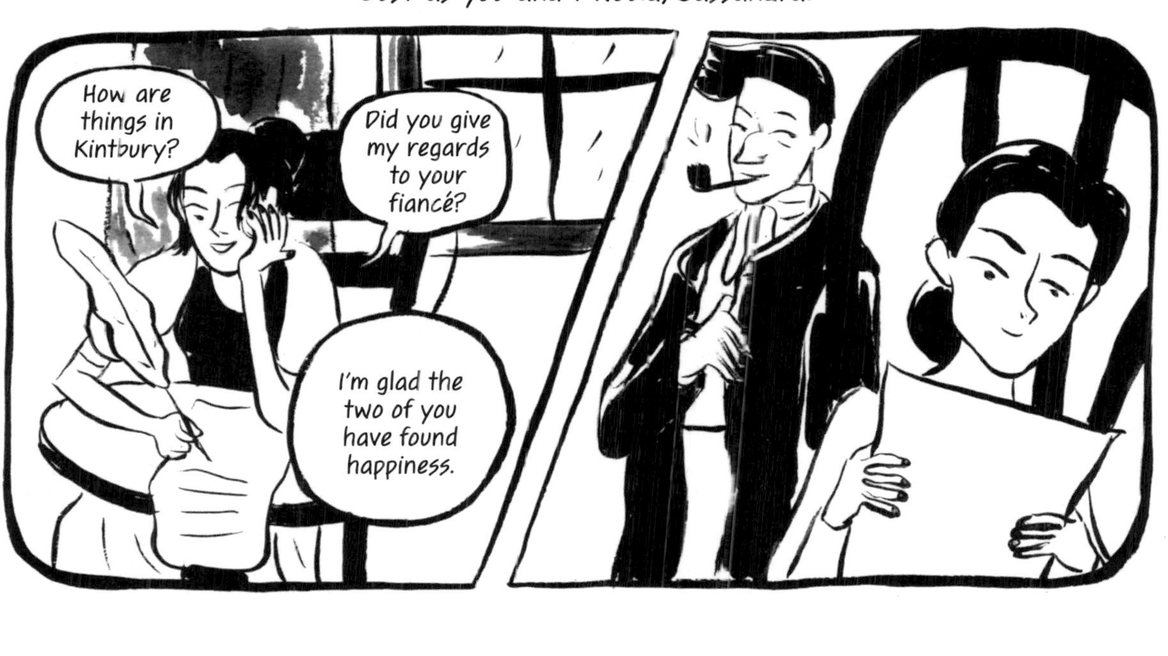
How are things in Kintbury?
Did you give my regards to your fiancé?
I'm glad the two of you have found happiness.

But love? What did I truly know about love?

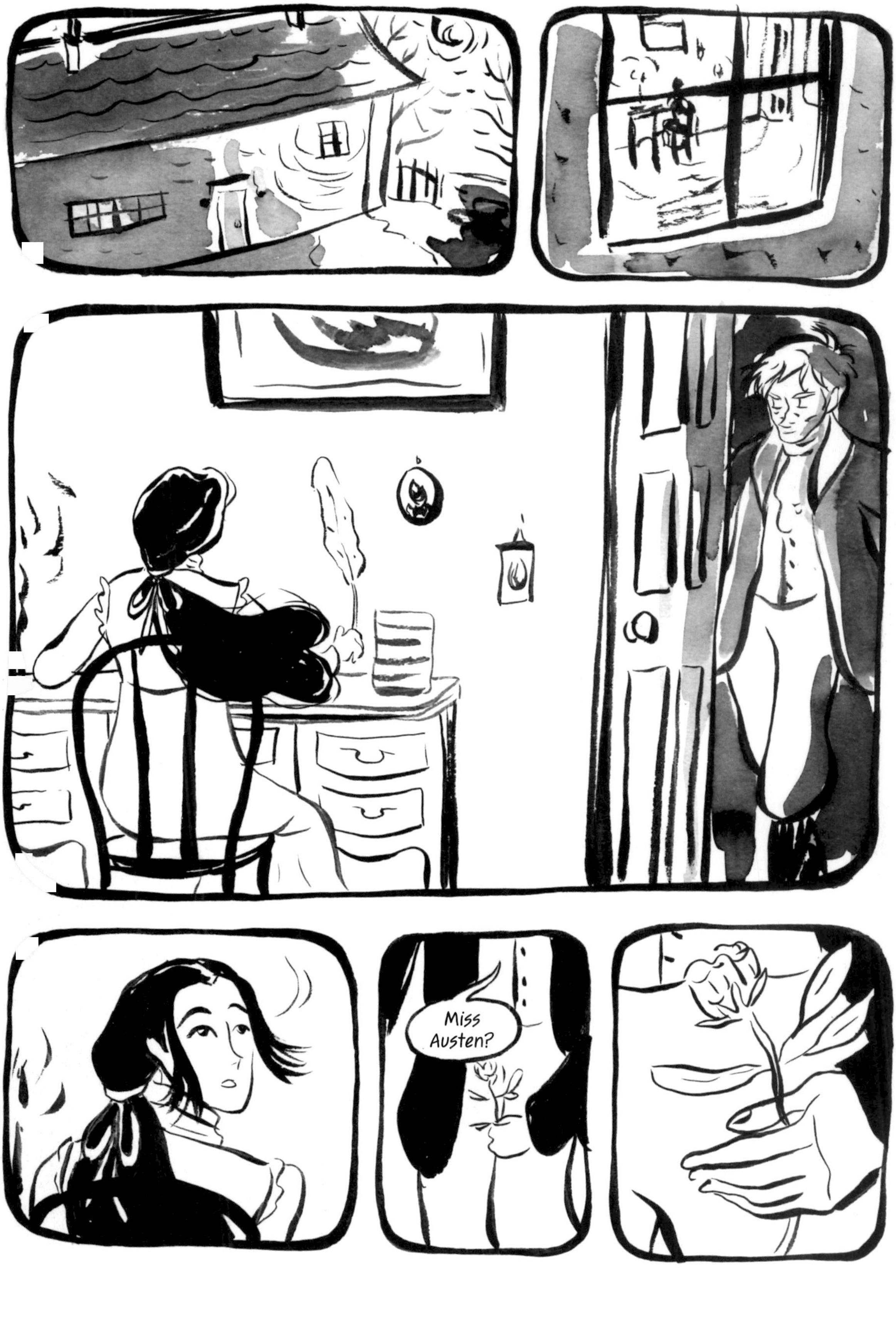
Miss Austen?

I was writing only of my expectations.

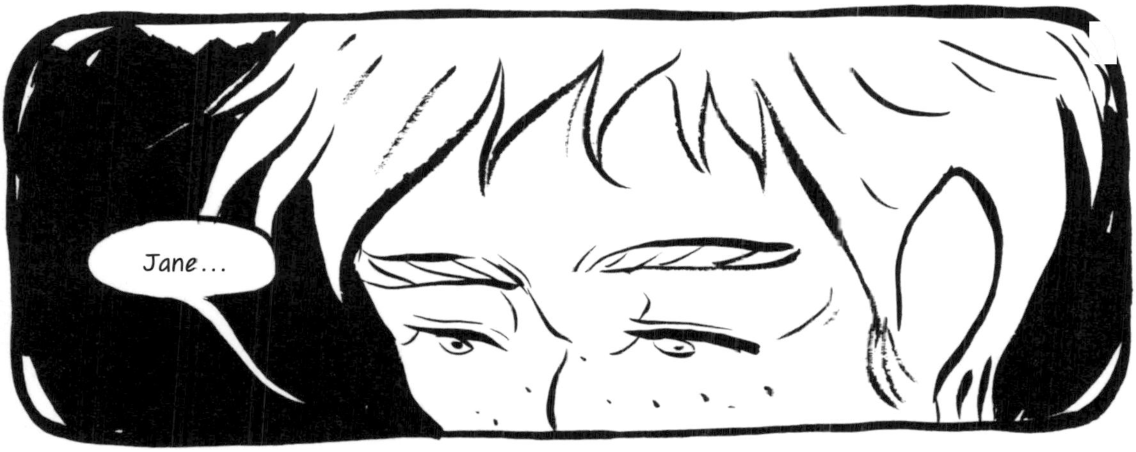
Jane…

All deep reasoning and calculation.

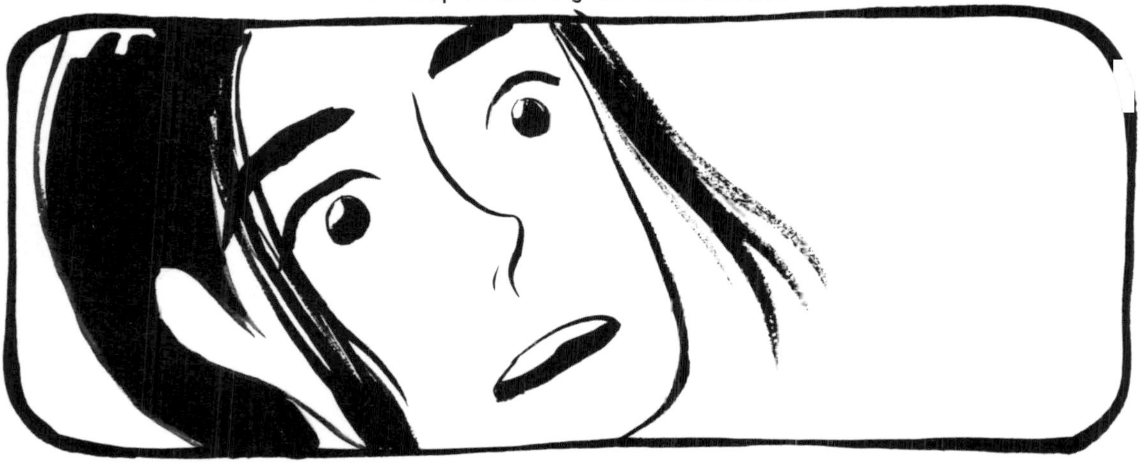

But where was the passion hiding?

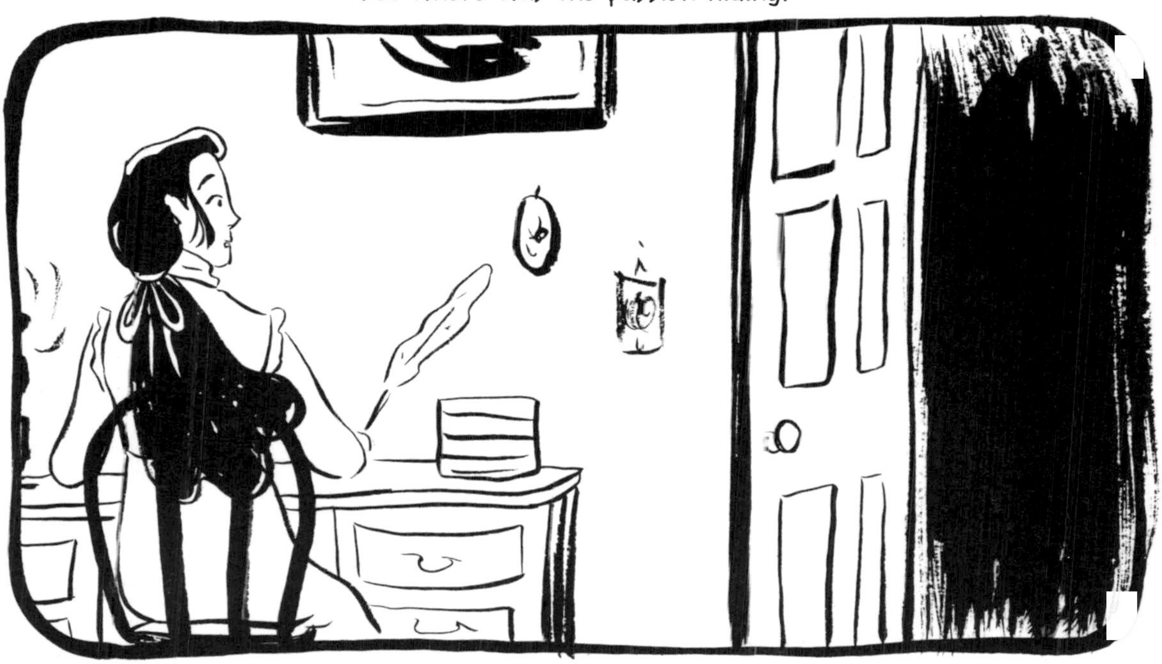

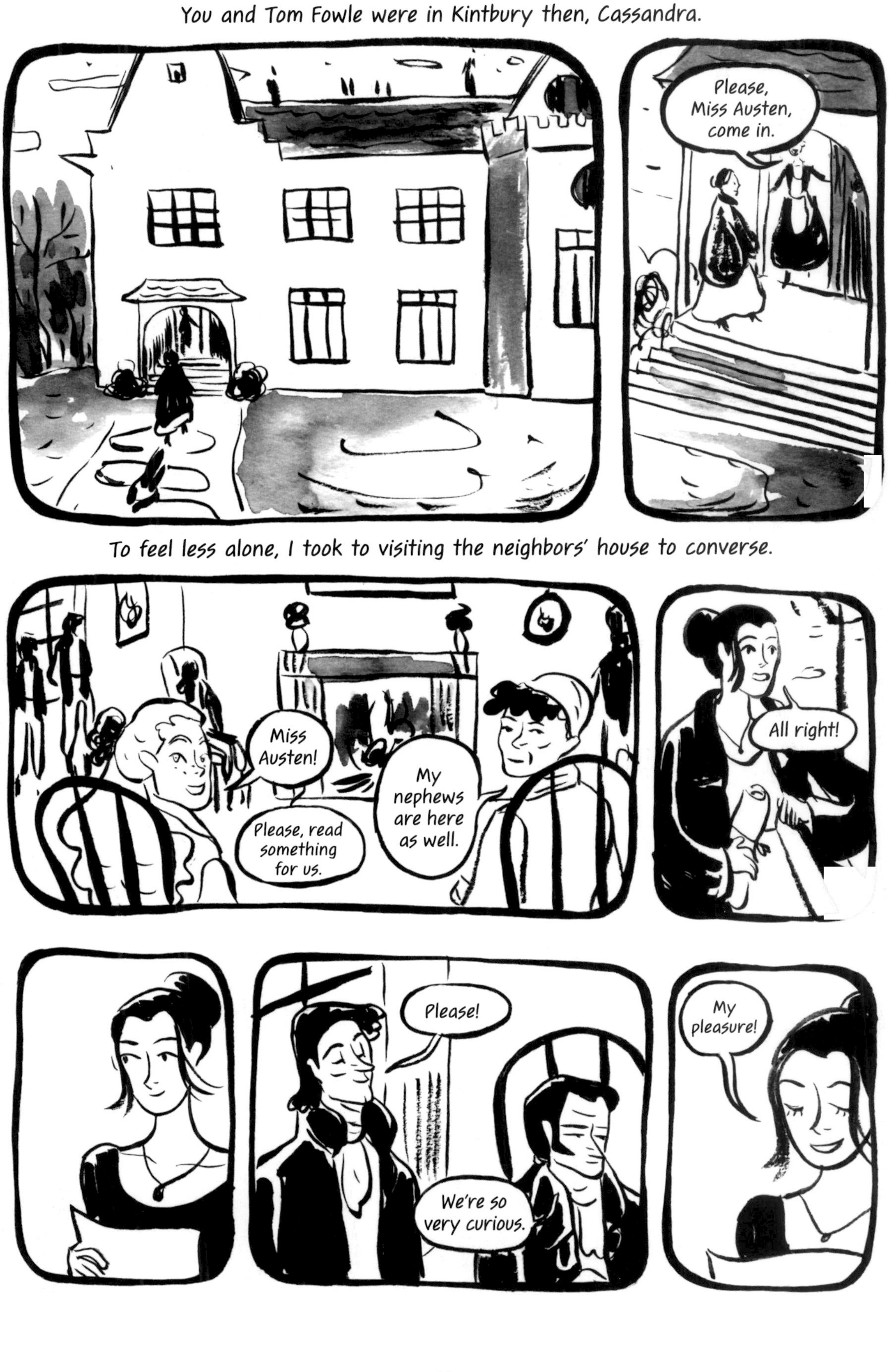
You and Tom Fowle were in Kintbury then, Cassandra.
Please, Miss Austen, come in.
To feel less alone, I took to visiting the neighbors' house to converse.
Miss Austen!
Please, read something for us.
My nephews are here as well.
All right!
Please!
We're so very curious.
My pleasure!

That day, I glimpsed a new face among the ones I already knew.

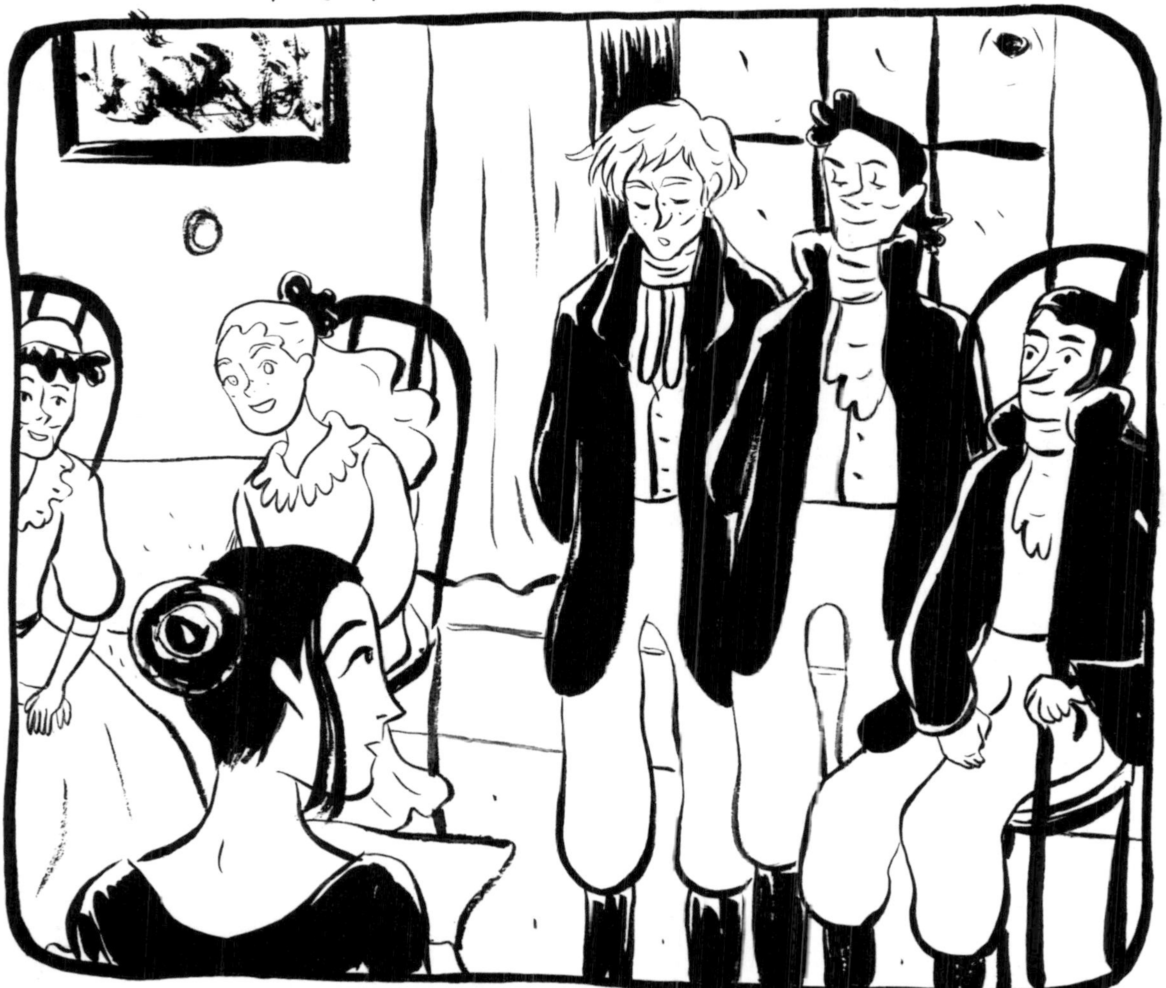

Who was the young man that didn't pay me any attention?

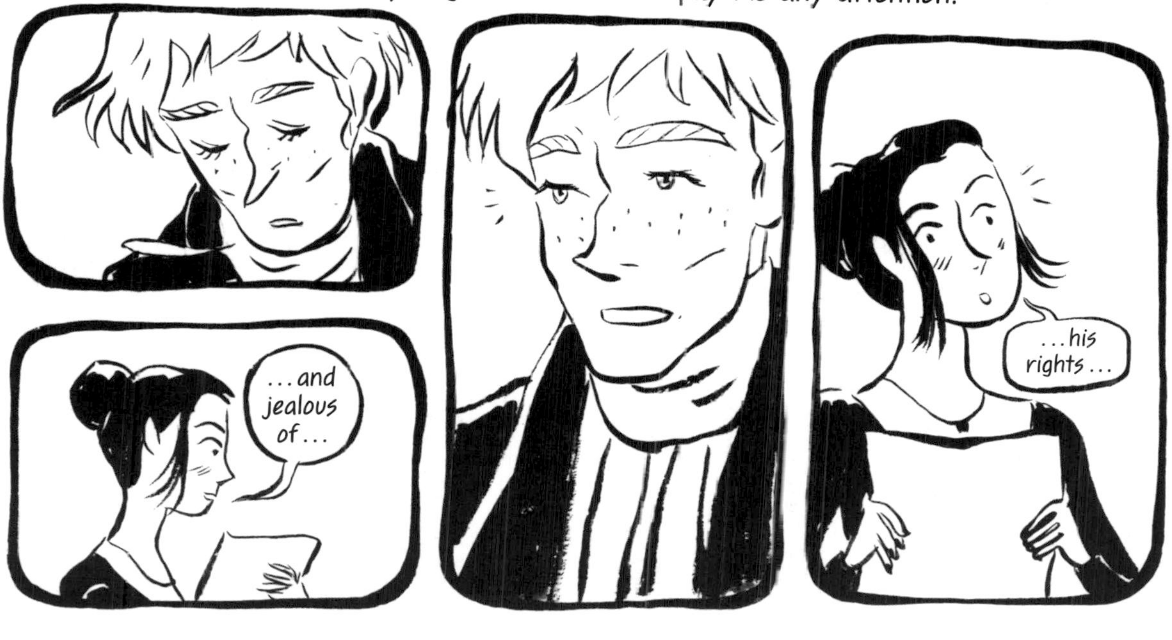
...his rights...
...and jealous of...

My wounded pride recovered when I looked at that smiling face.

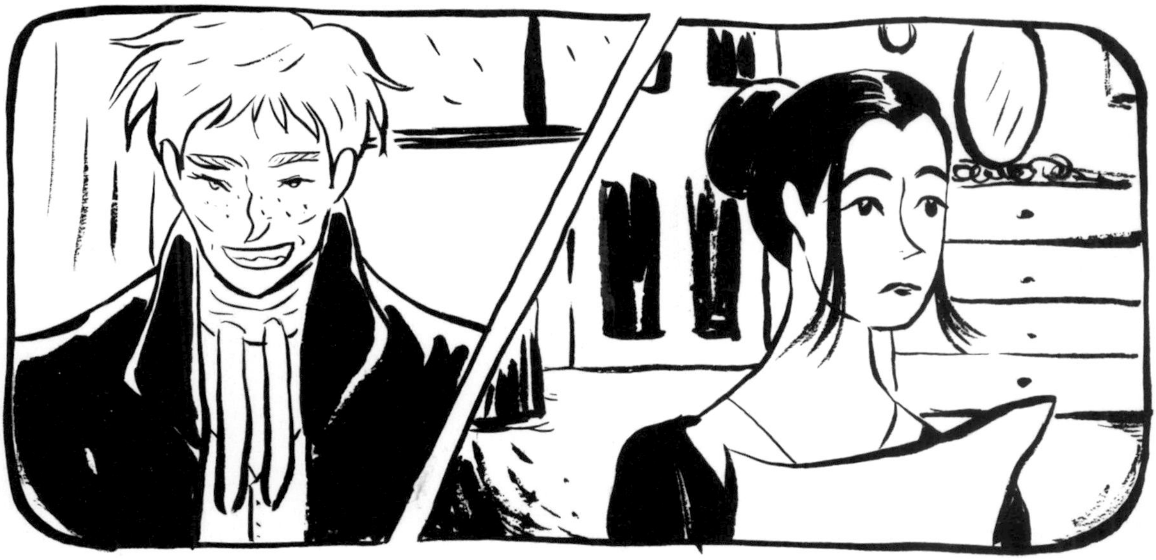

Why did I feel so strange?

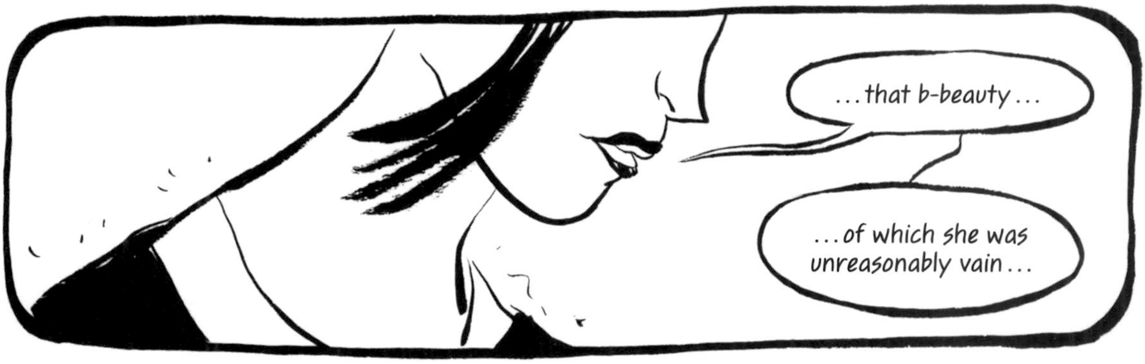
...that b-beauty...
...of which she was unreasonably vain...

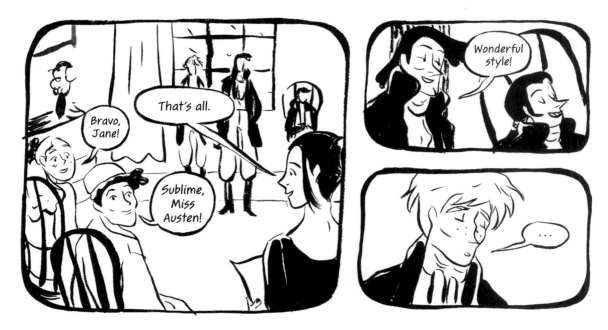

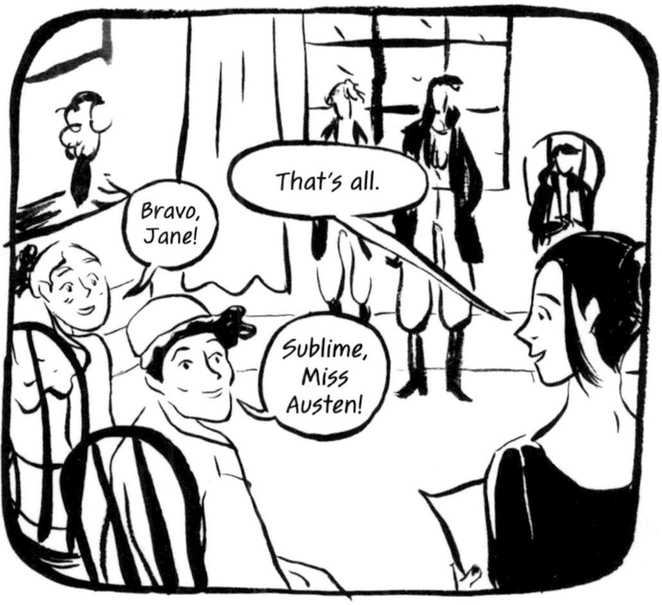
That's all.
Bravo, Jane!
Sublime, Miss Austen!

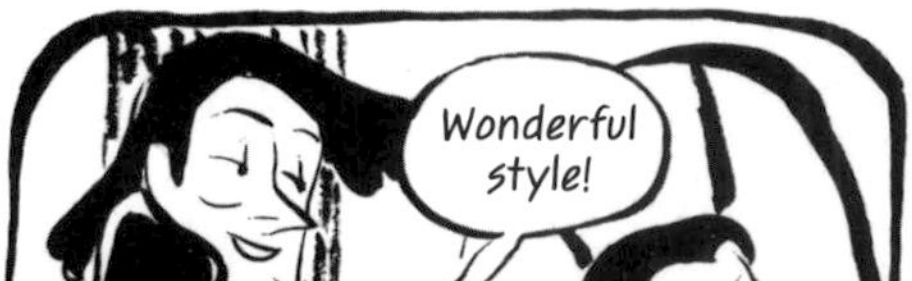
Wonderful style!

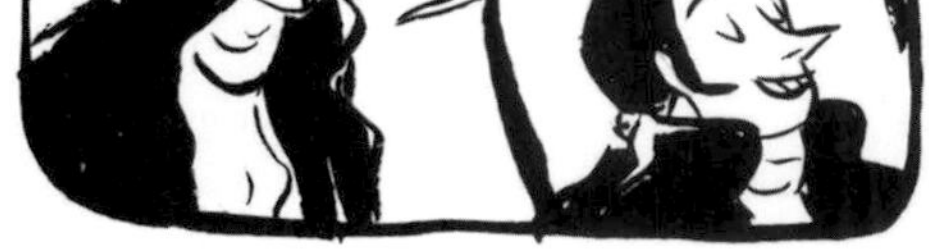
...

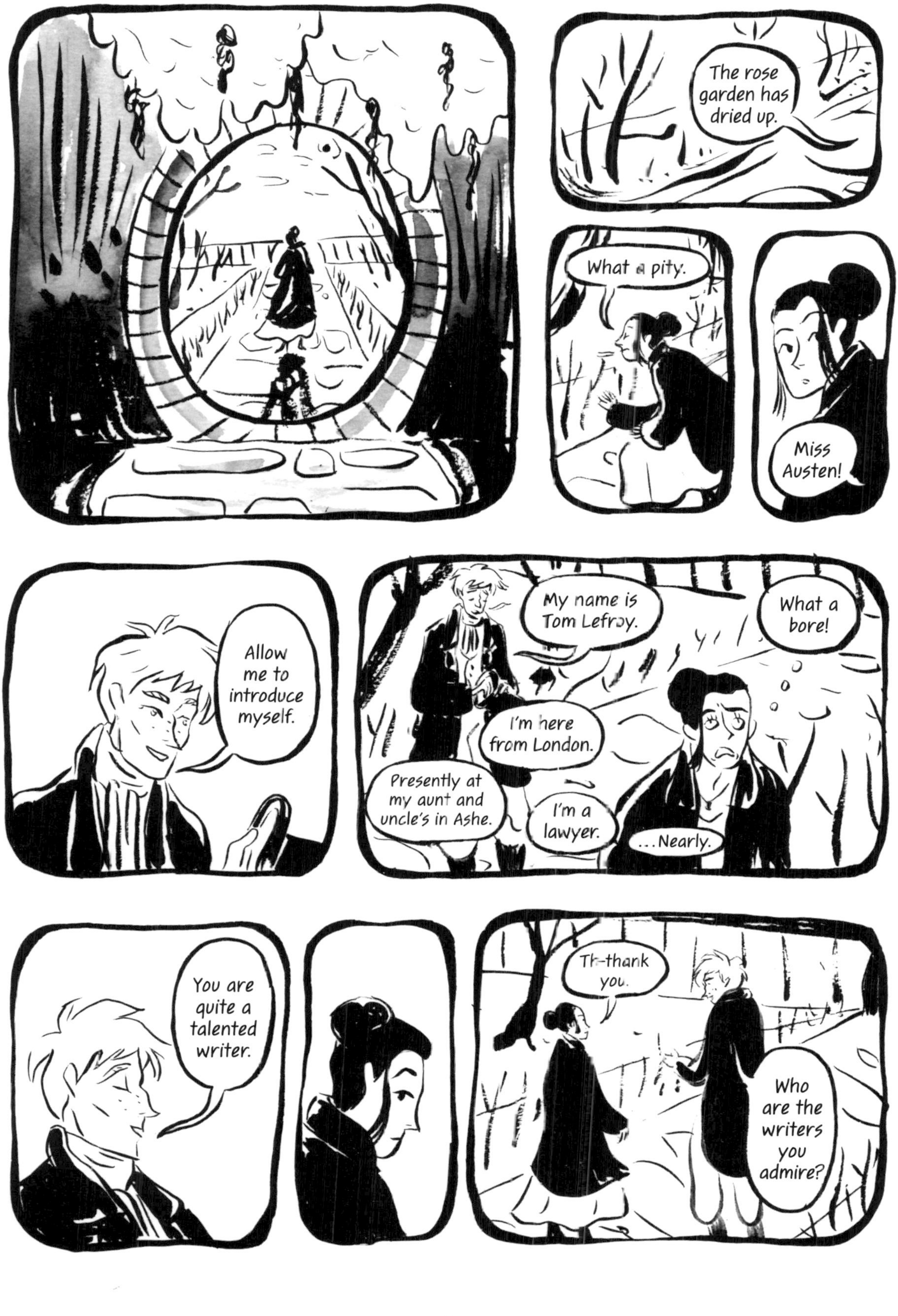

The rose garden has dried up.
What a pity.
Miss Austen!
Allow me to introduce myself.
My name is Tom Lefroy.
I'm here from London.
Presently at my aunt and uncle's in Ashe.
I'm a lawyer.
...Nearly.
What a bore!
You are quite a talented writer.
Th-thank you.
Who are the writers you admire?

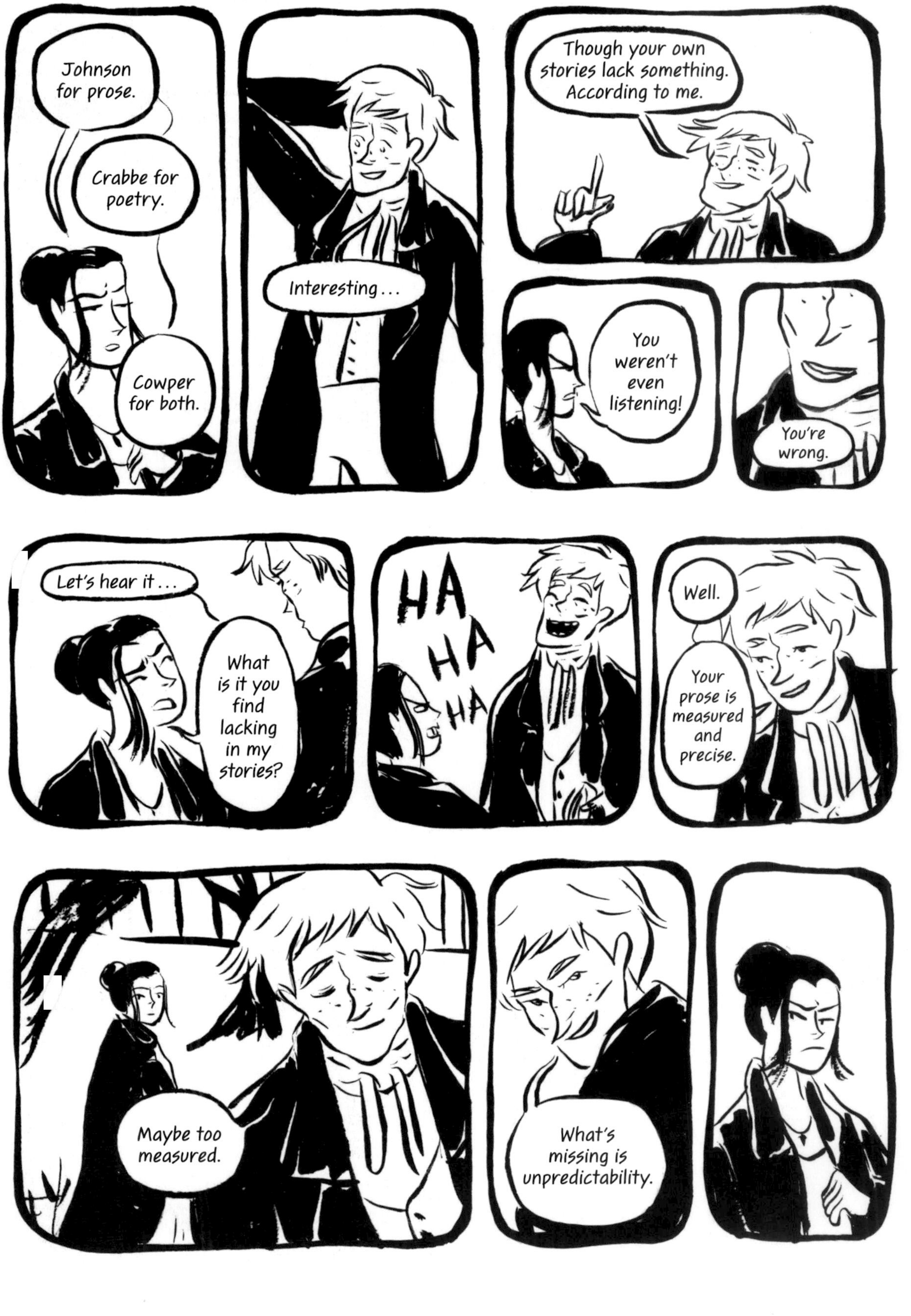
Johnson for prose.
Crabbe for poetry.
Cowper for both.
Interesting . . .
Though your own stories lack something. According to me.
You weren't even listening!
You're wrong.
Let's hear it . . .
What is it you find lacking in my stories?
HA HA HA
Well.
Your prose is measured and precise.
Maybe too measured.
What's missing is unpredictability.

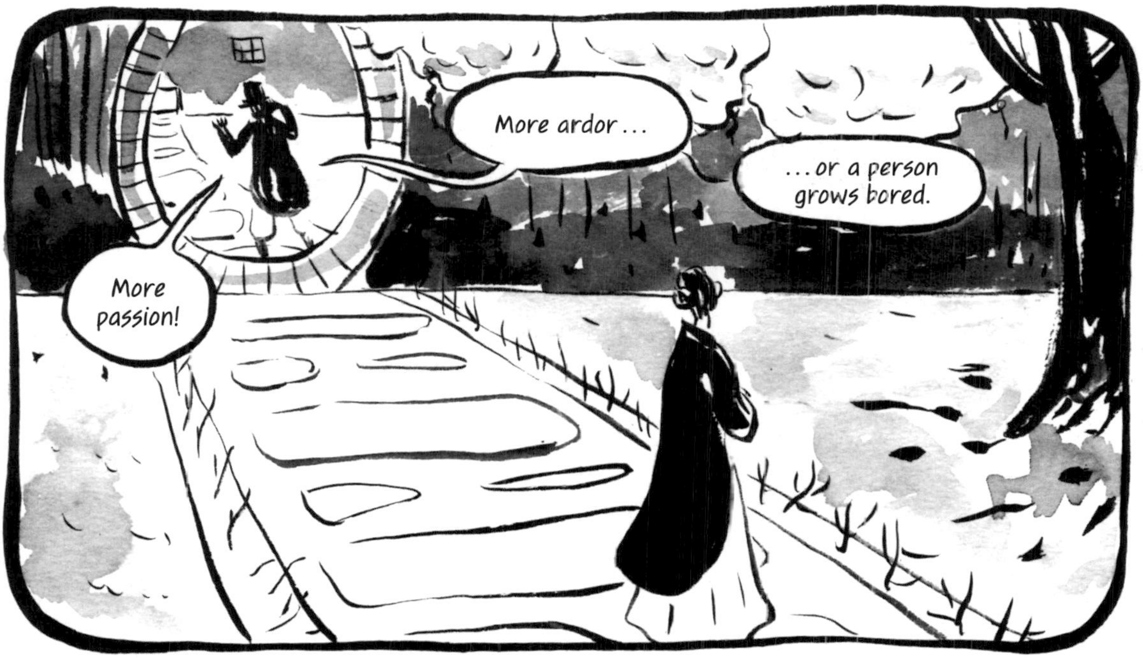
More passion!
More ardor . . .
. . . or a person grows bored.

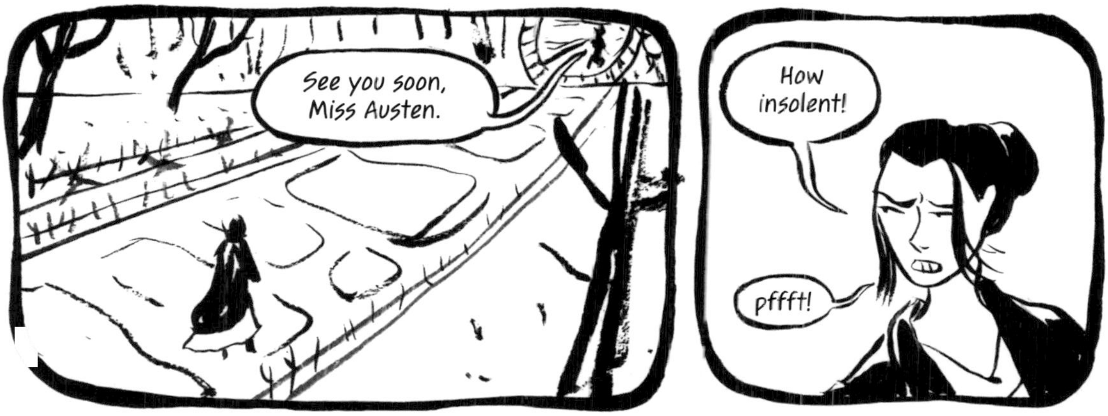
See you soon, Miss Austen.
How insolent!
pffft!

I returned home and sequestered myself in Father's office.

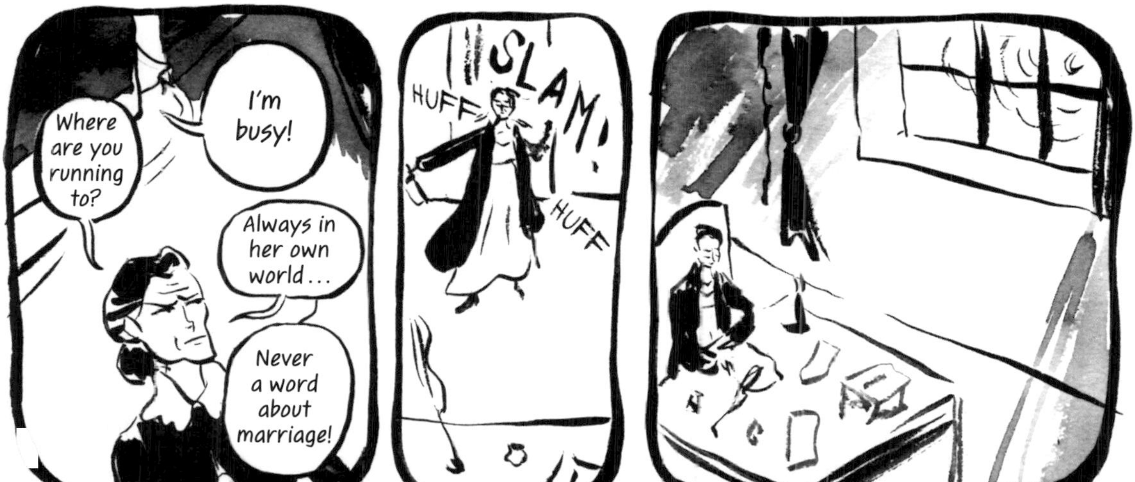
Where are you running to?
I'm busy!
Always in her own world . . .
Never a word about marriage!
HUFF
SLAM!
HUFF

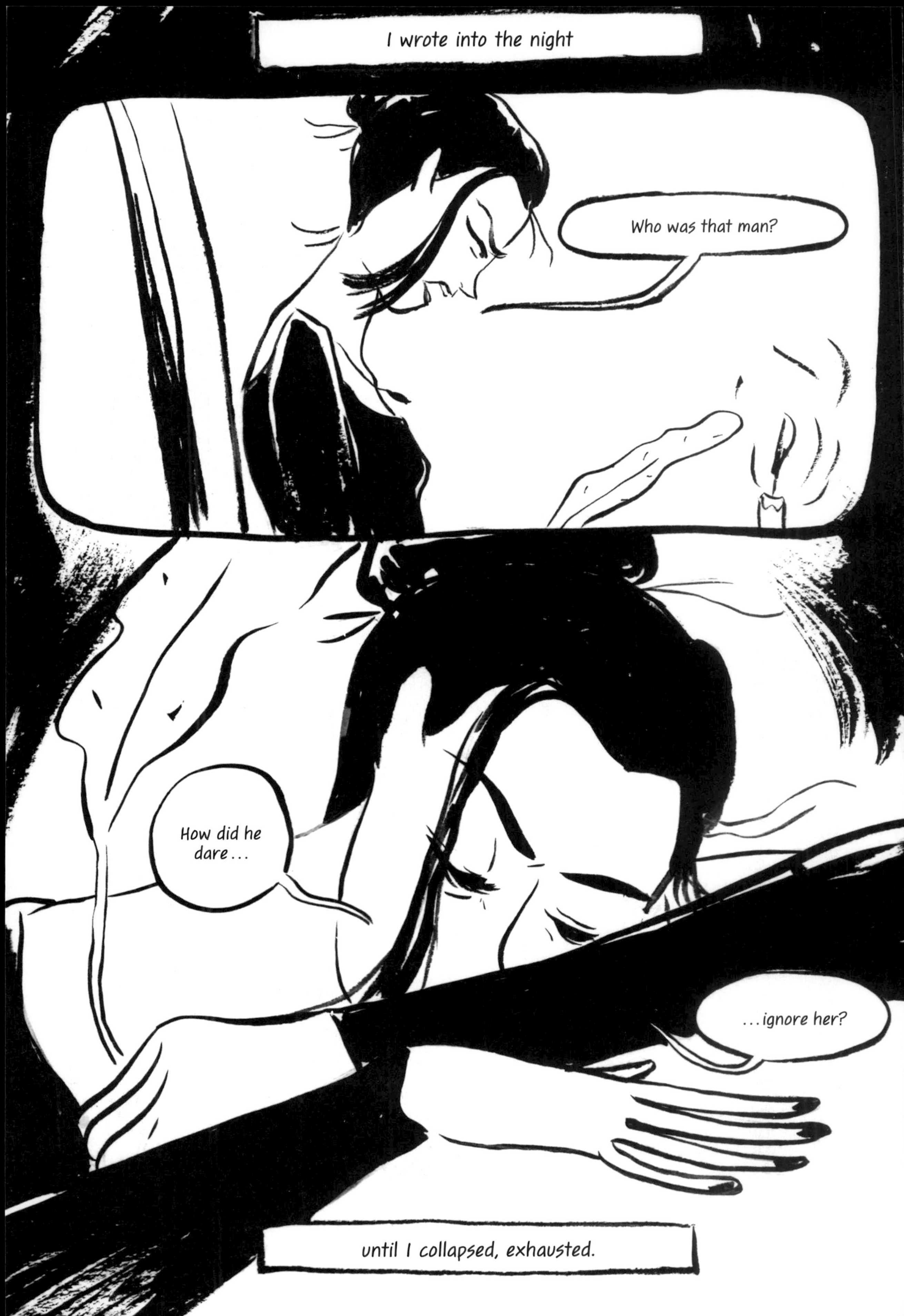
I wrote into the night
Who was that man?
How did he dare...
...ignore her?
until I collapsed, exhausted.

Christmas came and went quickly in our house.

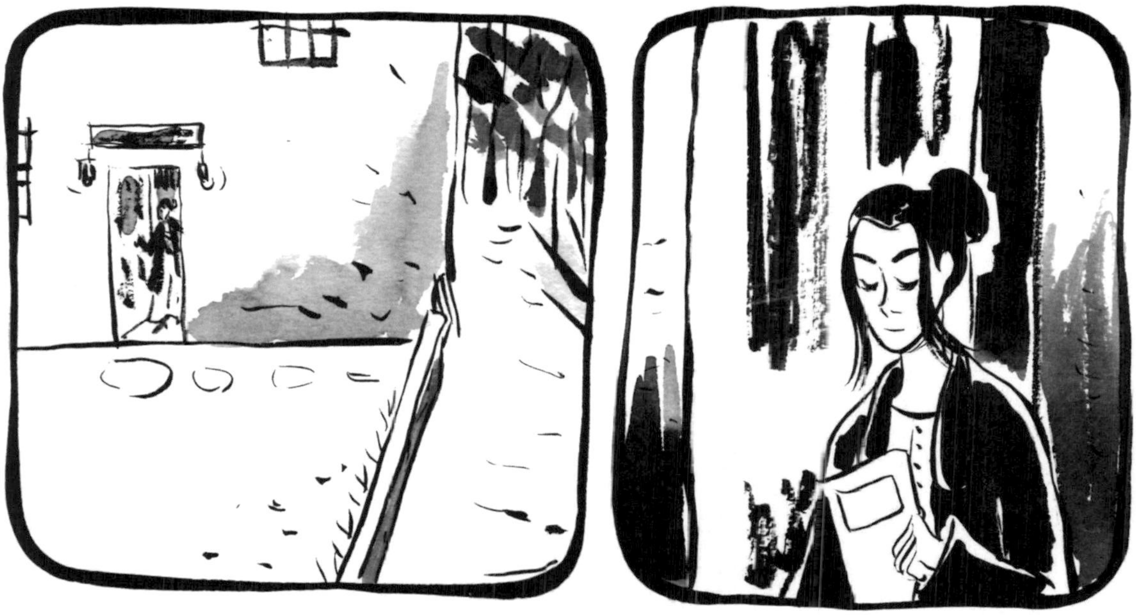

I felt restless, so I decided to go outside and read.

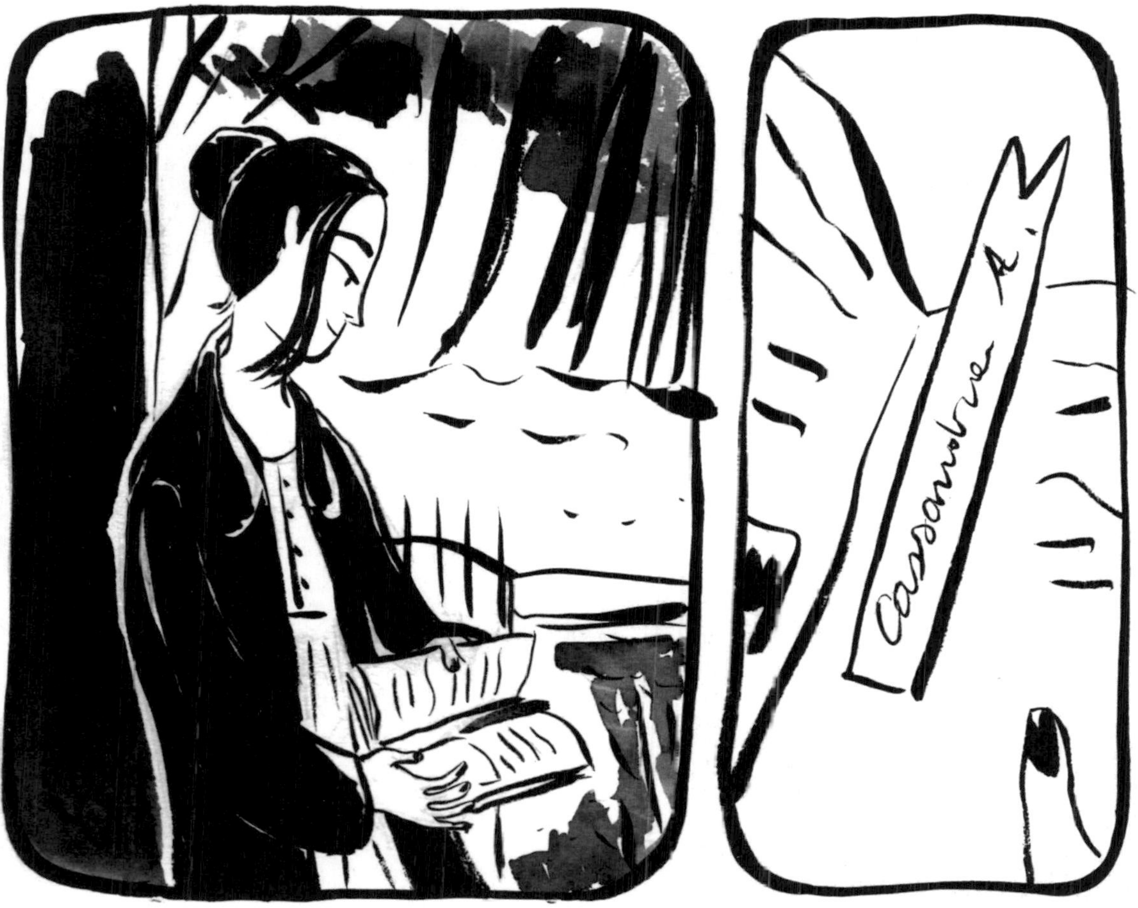
Cassandra A.

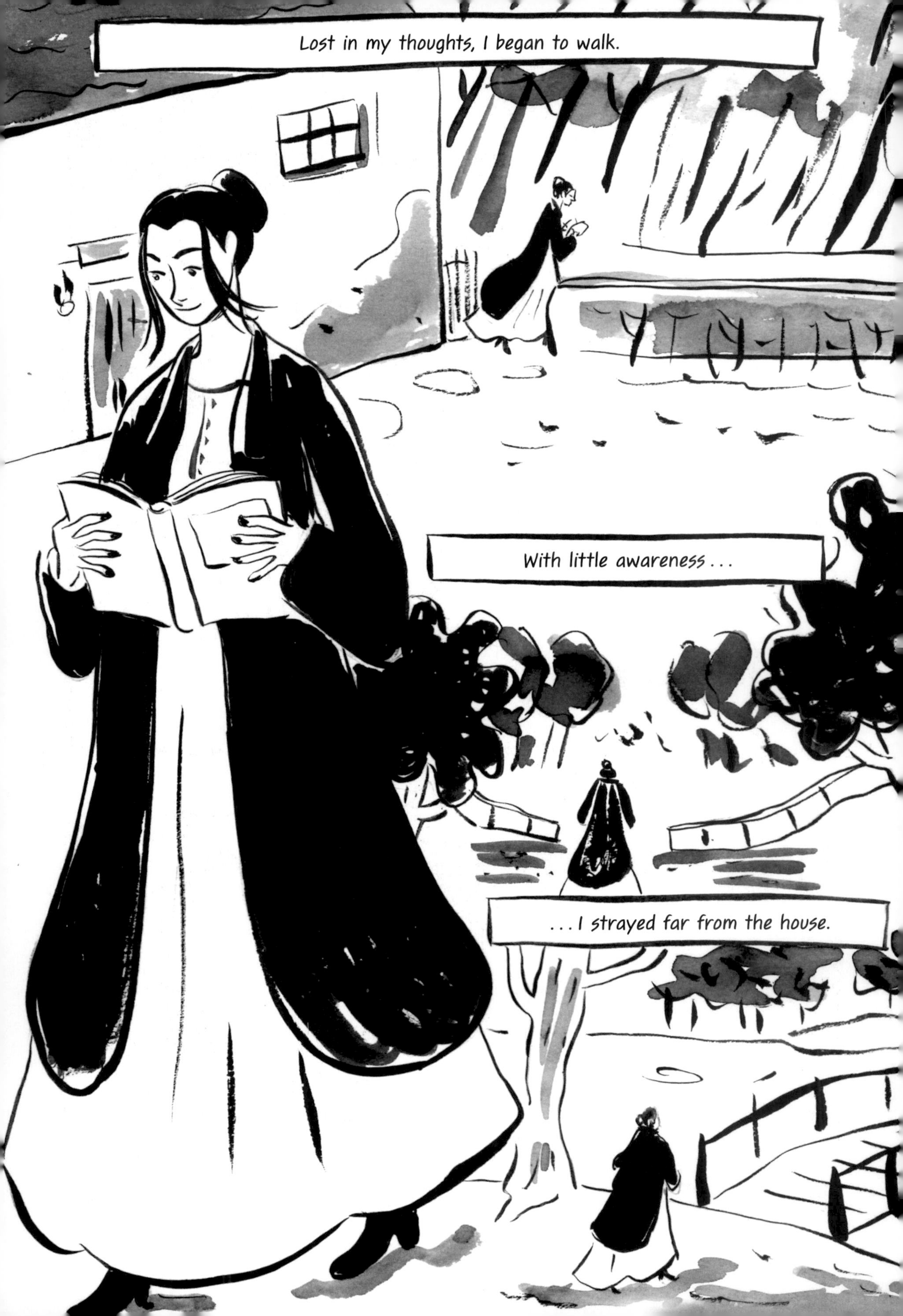
Lost in my thoughts, I began to walk.
With little awareness . . .
. . . I strayed far from the house.

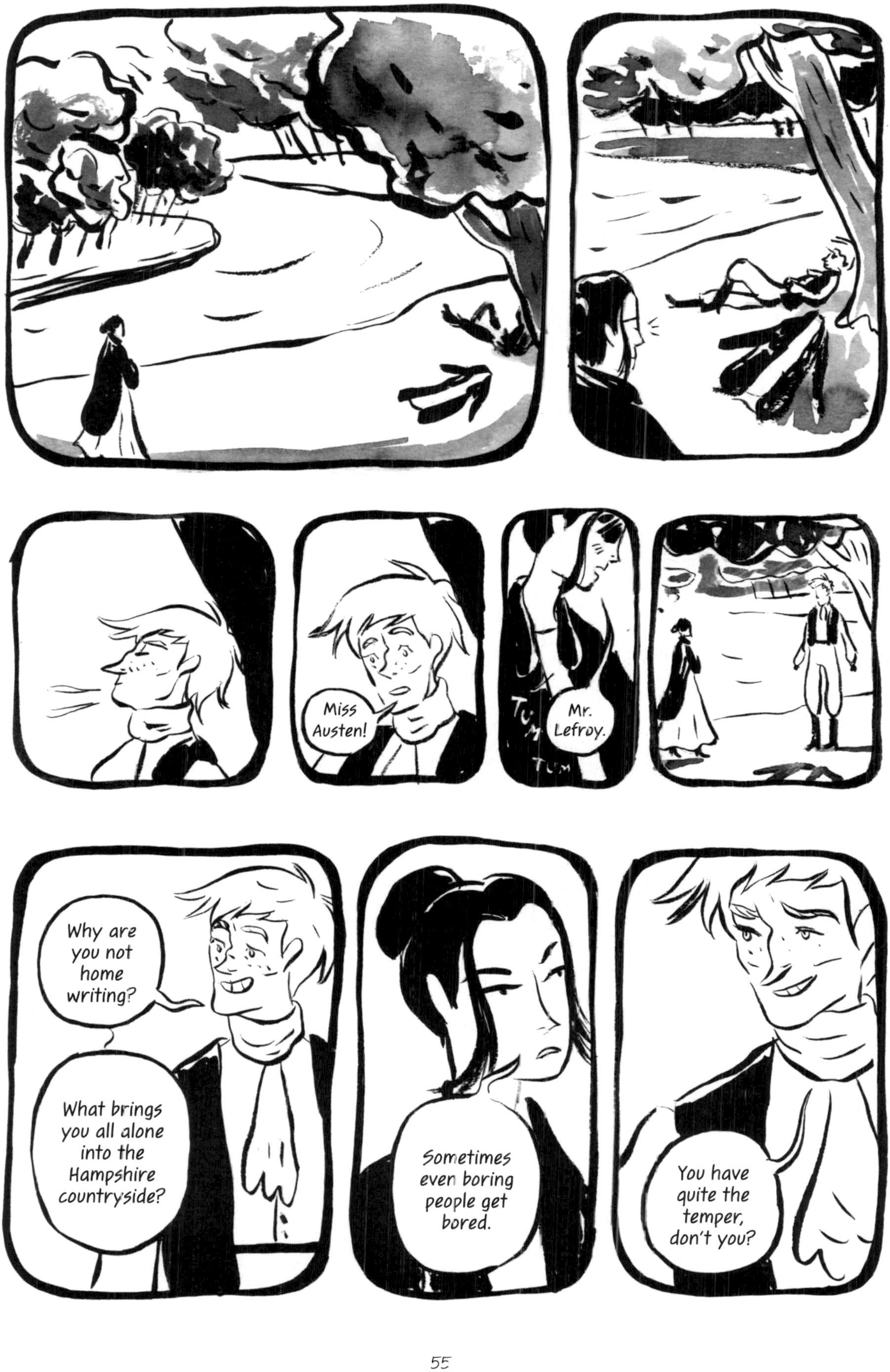
Miss Austen!
TUM TUM TUM
Mr. Lefroy.
Why are you not home writing?
What brings you all alone into the Hampshire countryside?
Sometimes even boring people get bored.
You have quite the temper, don't you?

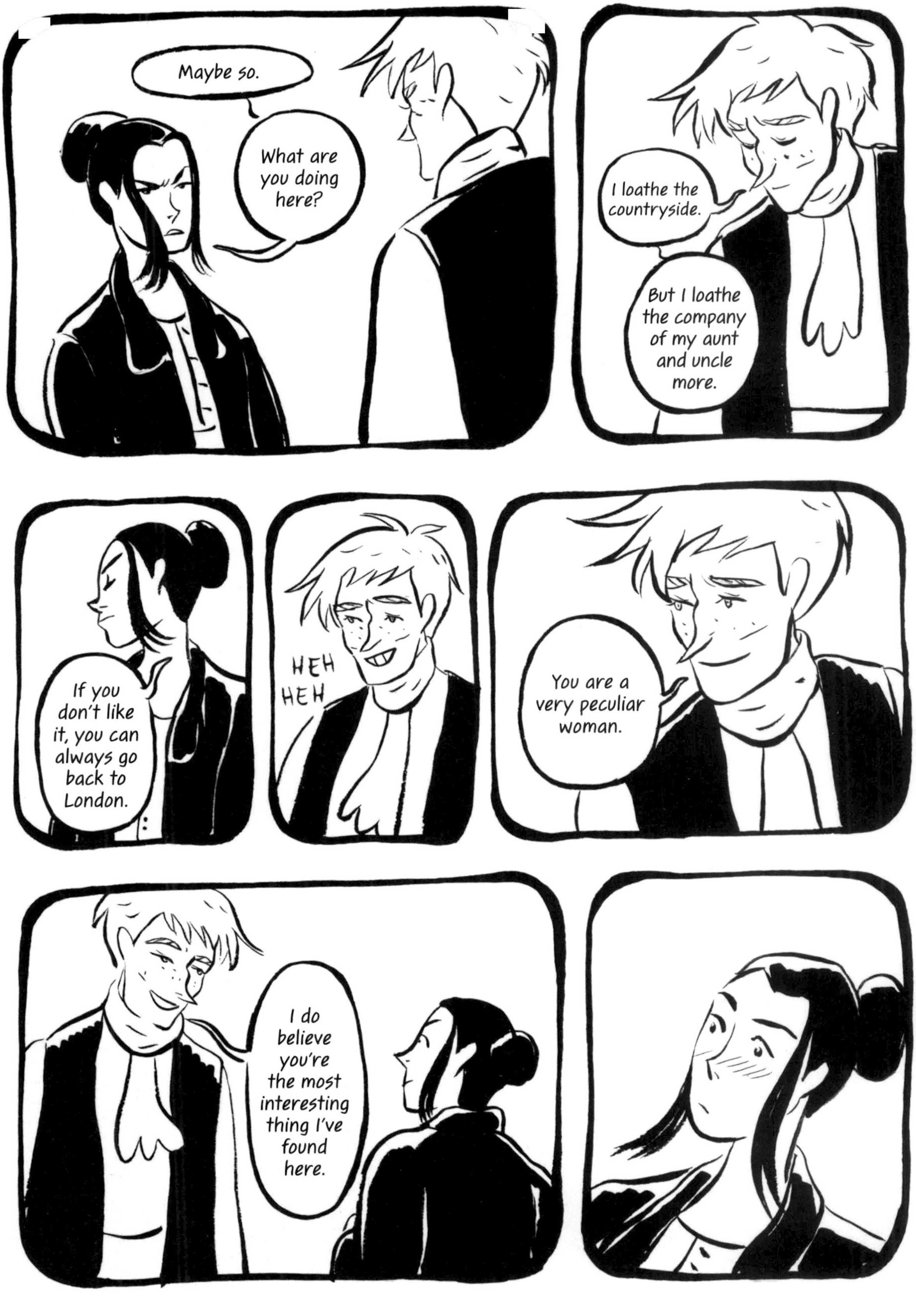
Maybe so.
What are you doing here?
I loathe the countryside.
But I loathe the company of my aunt and uncle more.
If you don't like it, you can always go back to London.
HEH HEH
You are a very peculiar woman.
I do believe you're the most interesting thing I've found here.

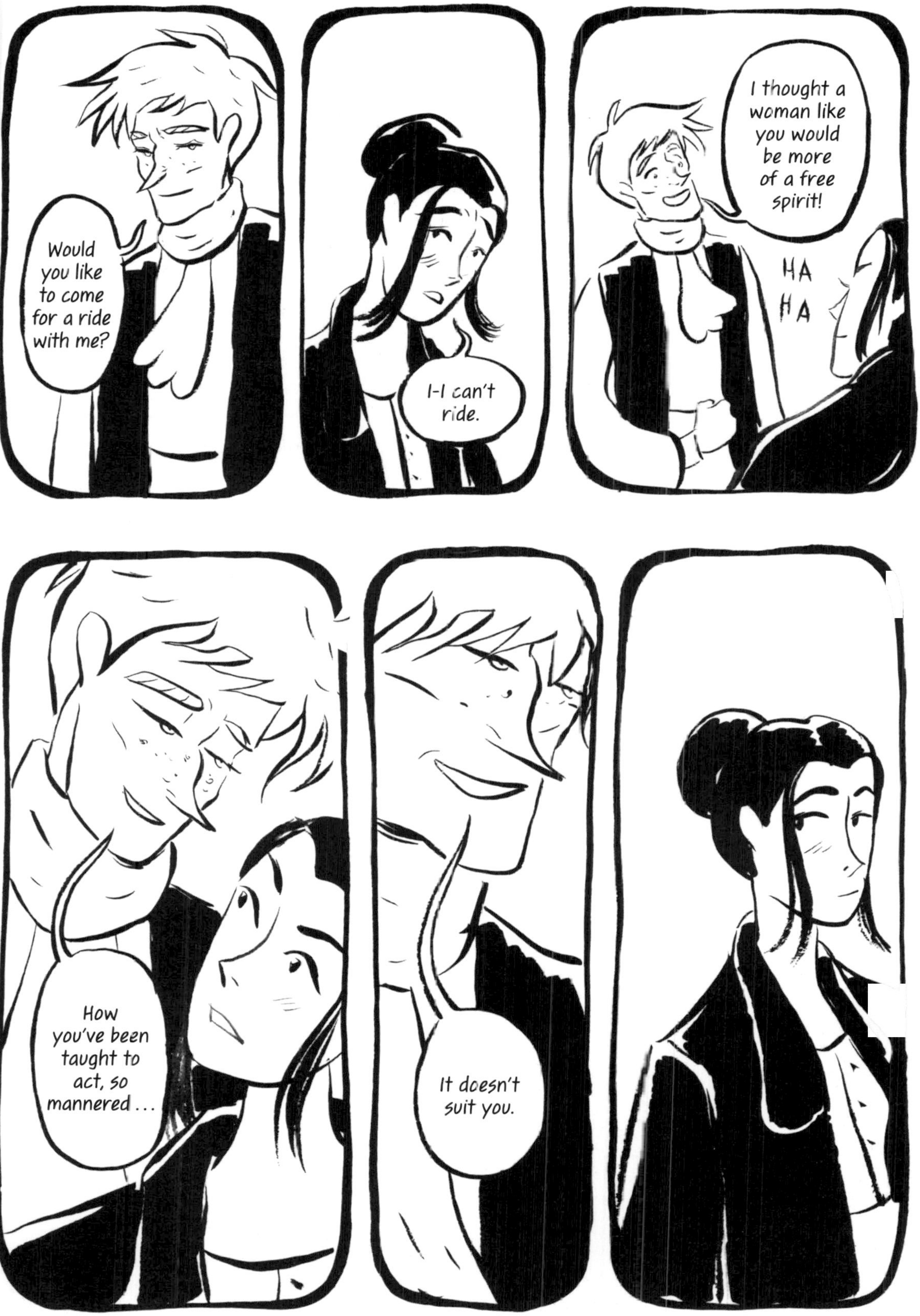
Would you like to come for a ride with me?
I-I can't ride.
I thought a woman like you would be more of a free spirit!
HA HA
How you've been taught to act, so mannered . . .
It doesn't suit you.

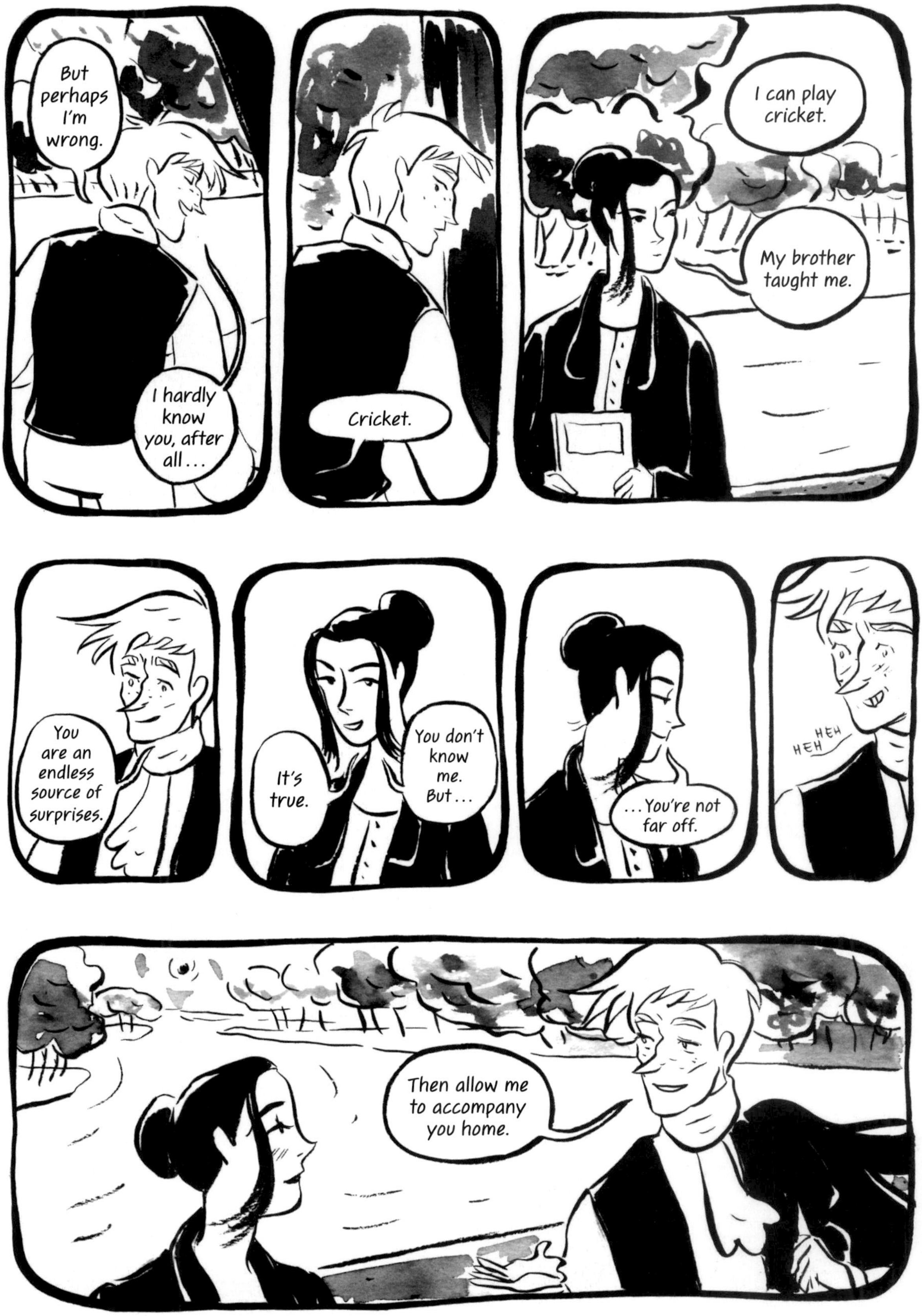
But perhaps I'm wrong.
I hardly know you, after all...
Cricket.
I can play cricket.
My brother taught me.
You are an endless source of surprises.
It's true.
You don't know me. But...
...You're not far off.
HEH HEH
Then allow me to accompany you home.

We started speaking almost frantically. In tune together.

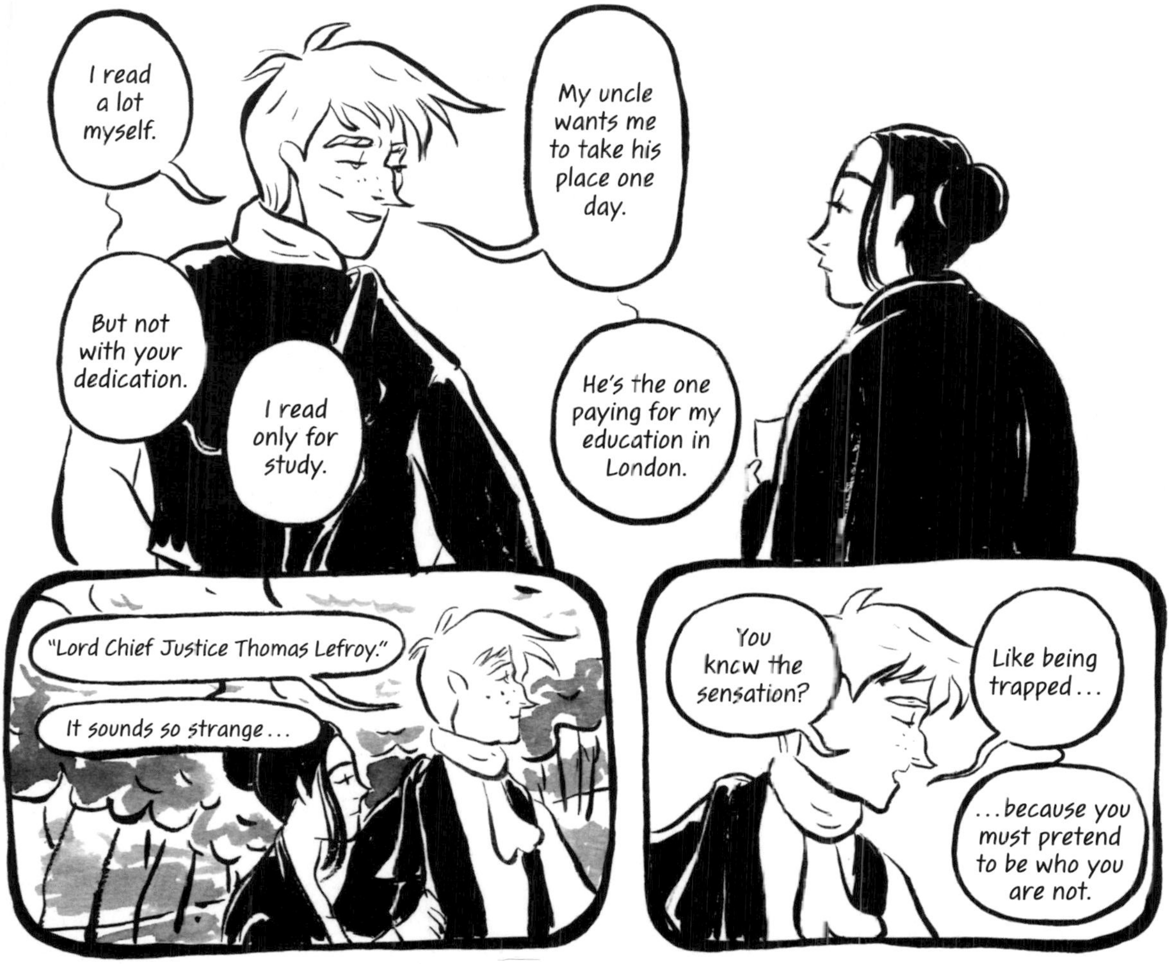

I read a lot myself.
But not with your dedication.
I read only for study.
My uncle wants me to take his place one day.
He's the one paying for my education in London.
"Lord Chief Justice Thomas Lefroy."
It sounds so strange...
You knew the sensation?
Like being trapped...
...because you must pretend to be who you are not.

Had my earliest impressions of him been wrong?

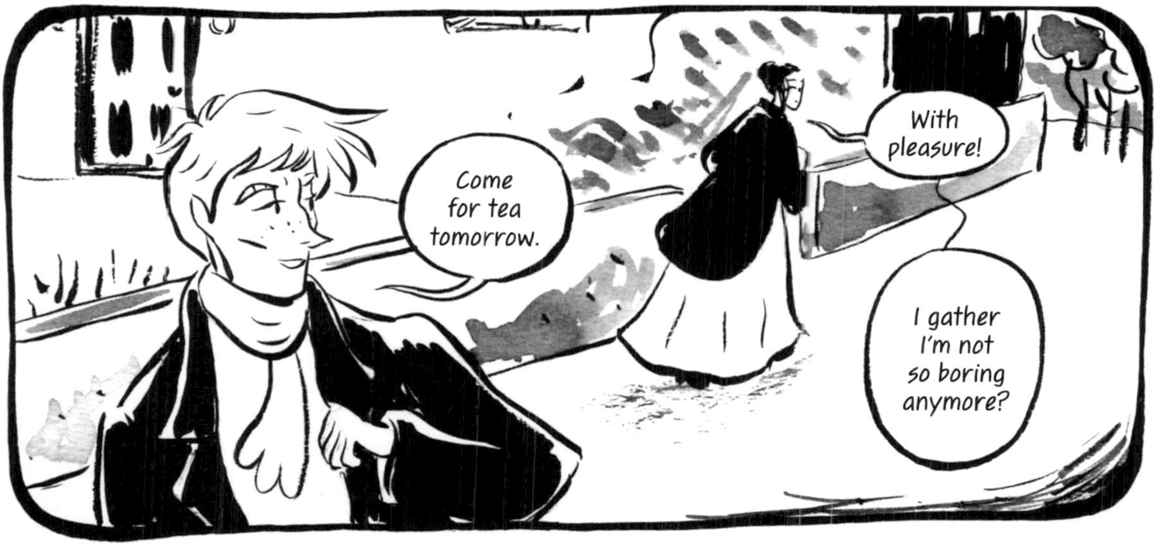

Come for tea tomorrow.
With pleasure!
I gather I'm not so boring anymore?

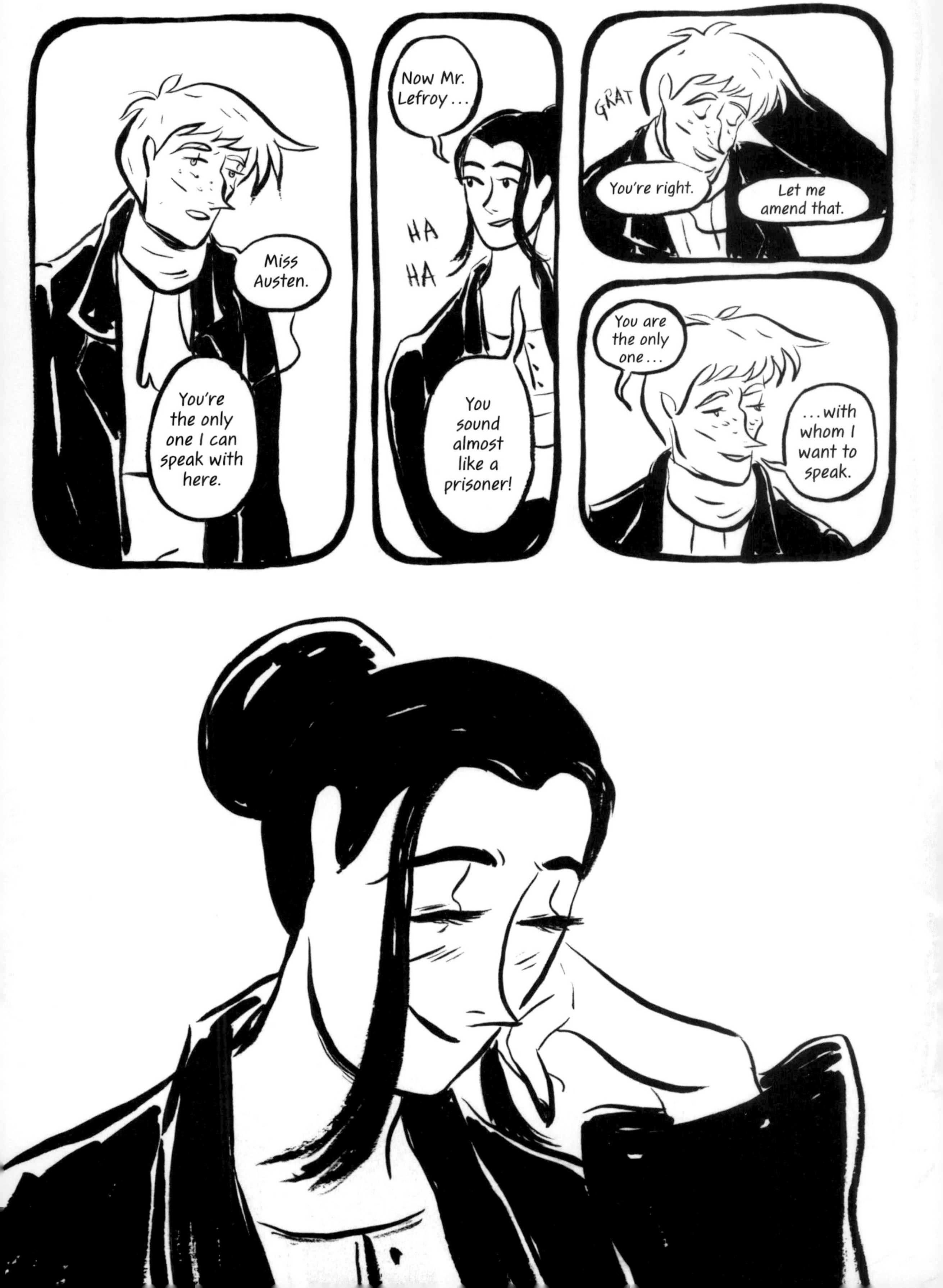
Miss Austen.
You're the only one I can speak with here.
Now Mr. Lefroy...
HA HA
You sound almost like a prisoner!
GRAT
You're right.
Let me amend that.
You are the only one...
...with whom I want to speak.

Soon thoughts of Tom became very persistent in my mind.

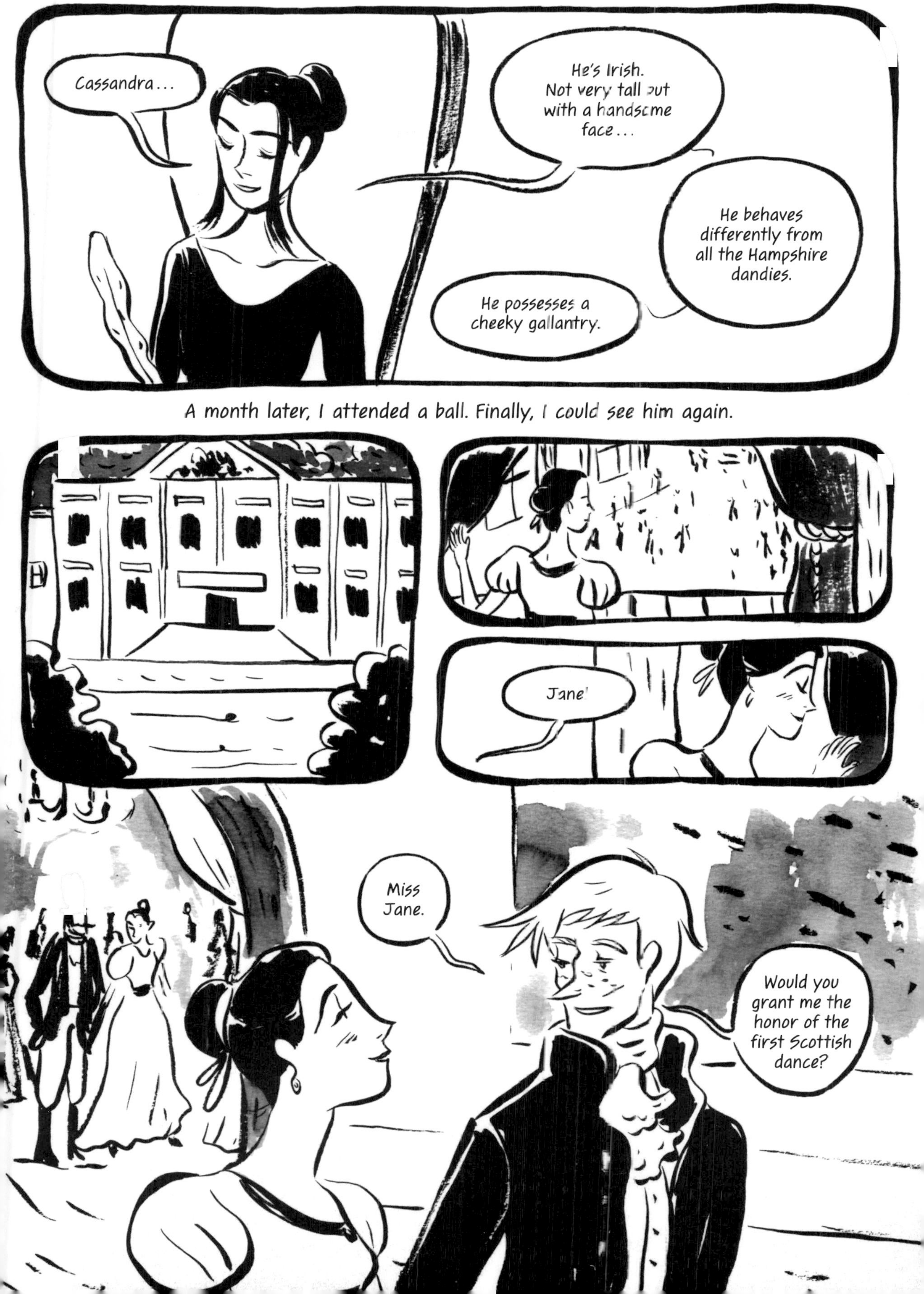
Cassandra...
He's Irish. Not very tall but with a handsome face...
He behaves differently from all the Hampshire dandies.
He possesses a cheeky gallantry.
A month later, I attended a ball. Finally, I could see him again.
Jane!
Miss Jane.
Would you grant me the honor of the first Scottish dance?

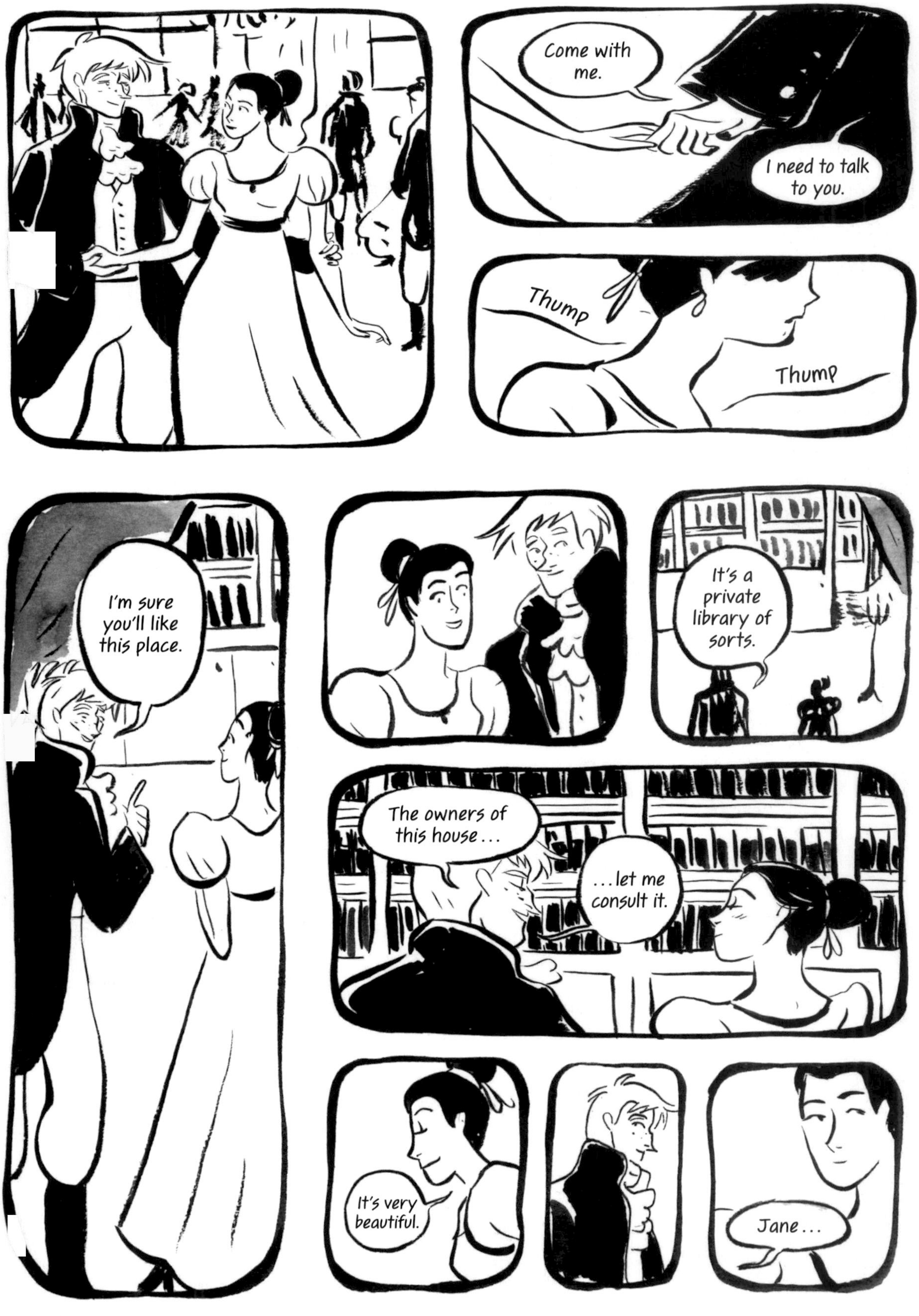
Come with me.
I need to talk to you.
Thump
Thump
I'm sure you'll like this place.
It's a private library of sorts.
The owners of this house...
...let me consult it.
It's very beautiful.
Jane...

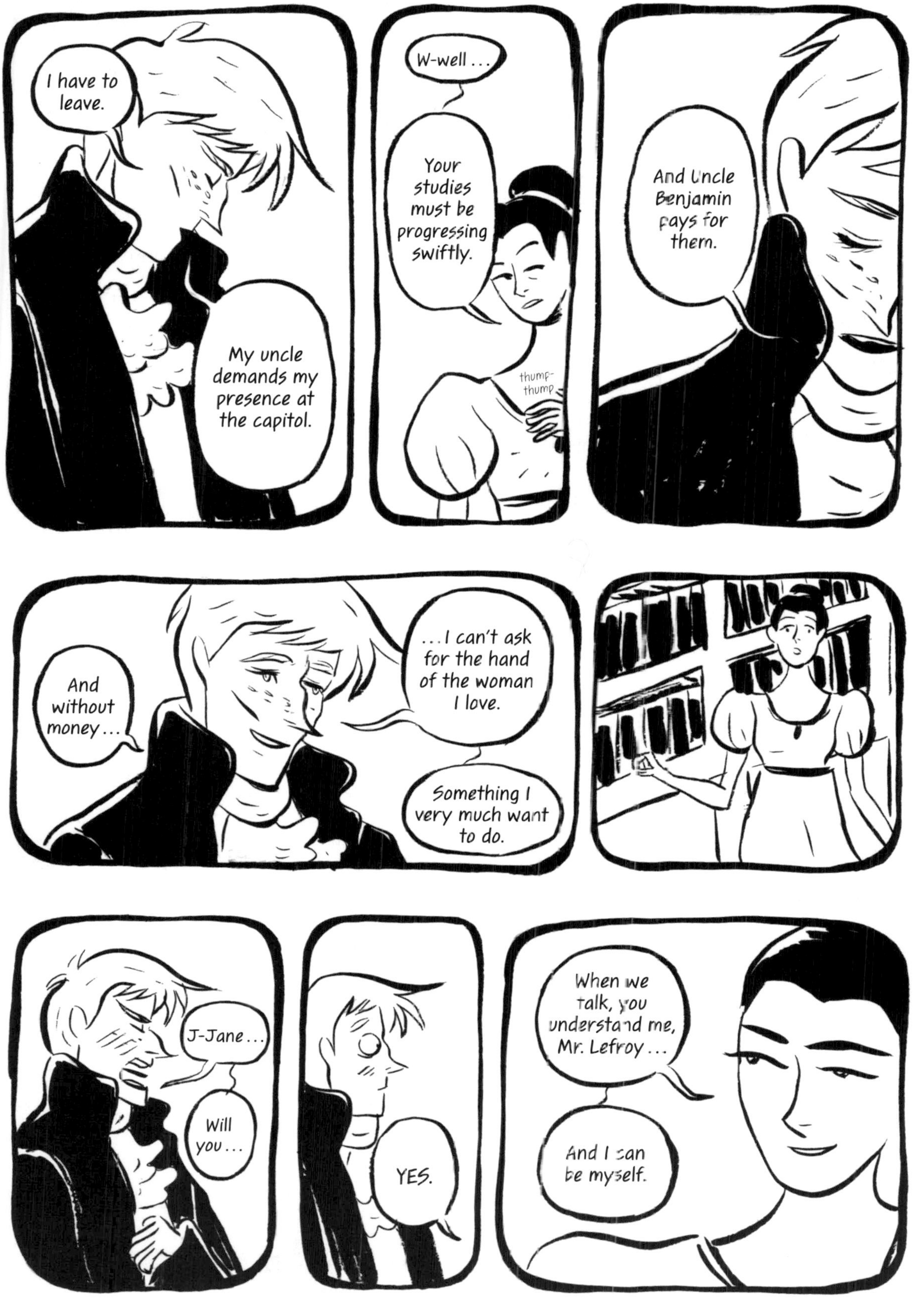
I have to leave.
My uncle demands my presence at the capitol.
W-well . . .
Your studies must be progressing swiftly.
thump-thump
And Uncle Benjamin pays for them.
And without money . . .
. . . I can't ask for the hand of the woman I love.
Something I very much want to do.
J-Jane . . .
Will you . . .
YES.
When we talk, you understand me, Mr. Lefroy . . .
And I can be myself.

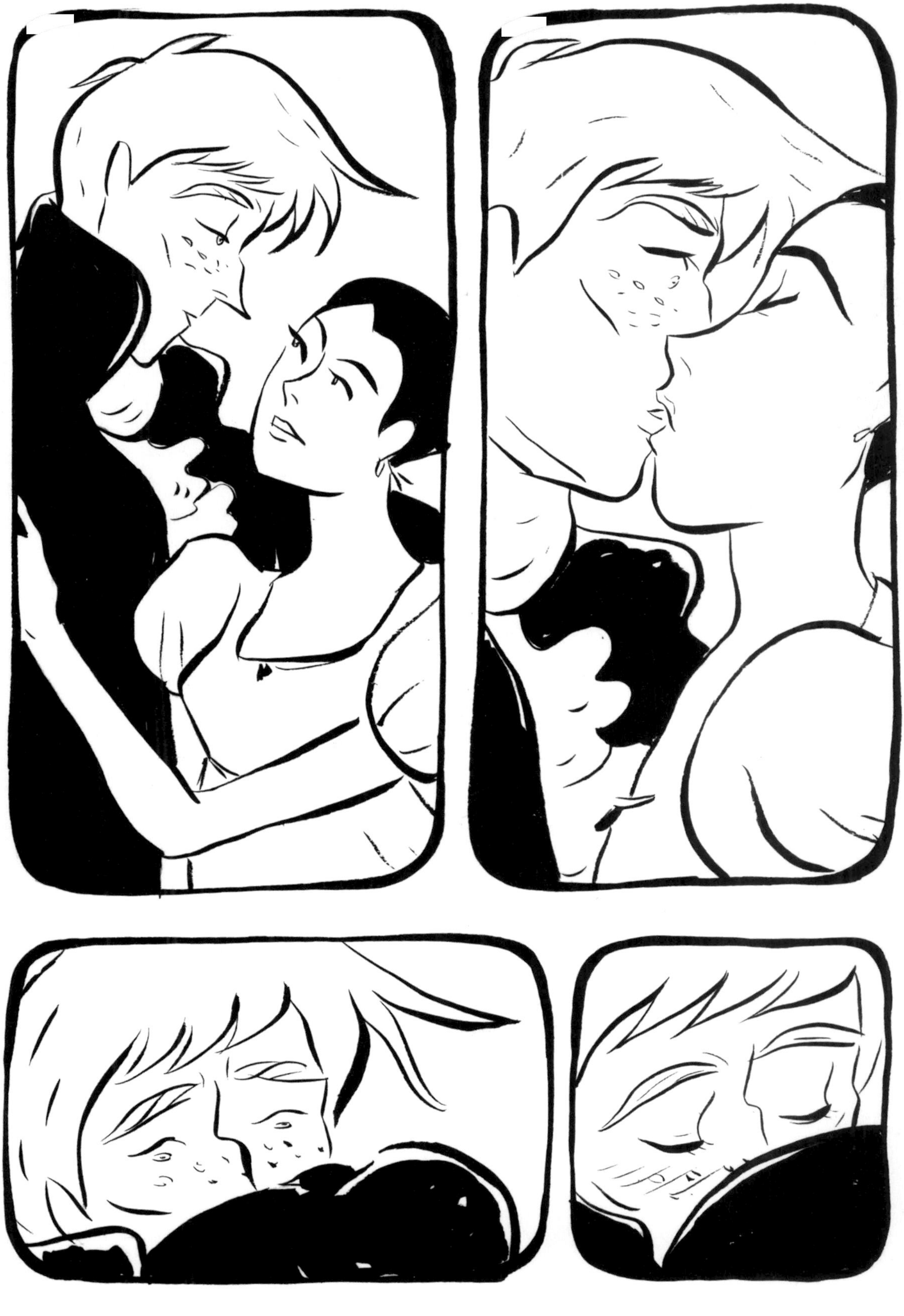

We spent the whole night in that room, far from everything and everyone.

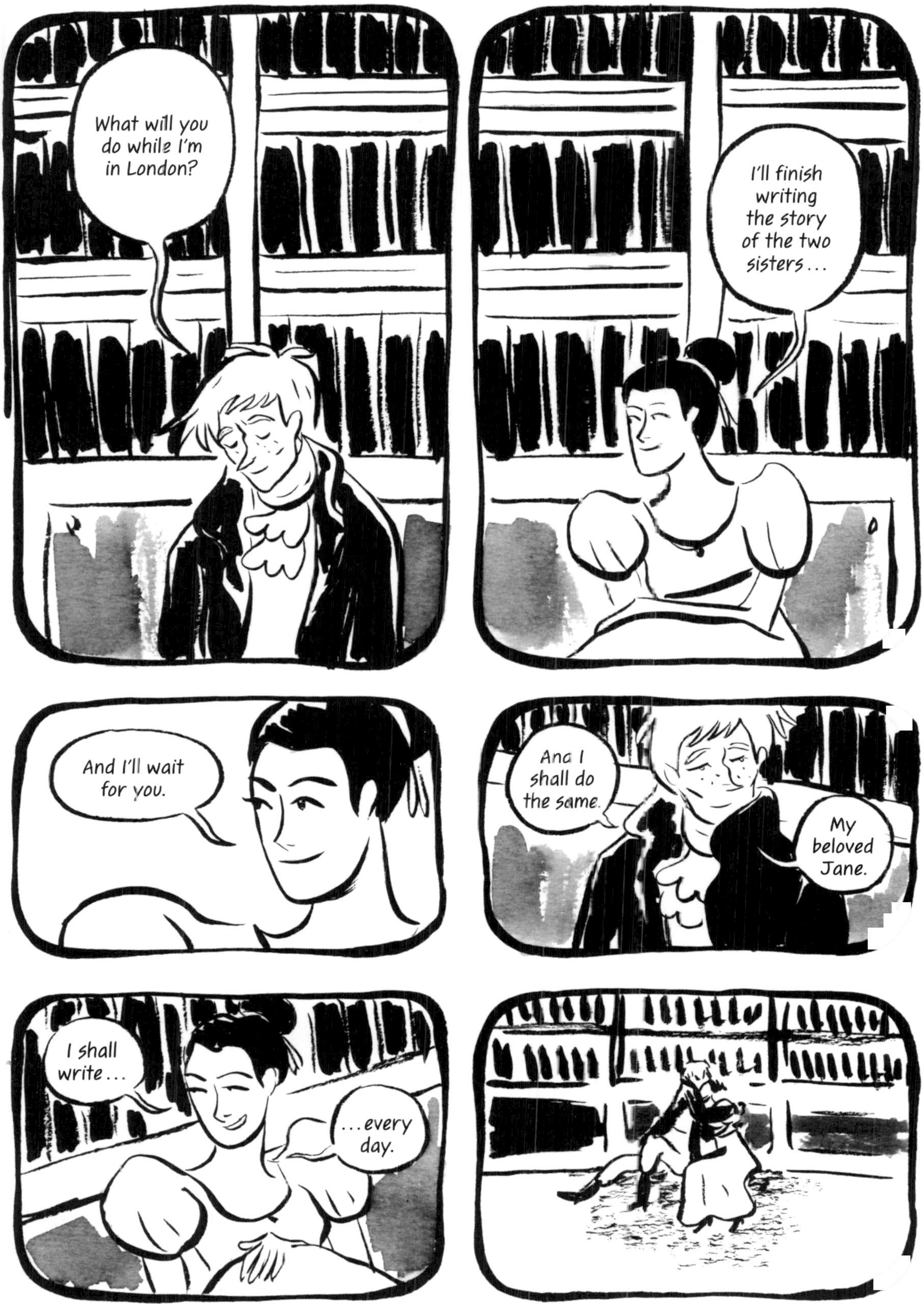

What will you do while I'm in London?
I'll finish writing the story of the two sisters...
And I'll wait for you.
And I shall do the same.
My beloved Jane.
I shall write...
...every day.

We wrote each other seventy-six letters in six months.

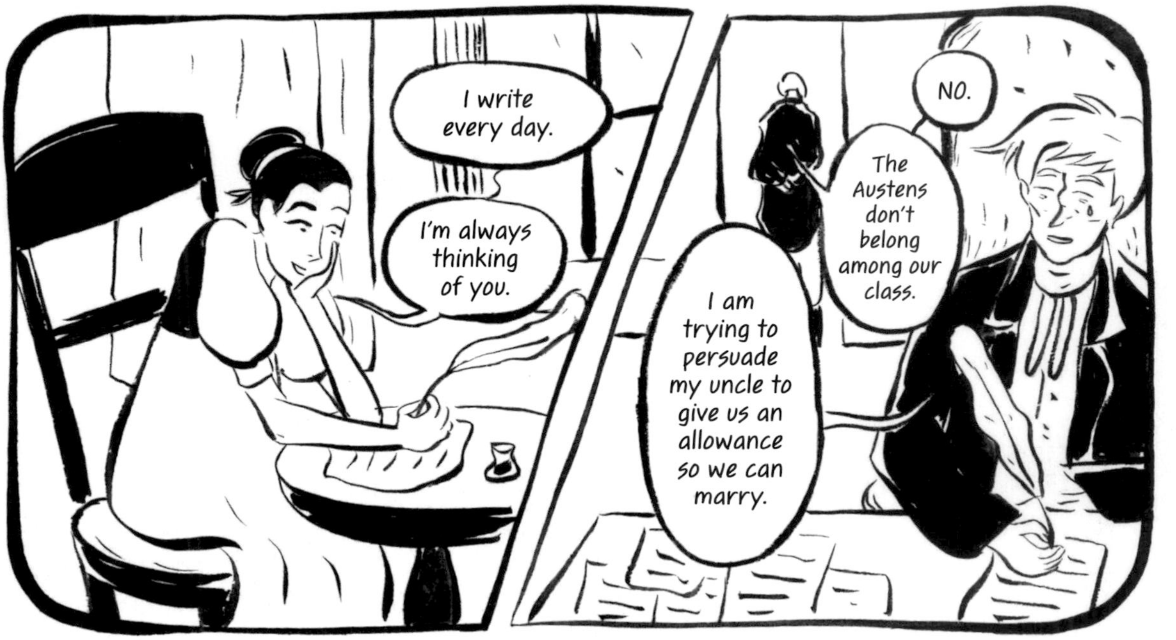
I write every day.
I'm always thinking of you.
NO.
The Austens don't belong among our class.
I am trying to persuade my uncle to give us an allowance so we can marry.

But with the passing of time . . .

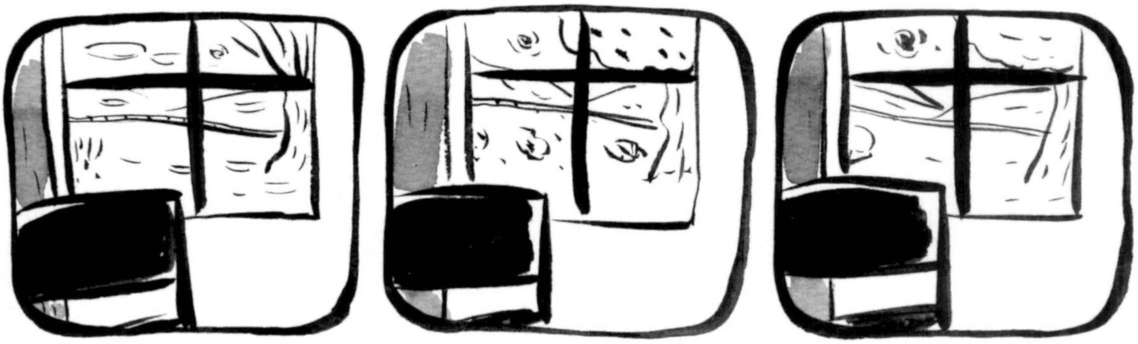

. . . Tom became more and more obscure to me.

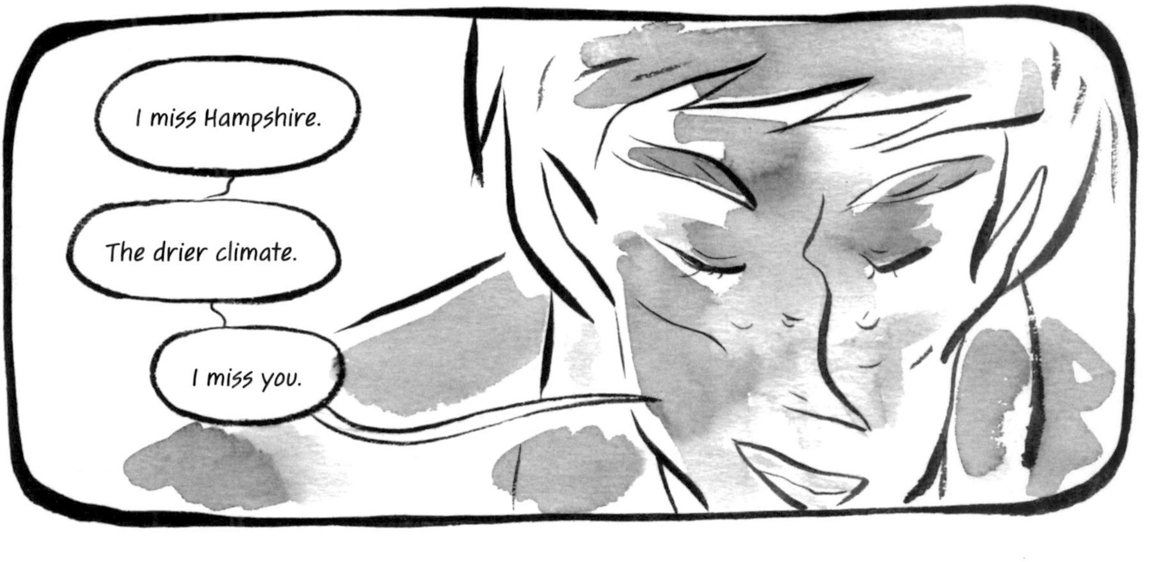
I miss Hampshire.
The drier climate.
I miss you.

One morning, I woke up and I couldn't remember his face.

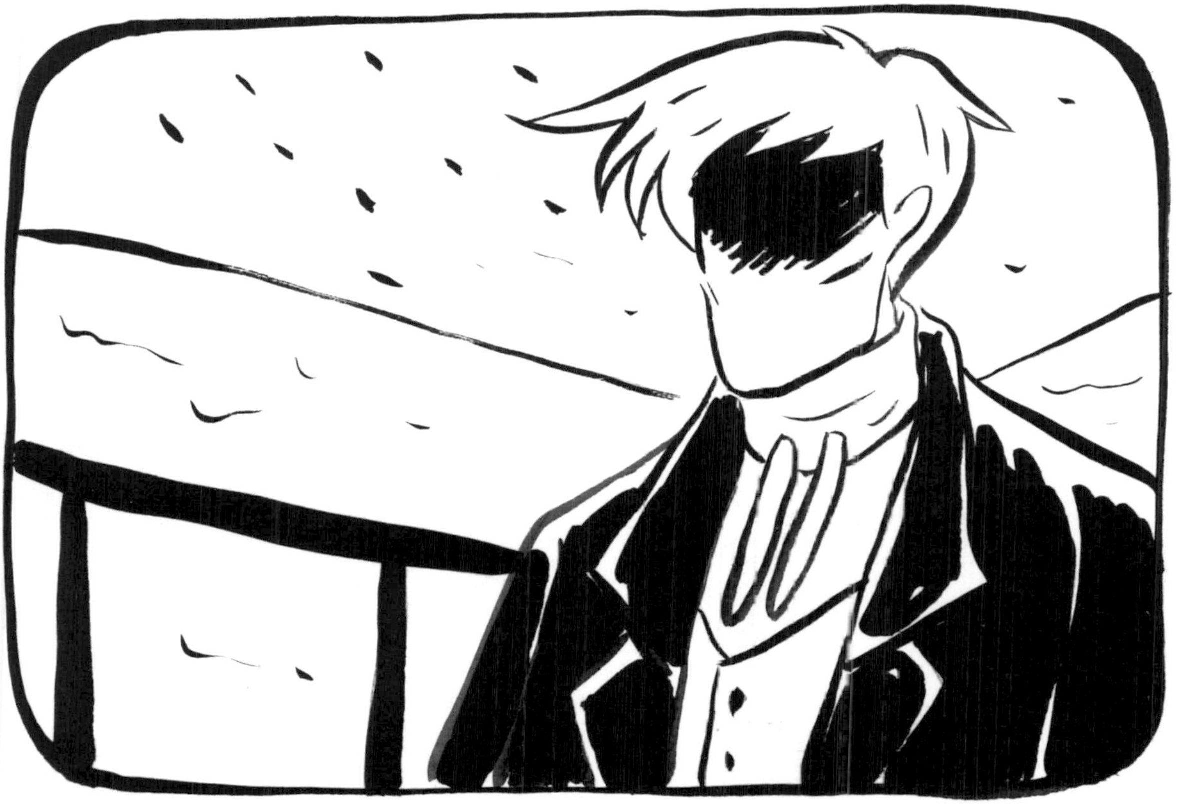

I found myself confusing it with other faces.

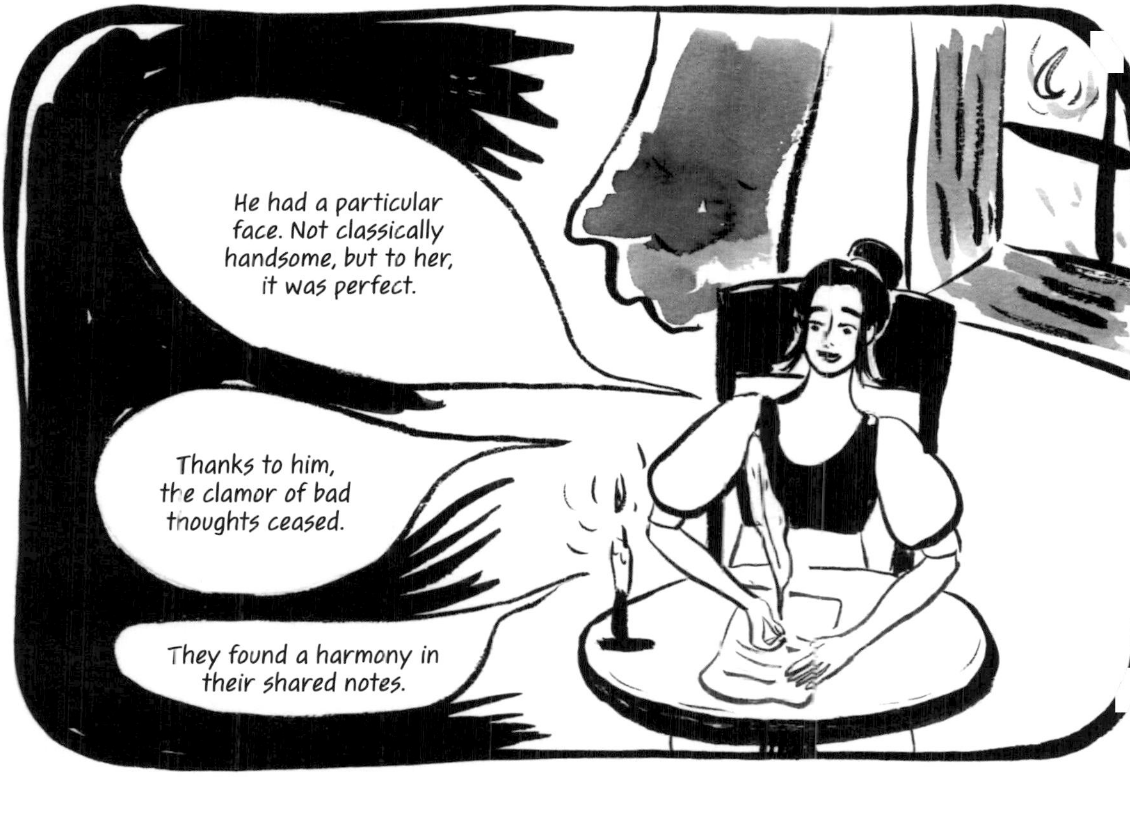
He had a particular face. Not classically handsome, but to her, it was perfect.
Thanks to him, the clamor of bad thoughts ceased.
They found a harmony in their shared notes.

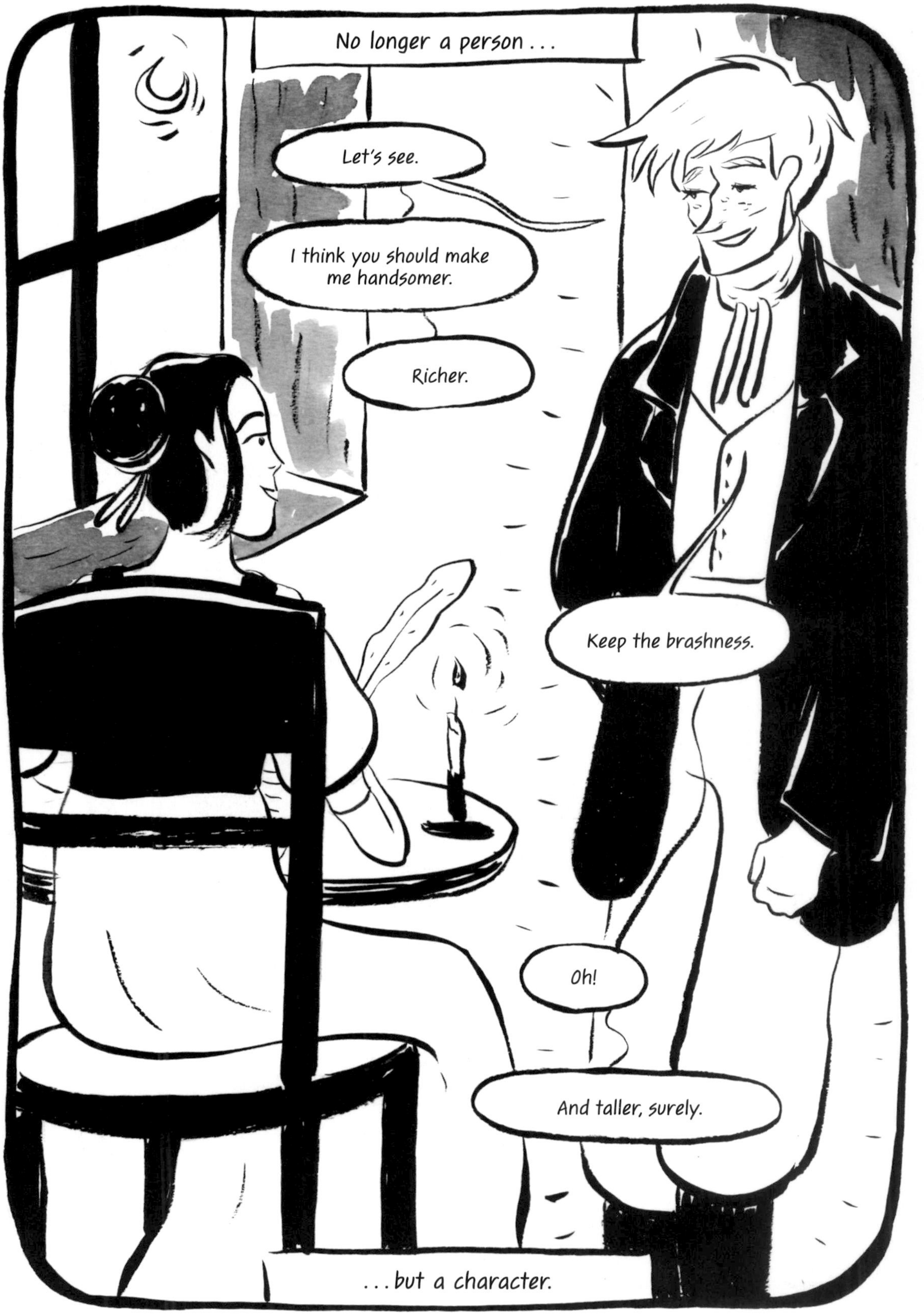
No longer a person . . .
Let's see.
I think you should make me handsomer.
Richer.
Keep the brashness.
Oh!
And taller, surely.
. . . but a character.

Then I received the invitation to go to London for the official marriage announcement.

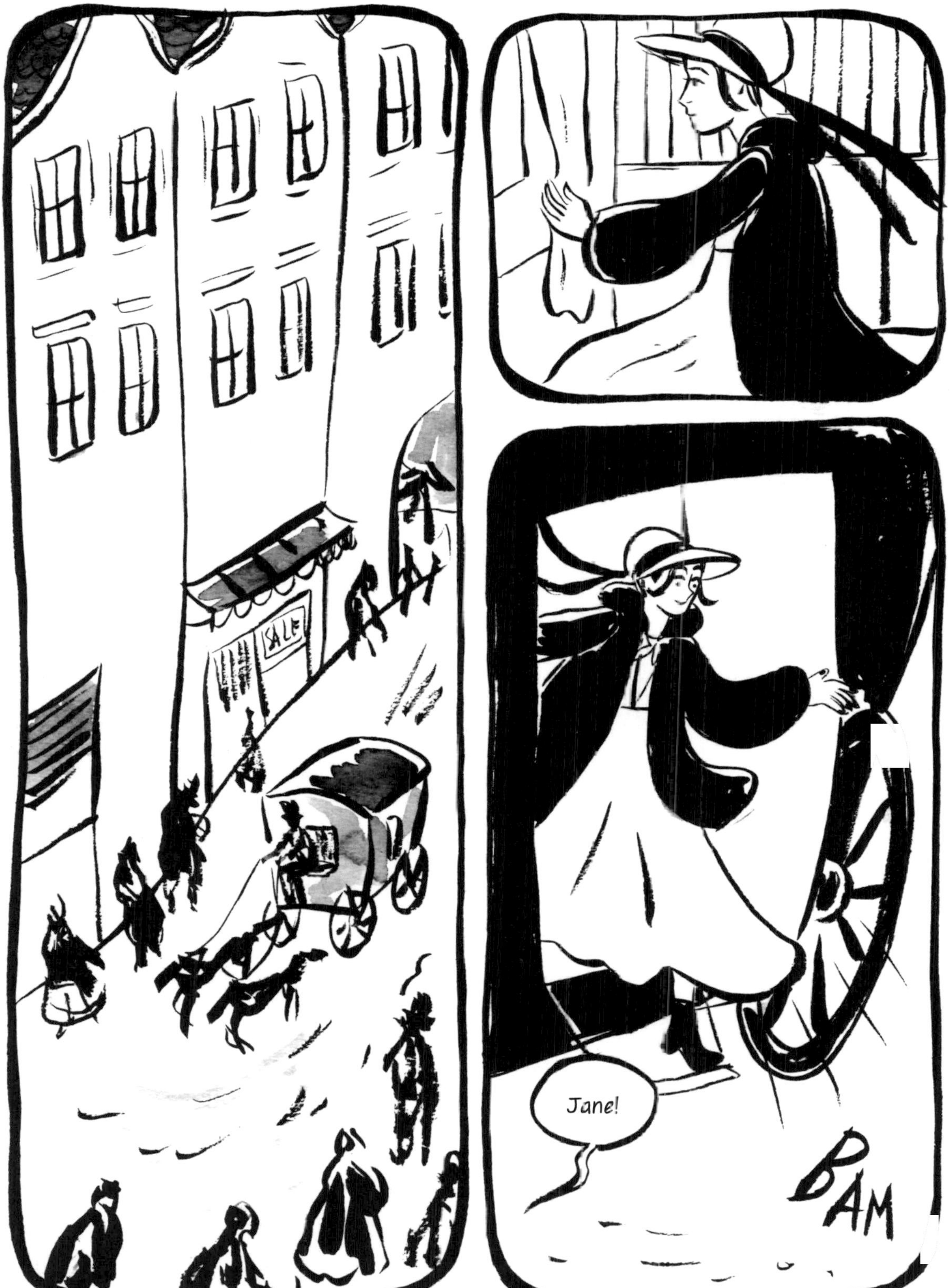
SALE
Jane!
BAM

My fate was about to be sealed.

I will be married and have children.

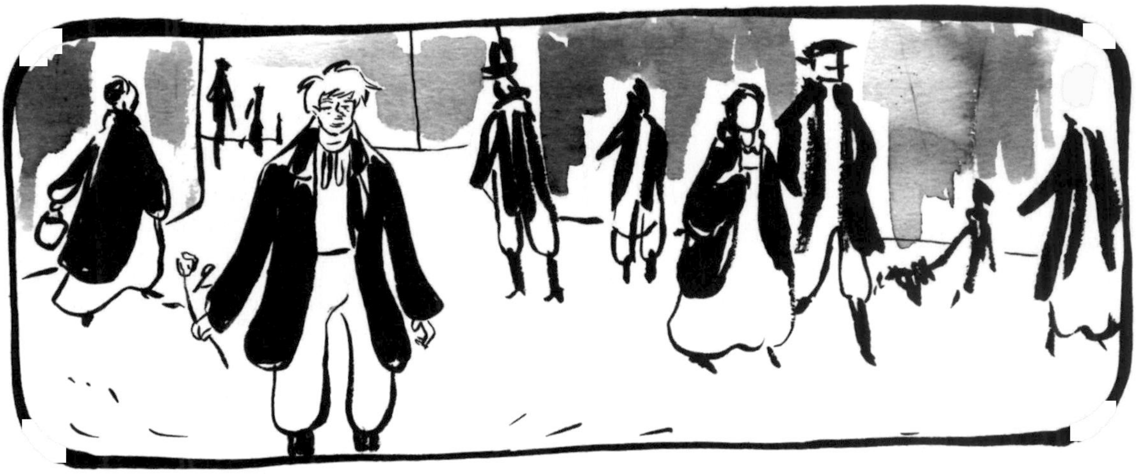

I will attend to my husband.

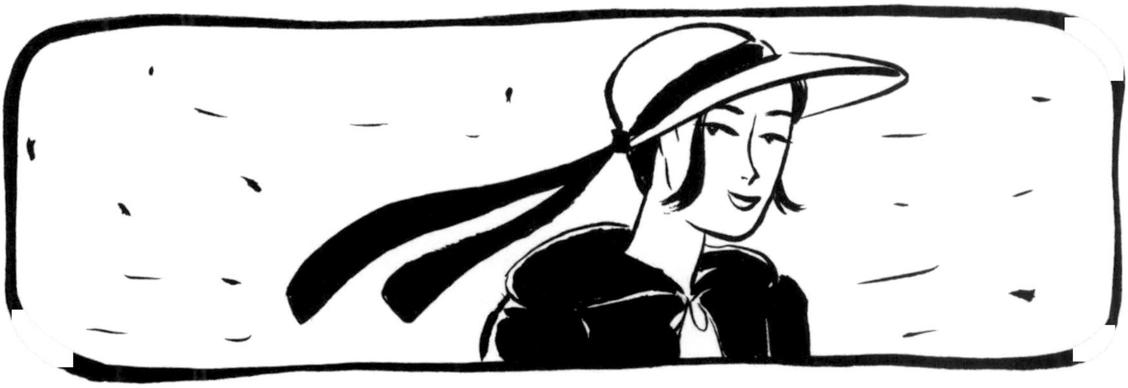

I will stop writing stories.

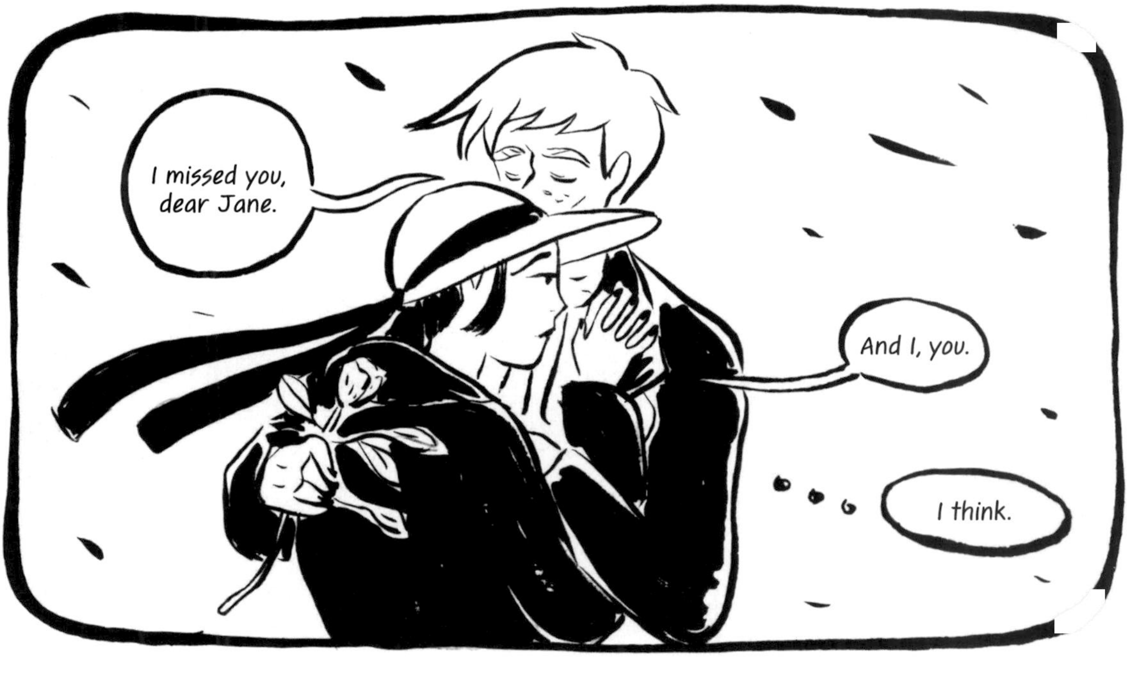
I missed you, dear Jane.
And I, you.
I think.

It unsettled me. I couldn't recognize him anymore.

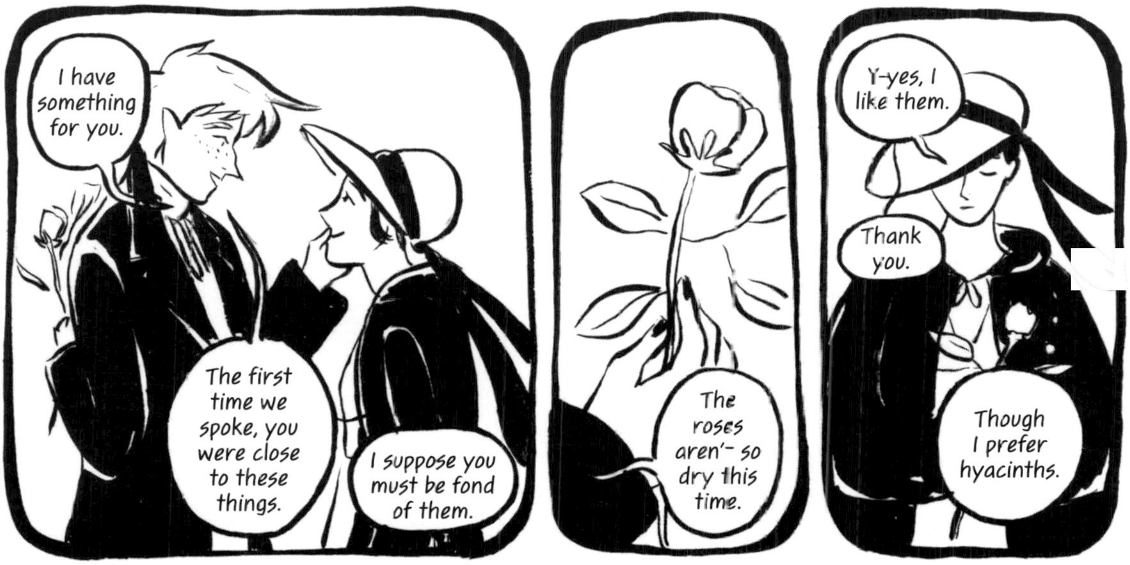
I have something for you.
The first time we spoke, you were close to these things.
I suppose you must be fond of them.
The roses aren't so dry this time.
Y-yes, I like them.
Thank you.
Though I prefer hyacinths.

I no longer felt anything for him.

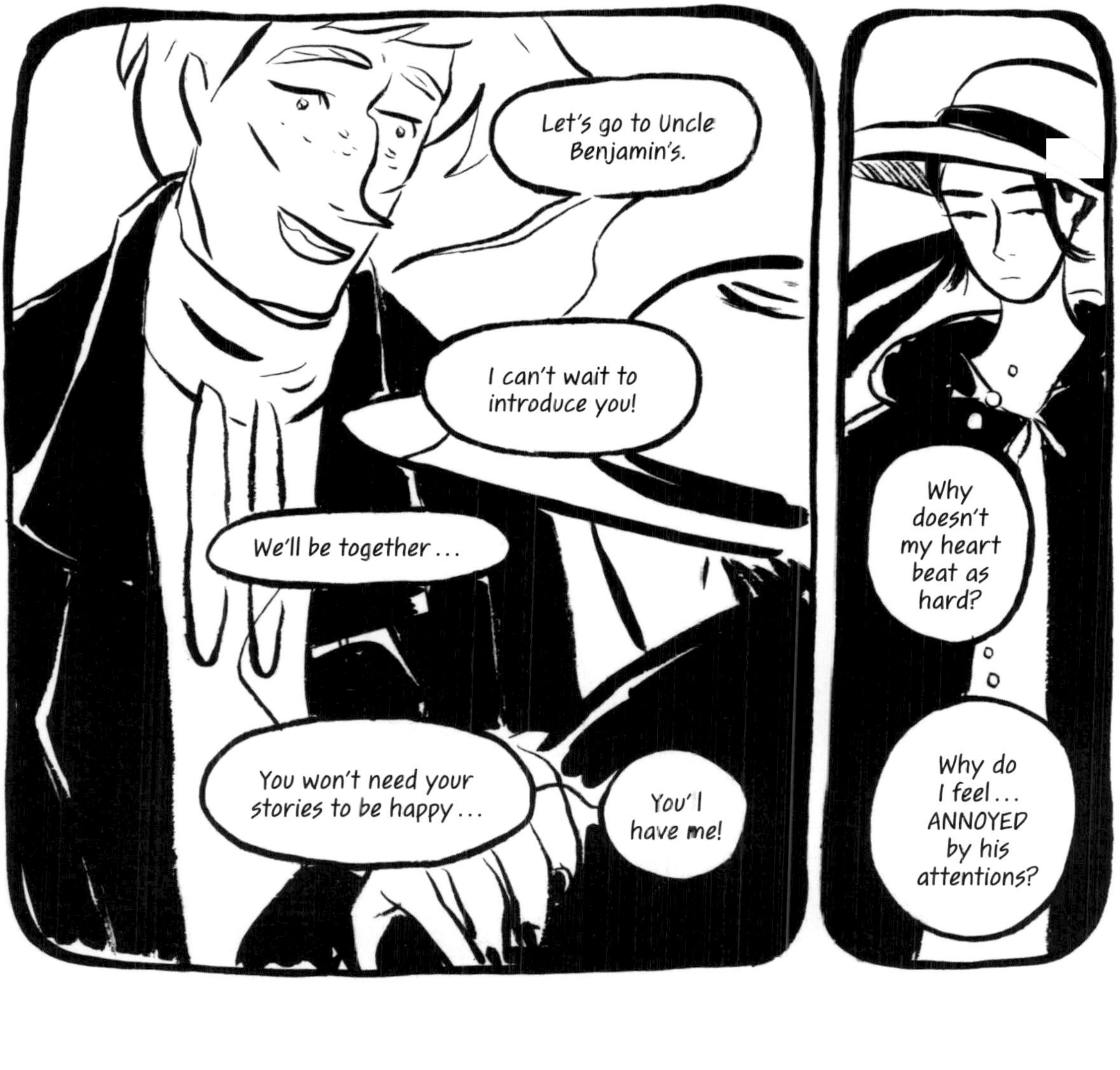
Let's go to Uncle Benjamin's.
I can't wait to introduce you!
We'll be together . . .
You won't need your stories to be happy . . .
You'll have me!
Why doesn't my heart beat as hard?
Why do I feel . . . ANNOYED by his attentions?

After four weeks, I knew what I had to do.

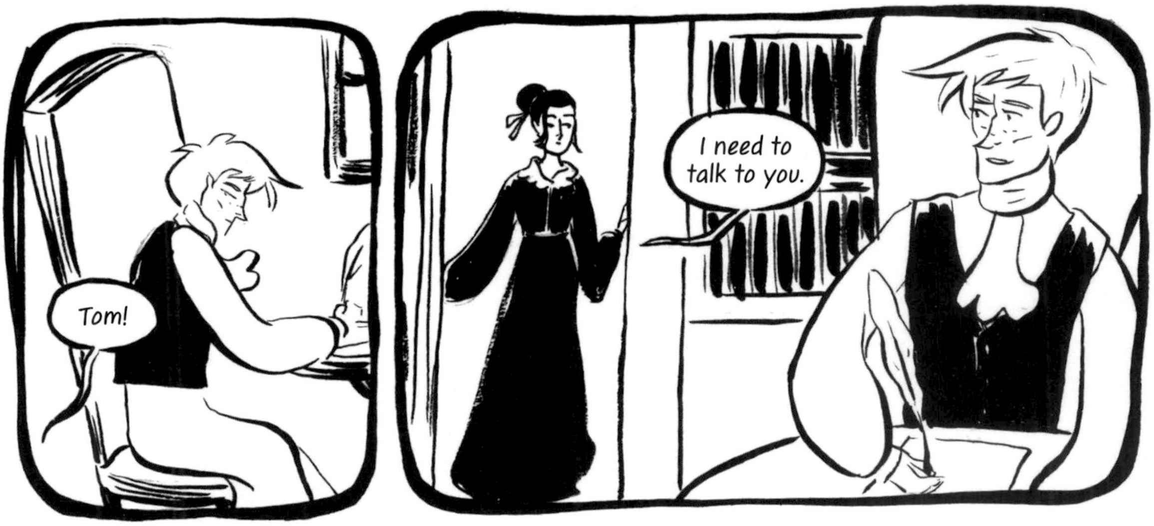
Tom!
I need to talk to you.

At the close of September, I ended our engagement.

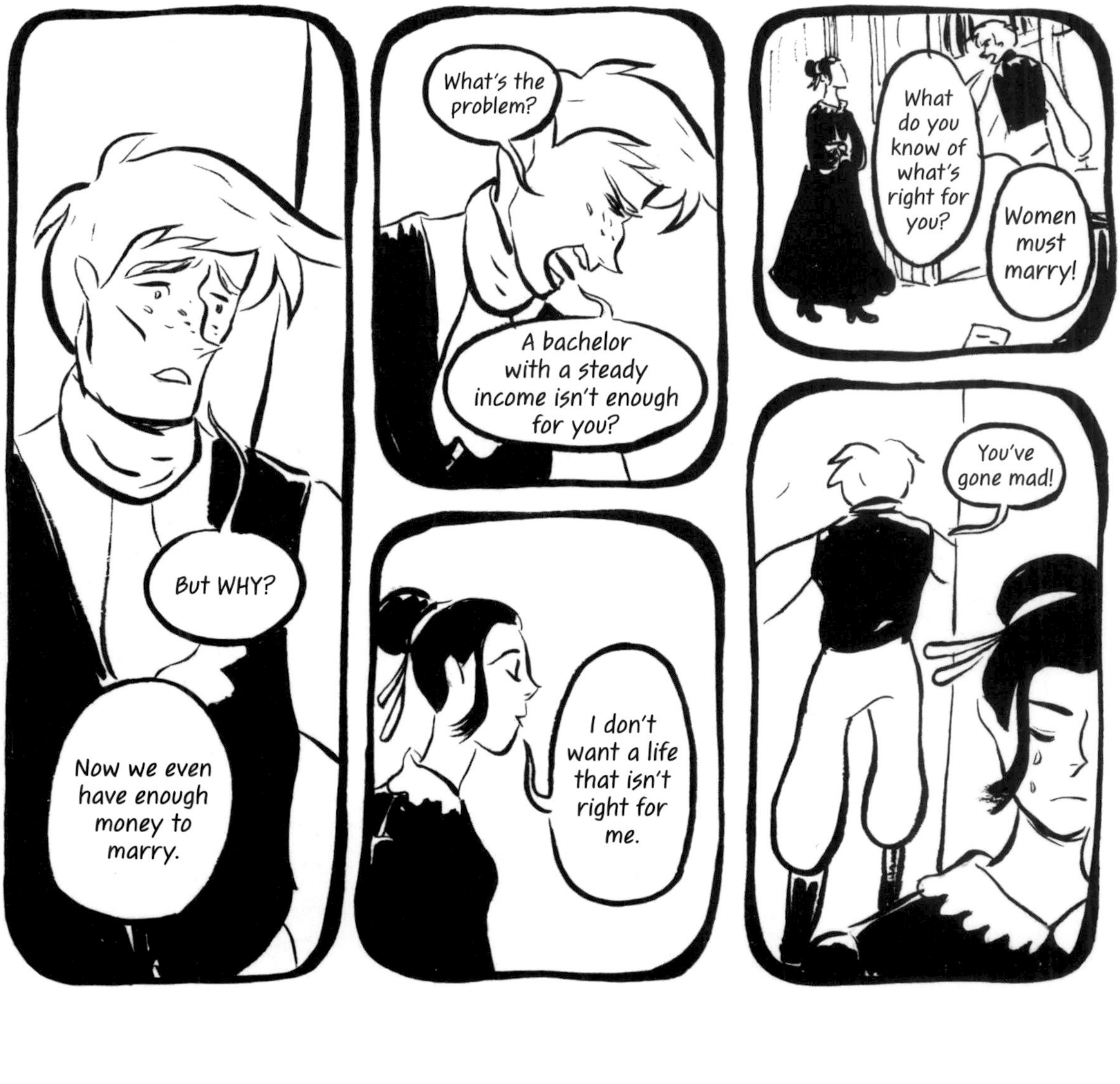
But WHY?
Now we even have enough money to marry.
What's the problem?
A bachelor with a steady income isn't enough for you?
What do you know of what's right for you?
Women must marry!
I don't want a life that isn't right for me.
You've gone mad!

The next day, I returned to Steventon.

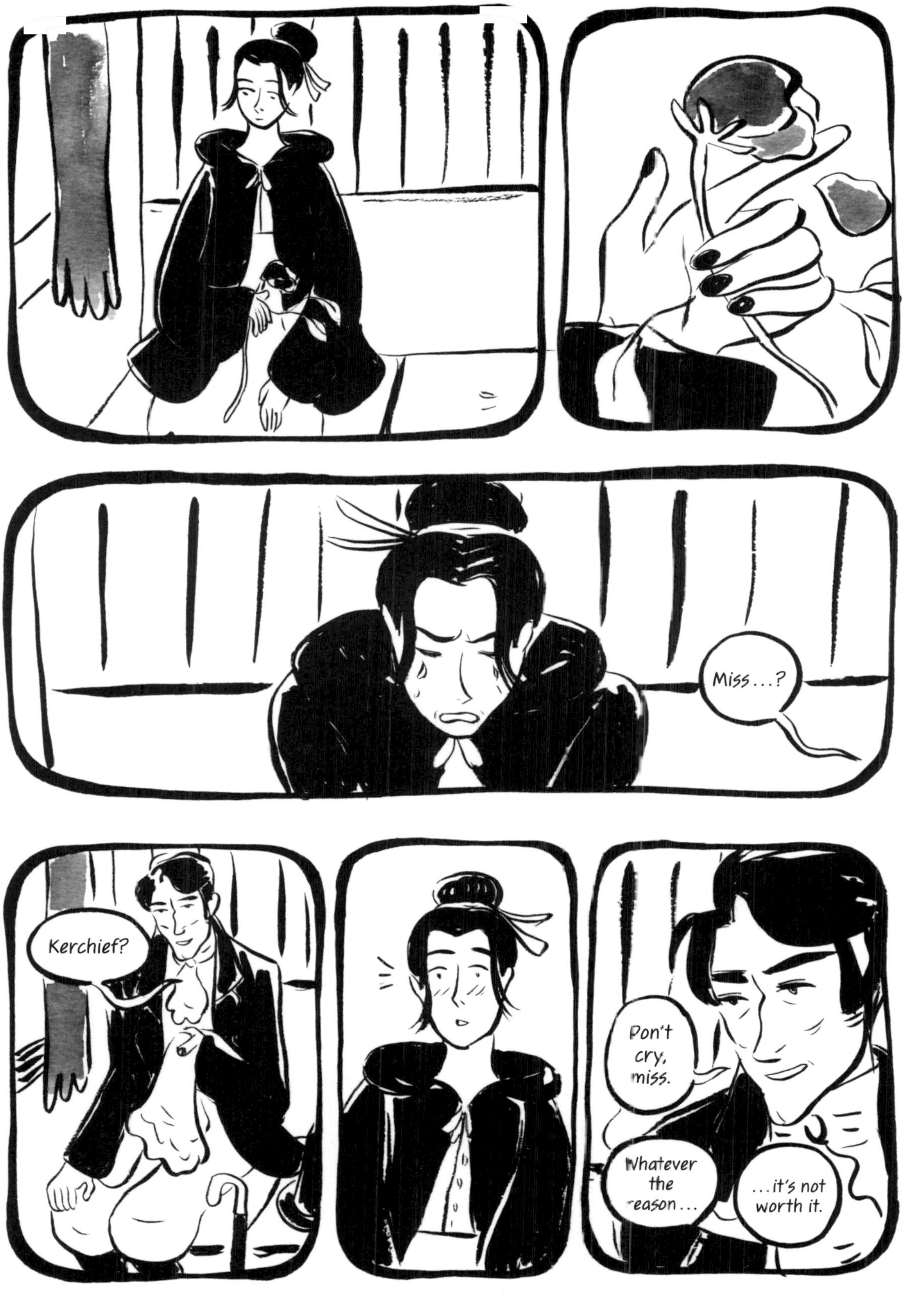
Miss . . . ?
Kerchief?
Don't cry, miss.
Whatever the reason . . .
. . . it's not worth it.

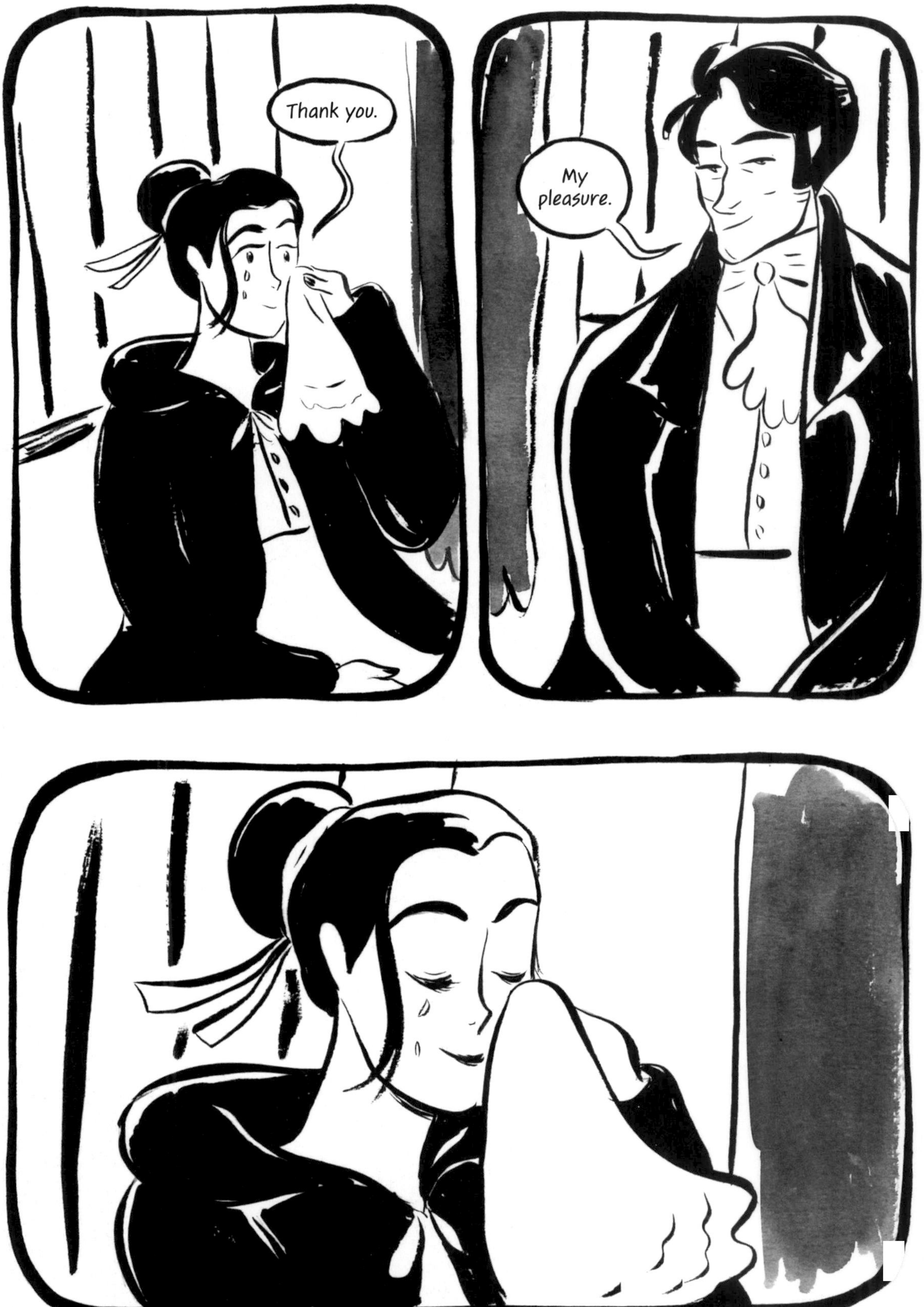
Thank you.
My pleasure.

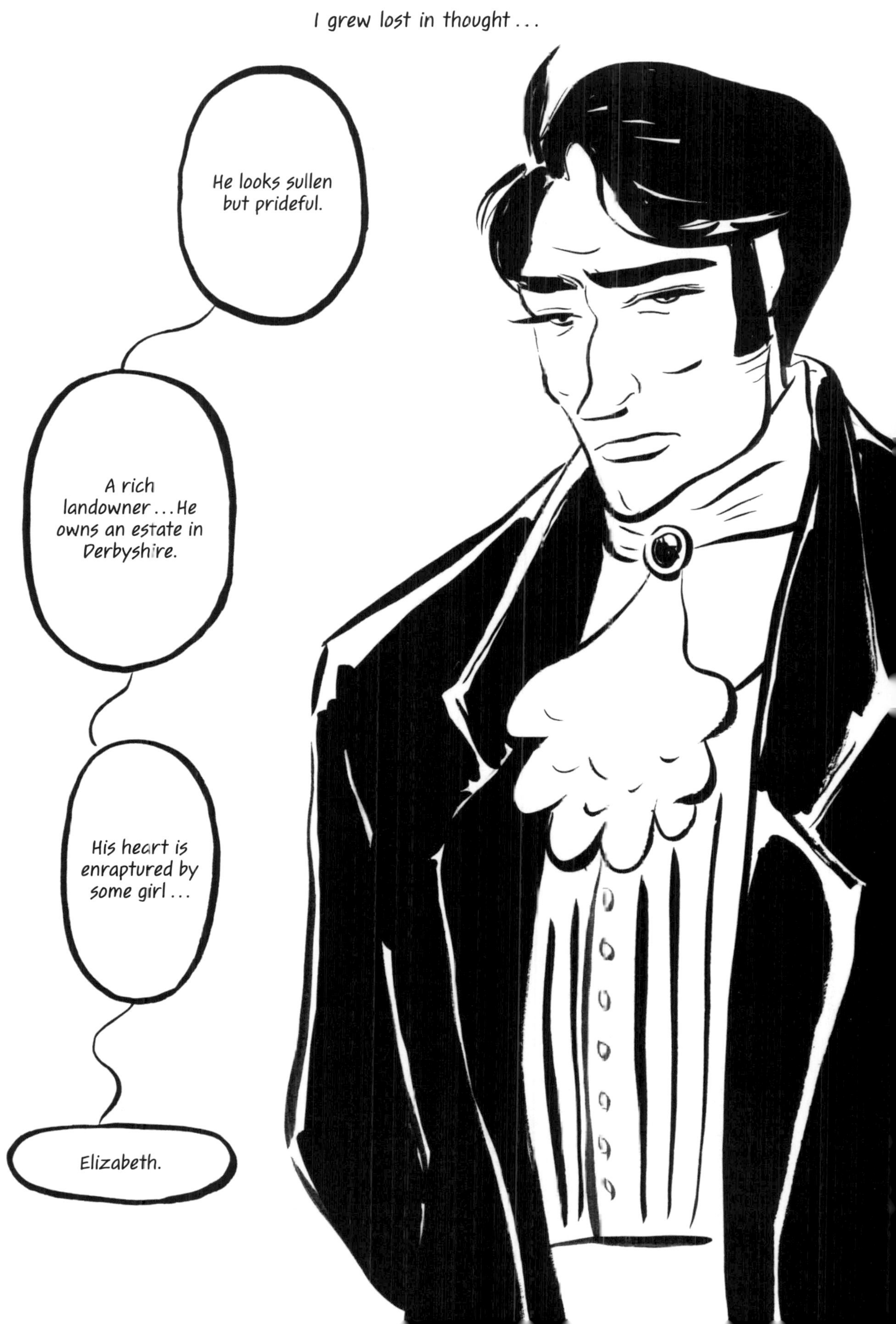
I grew lost in thought . . .
He looks sullen but prideful.
A rich landowner . . . He owns an estate in Derbyshire.
His heart is enraptured by some girl . . .
Elizabeth.

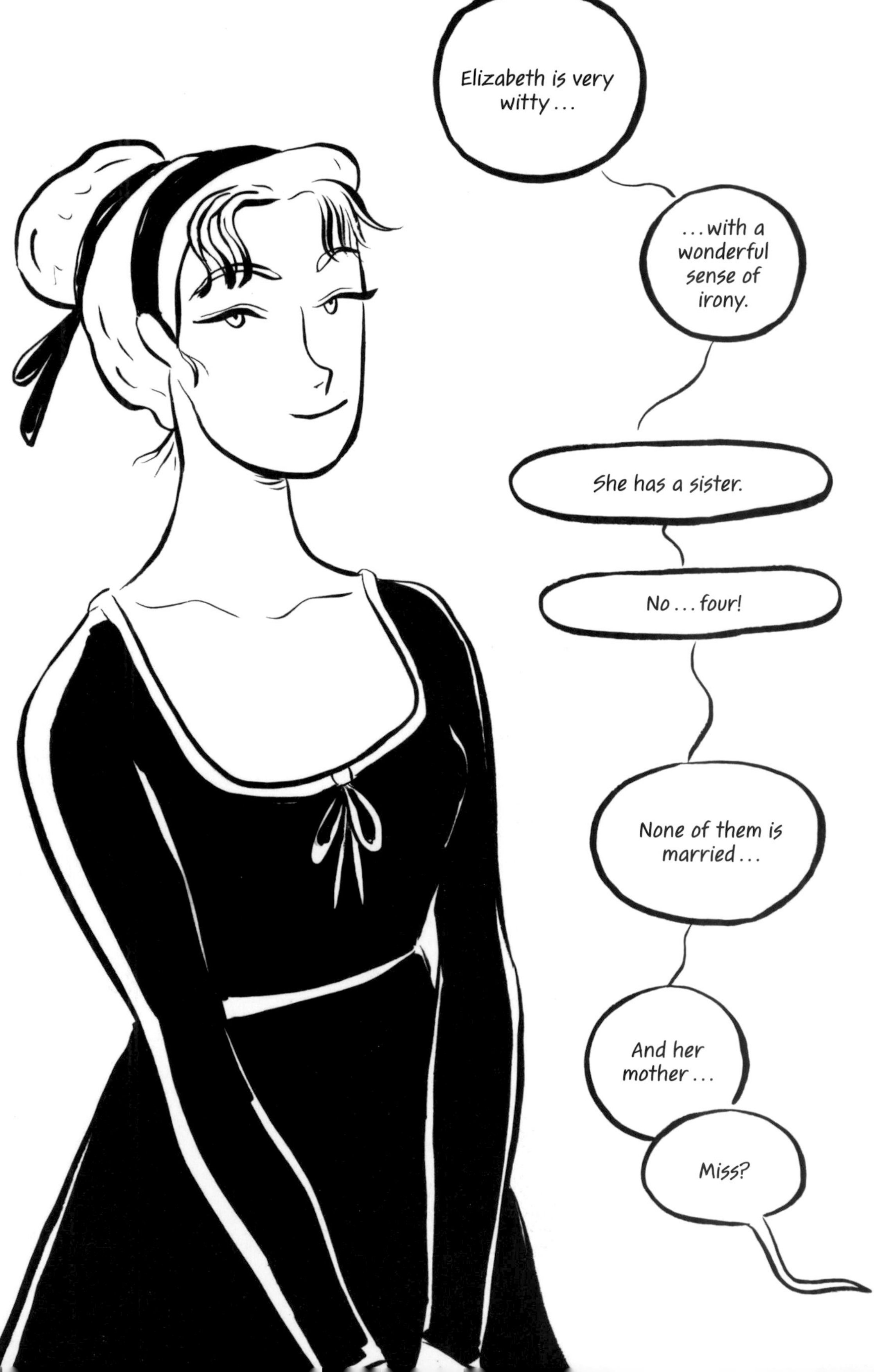
Elizabeth is very witty...
...with a wonderful sense of irony.
She has a sister.
No... four!
None of them is married...
And her mother...
Miss?

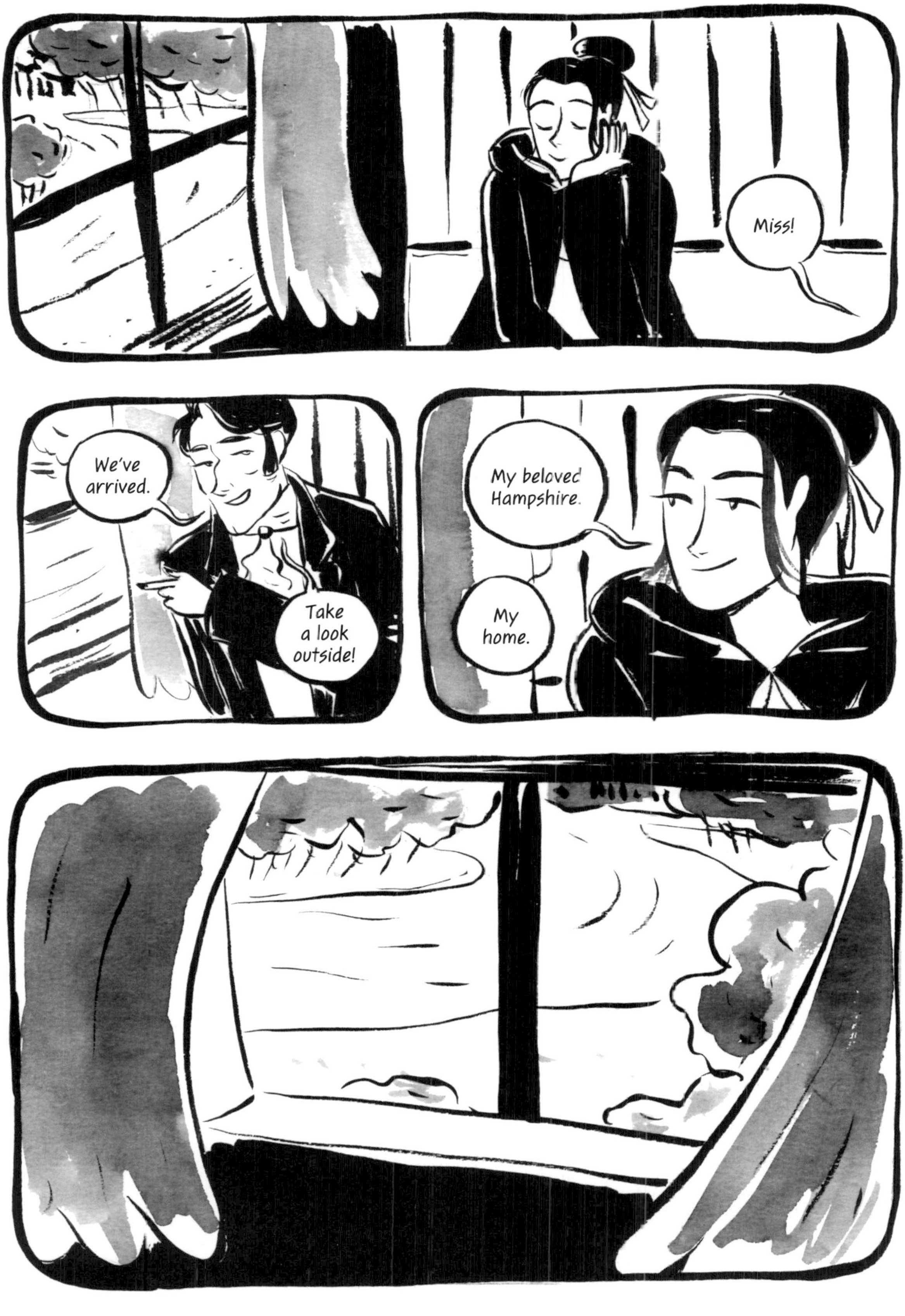

Miss!
We've arrived.
Take a look outside!
My beloved Hampshire.
My home.

As soon as I reached the house . . .

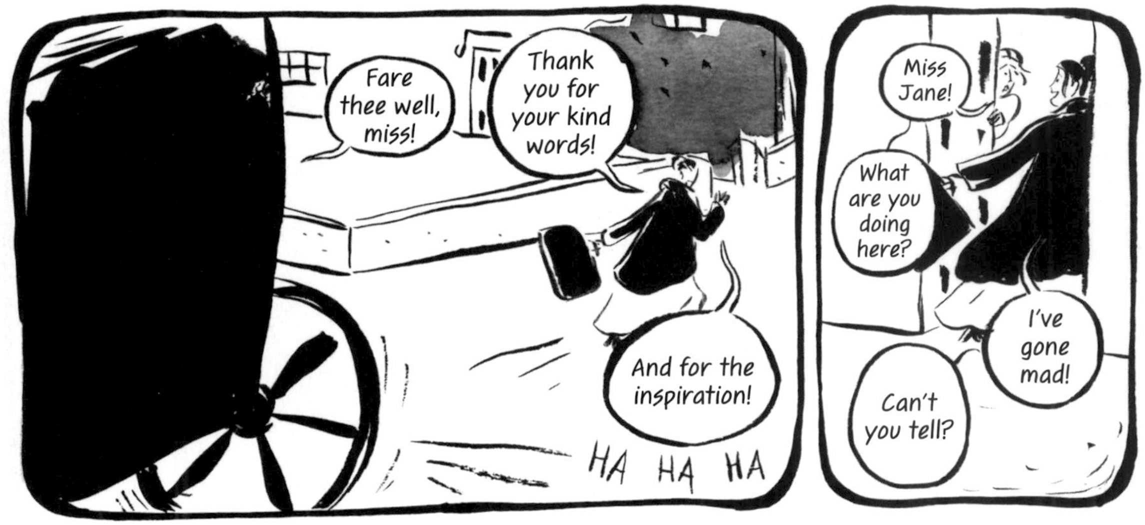
Fare thee well, miss!
Thank you for your kind words!
And for the inspiration!
HA HA HA
Miss Jane!
What are you doing here?
I've gone mad!
Can't you tell?

. . . I ran to my father's study.

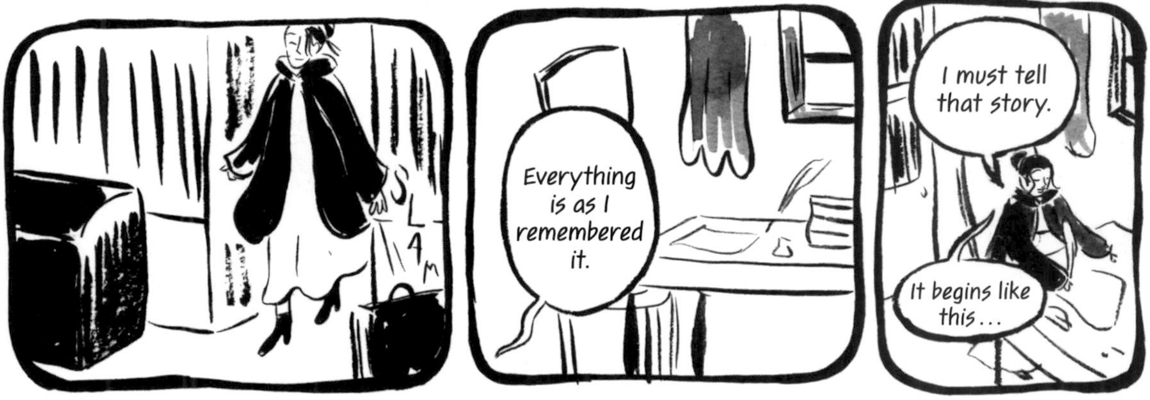
Everything is as I remembered it.
I must tell that story.
It begins like this . . .

And I did what I was born to do.

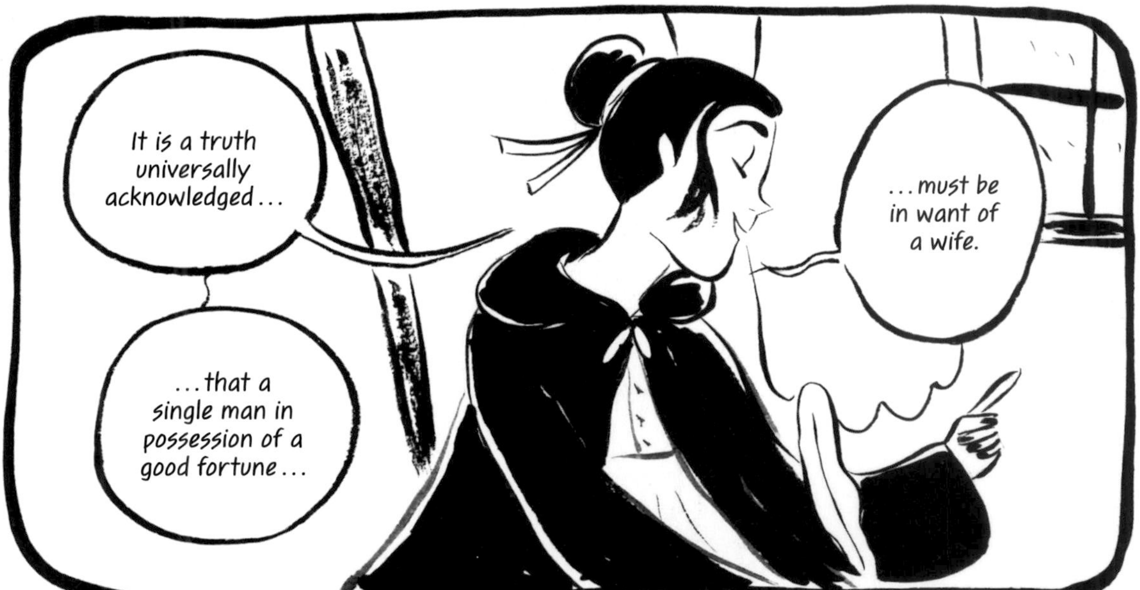
It is a truth universally acknowledged . . .
. . . that a single man in possession of a good fortune . . .
. . . must be in want of a wife.

That story in my head became a book . . .

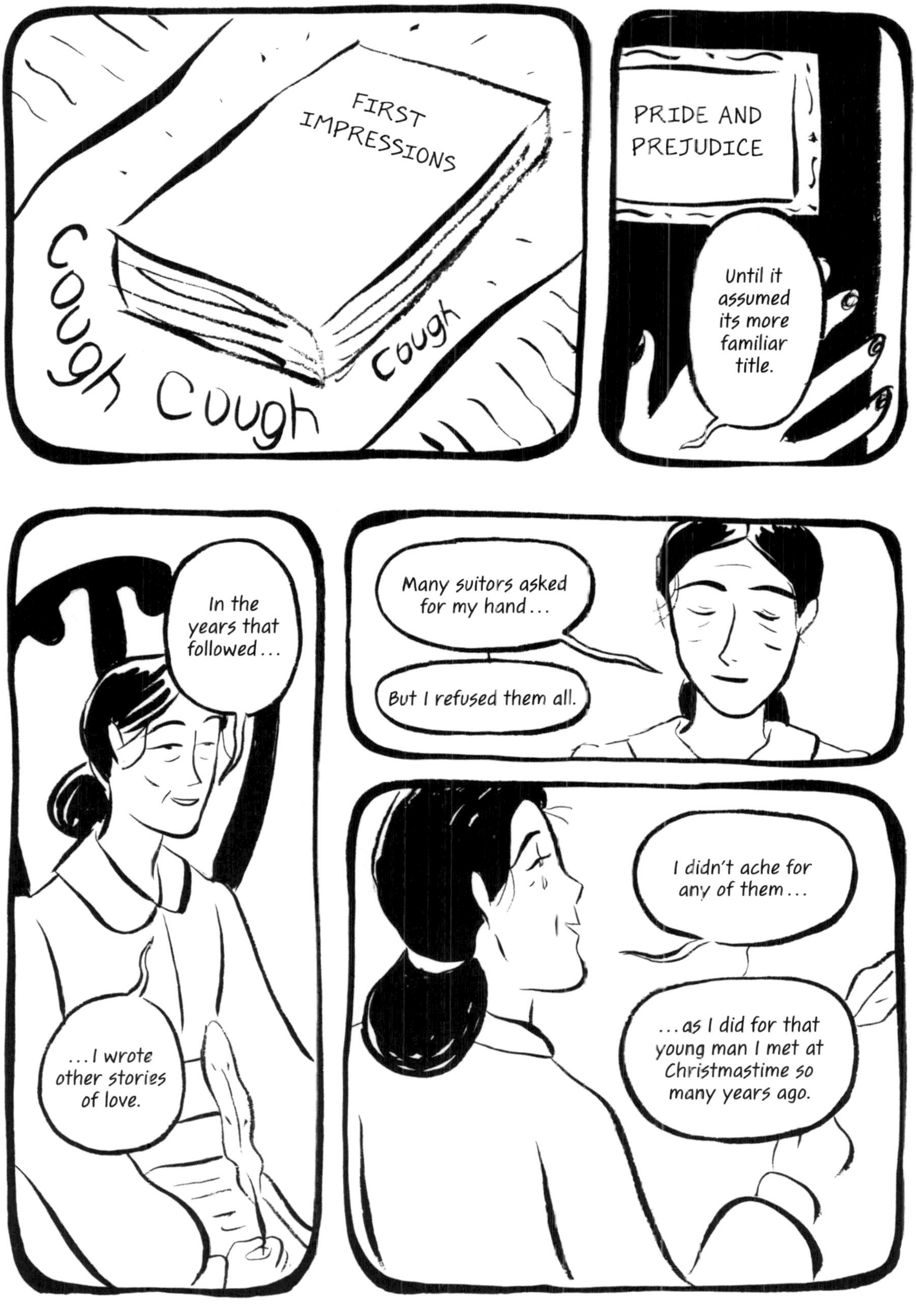
FIRST IMPRESSIONS
Cough Cough Cough
PRIDE AND PREJUDICE
Until it assumed its more familiar title.
In the years that followed . . .
. . . I wrote other stories of love.
Many suitors asked for my hand . . .
But I refused them all.
I didn't ache for any of them . . .
. . . as I did for that young man I met at Christmastime so many years ago.

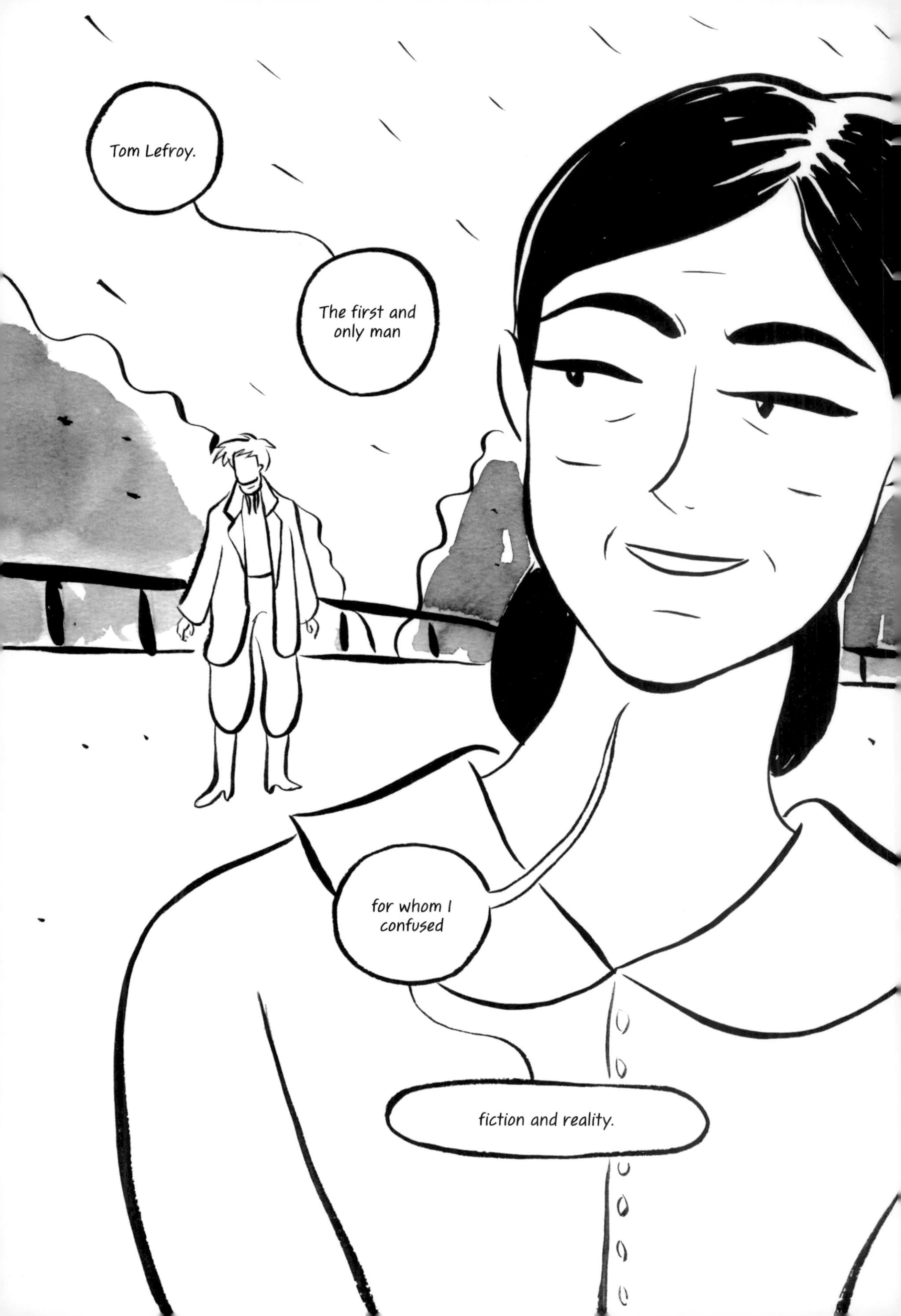
Tom Lefroy.
The first and only man
for whom I confused
fiction and reality.

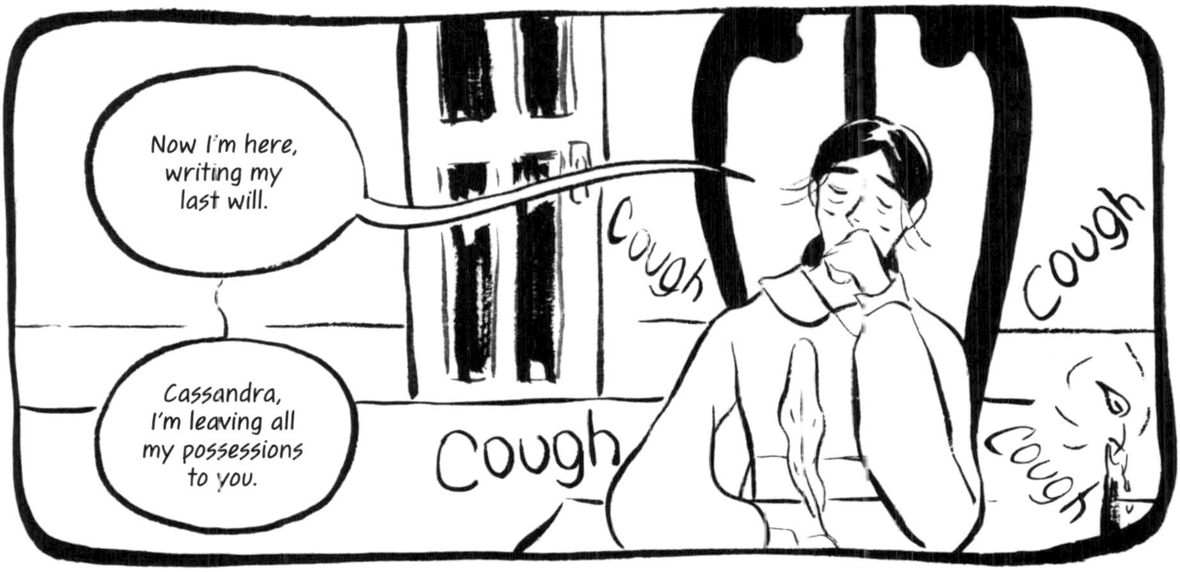
Now I'm here, writing my last will.
Cassandra, I'm leaving all my possessions to you.
Cough
Cough
Cough
Cough

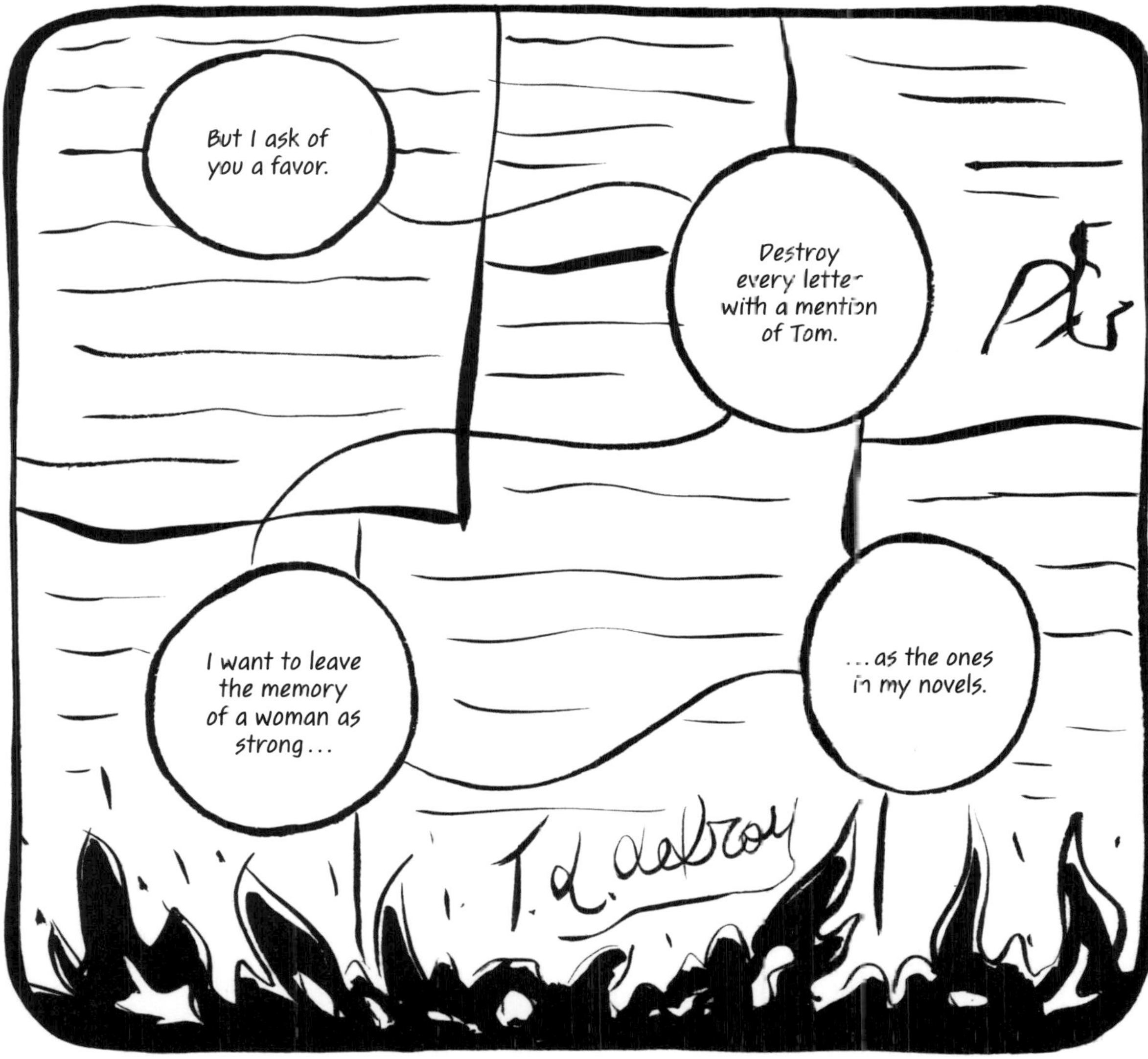
But I ask of you a favor.
Destroy every letter with a mention of Tom.
I want to leave the memory of a woman as strong...
...as the ones in my novels.

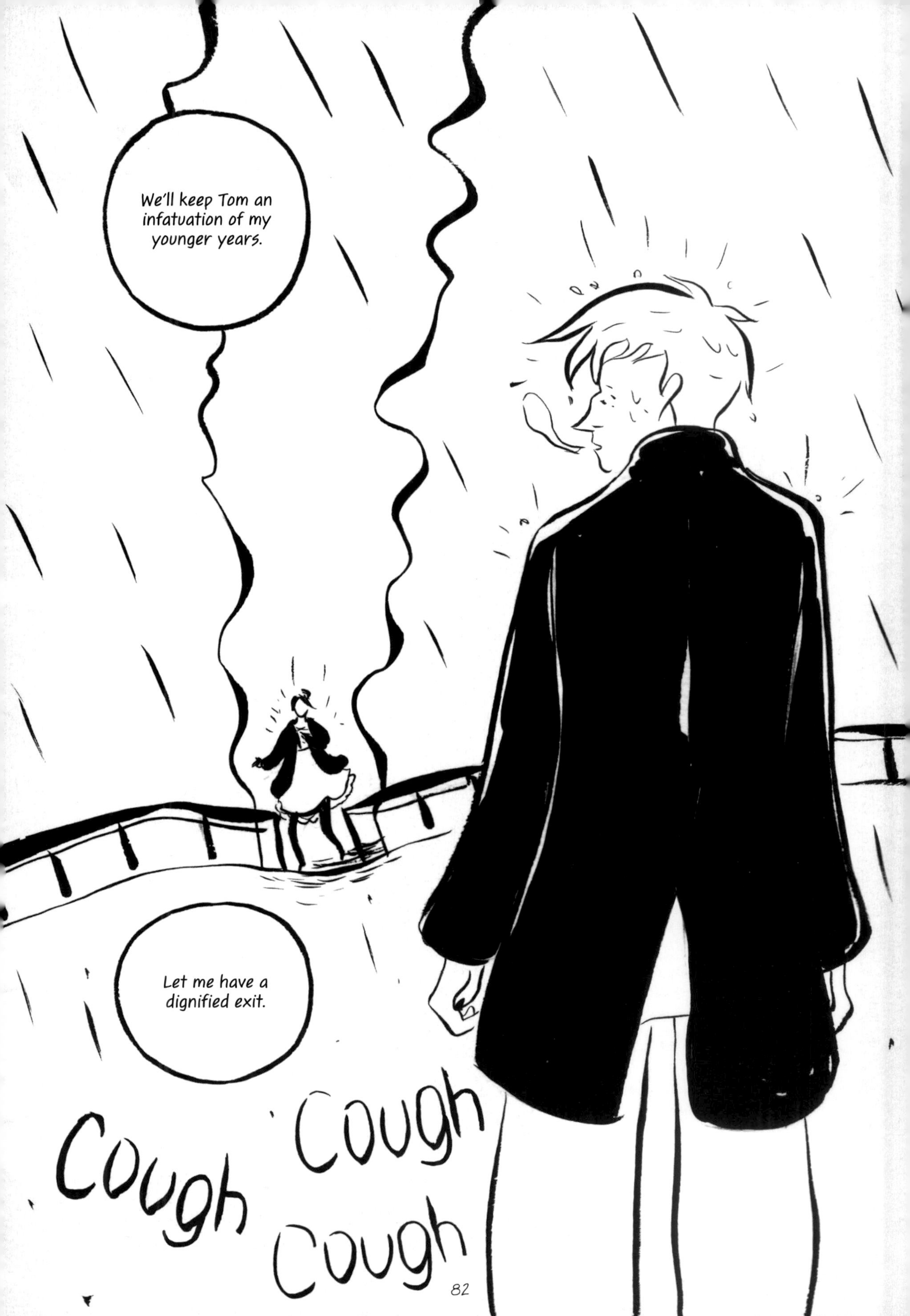

We'll keep Tom an infatuation of my younger years.
Let me have a dignified exit.
Cough
Cough
Cough

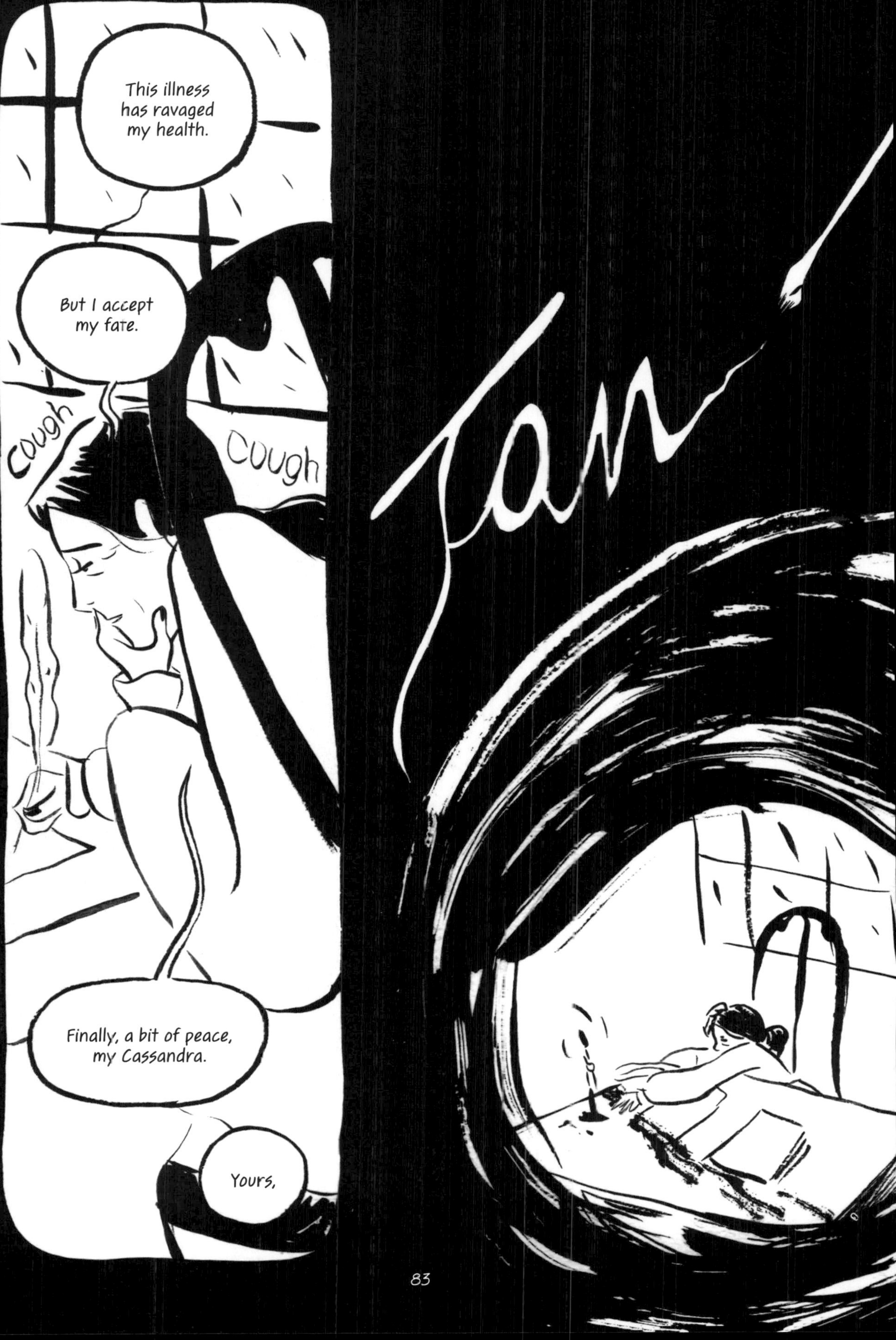
This illness has ravaged my health.
But I accept my fate.
Cough
Cough
Finally, a bit of peace, my Cassandra.
Yours,
Jan

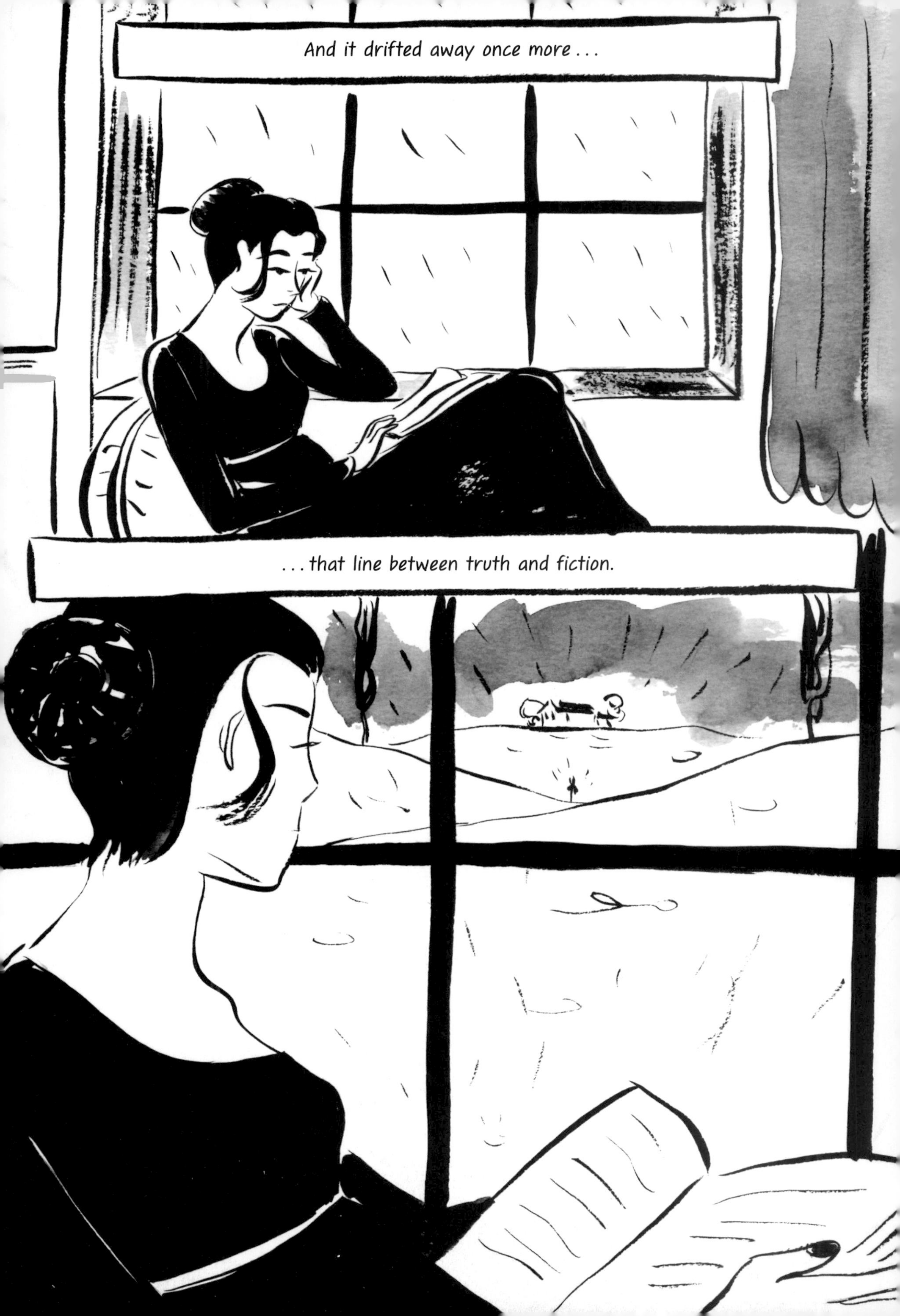
And it drifted away once more . . .
. . . that line between truth and fiction.

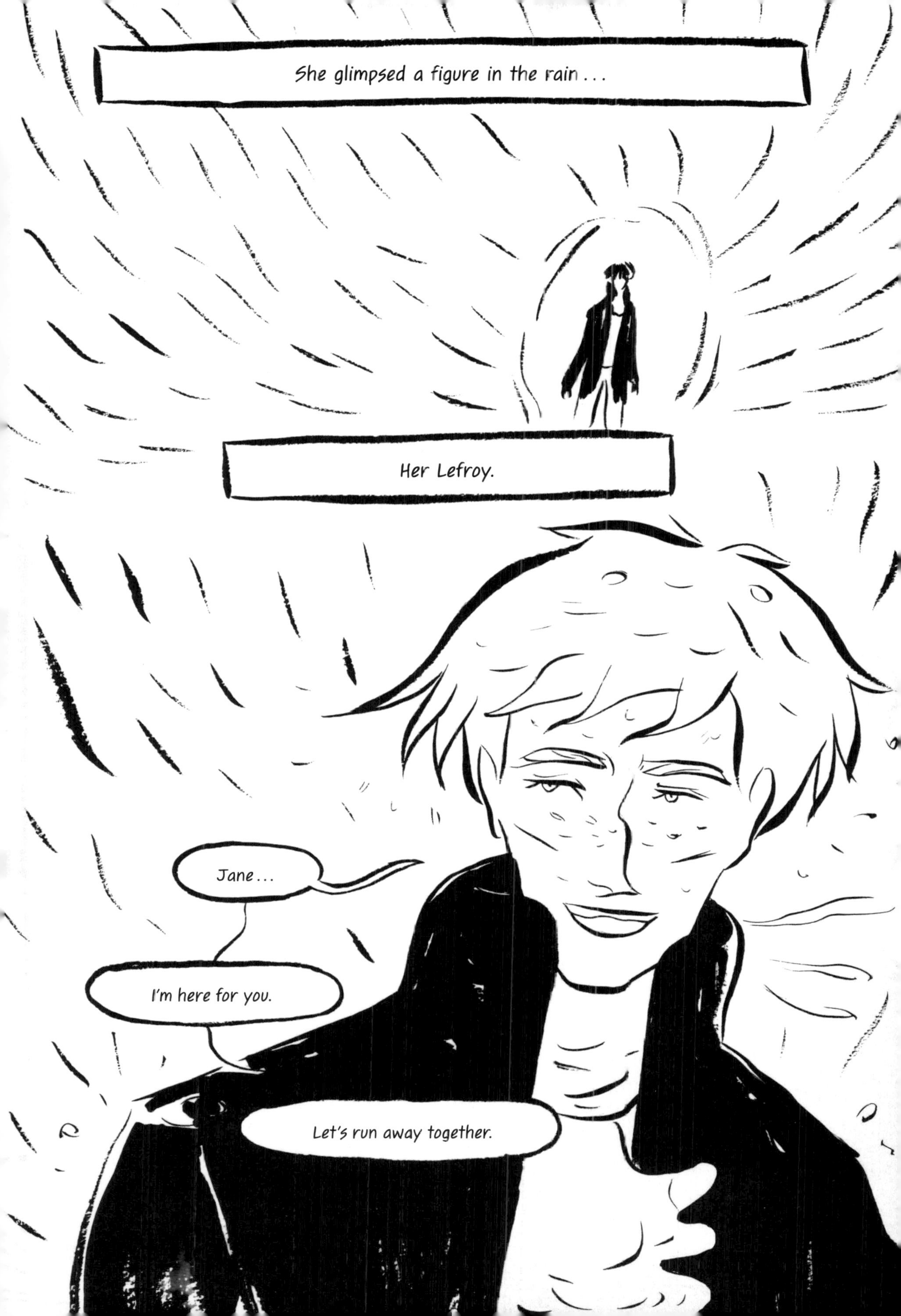
She glimpsed a figure in the rain . . .
Her Lefroy.
Jane . . .
I'm here for you.
Let's run away together.

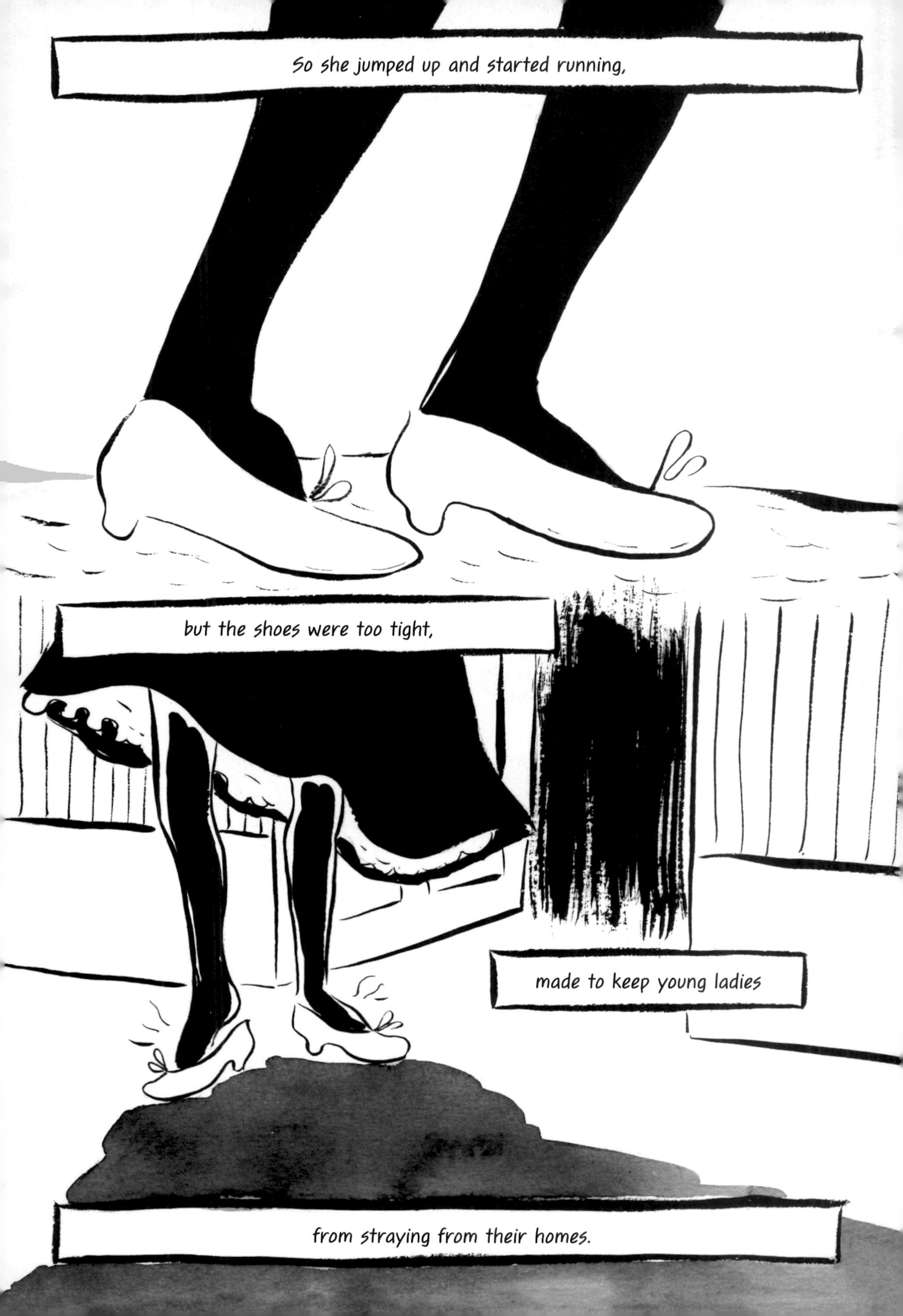
So she jumped up and started running,
but the shoes were too tight,
made to keep young ladies
from straying from their homes.

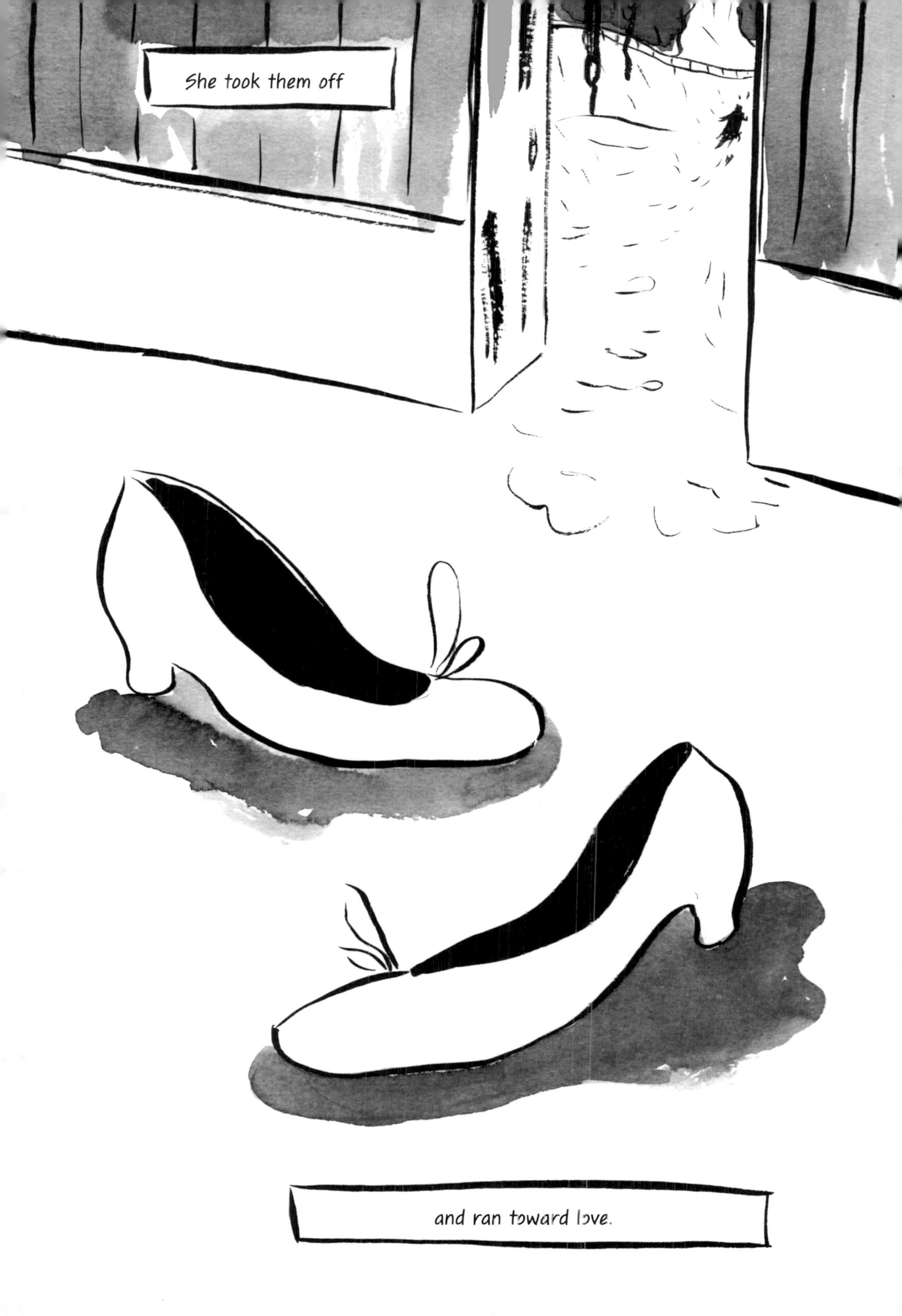
She took them off
and ran toward love.

An Extraordinarily Normal Life

It is a truth universally acknowledged that the world is divided into two groups: those who love to read Jane Austen and those who do not. The reasons for one's interest or disinterest in Austen are the same. They have to do with Austen's insistence on writing about confined spaces, creating scenes that are almost dioramic re-creations of lounges, dance parties, and conversations. These spaces are the sites in which Austen studies the inner lives of her characters and, even more so, their relationships.

We know much about Jane Austen's biography, but perhaps not enough. Some accounts from her family are available, but we can't take their reliability for granted. What's most important is the letters of Austen herself that have been preserved. These letters tell us of an extraordinarily normal life. Like Austen's novels, they are full of chatting, gossip, dances, vacations, and carriage trips, and they give a bright touch even to the upheavals in Austen's life.

Life and Home

Jane Austen was born in 1775 in Steventon, a Hampshire village where her father, George Austen, served as the rector of the church. She died in 1817 at the age of forty-one. She spent this short life entirely in England. Hampshire is a county on the southern coast of England with a mild climate and hills that descend gently to the sea. Jane Austen lived within this quiet landscape until 1801, when her father transferred the family to the town of Bath.

Following the death of George Austen in 1805, Jane, Cassandra, and their mother moved to Southampton, the home of Jane's brother Frank. In 1809 Jane moved again, to a cottage in Chawton (also in Hampshire County), which another brother, Edward, had made available to her. The cottage, a peaceful home surrounded by greenery, is perhaps the most important place in Austen's life as a writer. Here, she revised or wrote from start to finish her most famous works.

As soon as she arrived at Chawton, Austen returned to work on manuscripts she had composed when she was younger. The result was two novels: *Sense and Sensibility*, which received only modest attention, and *Pride and Prejudice*, which enjoyed some success during Austen's life but later became one of the most read, admired, translated, and reworked books in the world. She then wrote *Mansfield Park* and *Emma* and began work on *Northanger Abbey* and *Persuasion*.

Burned Letters and Tom Lefroy

Although many of Austen's letters are available to readers, Cassandra burned a substantial number of them following Jane's death, obeying Jane's express wishes. The flames that destroyed these correspondences have given rise to countless

theories and debates concerning the life of Jane Austen. Speculating about Austen has become a boundless passion for millions of readers around the world. In recent years, many scholars and novelists have attempted to reconstruct the missing parts of Jane Austen's biography, referring to the remaining letters and the striking clues they contain.

Among the aspects of Austen's life that have attracted attention are her decision not to marry—a transgressive choice for her era—and of course the stories of romance she tells in the first person. One subject of these stories—who Austen mentions in a couple of letters to her sister—is a young man named Tom Lefroy, who seems to have made her lose her head. By the end of Austen's mentions of Lefroy, readers don't know how much pain he might have caused her or she him. But since there is no conclusive information on what happened between the two and how things ended, Austen's fans can—and often do—imagine the courtship as they like, as is the inalienable right of a reader.

Social Lives and Class Struggles

The social lives of Austen's characters are some of the most distinctive aspects of her literary world. In her era and within her social class, conversations, shared walks, and visits to friends were among the most anticipated parts of everyday life. The most glamorous events were the dances, during which people made new friends and enjoyed themselves late at night. Above all else, young women at a dance had the chance to find a husband.

Women's freedom was limited in Austen's era. For instance, the rules of English society did not allow a woman to walk alone in the city or write a letter to a man who was not a relative or a boyfriend. Dances provided an extraordinary opportunity not only to get acquainted but to cope. For a woman who could not work, did not own property, and needed male company to maintain her reputation, marriage was the only option. Austen's choice to refuse marriage—and thus the natural destiny of a woman of her era—led to difficulties for her family. Her brothers had to provide for the needs of Jane's sister Cassandra—who also never married after the death of her fiancé, Tom Fowle—and their widowed mother.

The Problem of Money

Jane Austen's family lived in genteel poverty and was forced to pay great attention to expenses. The value of—and need for—money is felt with urgency in Austen's life story. A reader can't overlook the economic conditions of characters and their families throughout her works either. At least not without losing a significant part of the meaning Austen wanted to communicate. Her novels offer very precise economic information about their characters, and the information is absolutely necessary to a story's premise, its development, and its conclusion.

In Austen's first novel, *Sense and Sensibility*, a certain Mr. Dashwood dies, leaving his inheritance to his son John. Exhaling his last breath, he asks that John provide for his half sisters: Elinor, Marianne, and Margaret. But John's wife, Fanny, drives the girls and their mother from the family home, now owned by John. After this harsh change, Elinor and Marianne begin to lead a very different life in their new home of Devonshire. Their economic constraints lead them to demonstrate their most distinctive qualities: Elinor hides her pain, while Marianne expresses all her romantic passion, at the price of her reputation, especially in a love plotline with a neighbor, Mr. Willoughby.

In the most beloved of Austen novels, *Pride and Prejudice*, the Bennet family—made up of two parents and five daughters—is struck by the news that a rich young gentleman, Mr. Bingley, has rented a sumptuous residence, Netherfield, near them. Because the Bennet girls have a rather miserable dowry to offer and they aren't able to inherit their father's property if he passes away, their exuberant mother tries to create the conditions that will make one of her girls the newcomer's bride. At a dance in the village of Meryton, the oldest sister, Jane, catches the eye of Mr. Bingley, while Bingley's even wealthier friend, Mr. Darcy, annoys the second-oldest daughter, Elizabeth, with his brazen and proud character. Later, Bingley's sister persuades him to leave Netherfield, with the aim of moving him away from Jane Bennet; her motivation is that Jane would not be a suitable wife for him. Elizabeth, meanwhile, has more opportunities to meet Mr. Darcy and begins to have more complicated feelings toward him (to say the least).

In *Mansfield Park*, Austen's next novel, economic status is once again a key aspect of character and setting. Fanny Price leaves her struggling family to be adopted by her wealthy aunt and uncle, the Bertrams, the owners of the luxurious residence that gives the novel its name. *Emma* tells the story of Emma Woodhouse, a young, beautiful, and rich woman who does not intend to find a husband but who likes the idea of marrying off others. Her vanity and blasé attitude create many misunderstandings within the small company she attends, risking the ruin of friendships and the hurt feelings of others.

Later Novels

Similar to *Emma*, *Northanger Abbey* also takes the sometimes dangerous power of fantasy as a central theme. The novel's protagonist, Catherine Morland, is a young woman of modest trappings and one of a county clergyman's ten children. She often imagines that real life resembles the books she loves: stories of mysteries and crimes set in ancient, ghostly ruins. During a visit to the town of Bath, Catherine strikes up a friendship with two brothers who try to drag her into expensive and unkempt habits, and meets Henry Tilney, whom she falls in love with. Tilney's father invites Catherine to their home, Northanger Abbey. During that stay, Catherine's wild imagination causes a series of misunderstandings both humorous and dramatic.

Persuasion begins in the rural county of Somersetshire and in another place of economic hardship. Due to her father's debts, Anne Elliot and her family are forced to leave their beloved house, Kellynch Hall. The family then rents out the home, which awakens painful memories for Anne, as she realizes that one of the renters is the sister of Captain Frederick Wentworth, an old love. Seven years earlier, Anne refused Wentworth's marriage offer, and throughout the novel, Anne has a chance to meet frequently with Wentworth, who has become a wealthy official in the meantime and has not forgotten their history.

A Range of Characters

The variety of characters within Jane Austen's work—and the psychological and emotional portraits that the author paints—is another unforgettable trait of her writing. Women and men of exemplary behavior, tormented souls that arouse a strong sense of empathy in readers, characters of both great tenderness and elements that don't always attract a reader's sympathies. Austen's writing lays out the merits and defects of characters with precise description and often enthusiastic irony.

Jane Austen's ladies are the real and grand protagonists of her literature and are figures so full of life, feelings, and character as to be distinctly different from one another. There are women distinguished by the strength and constancy of heart, who live fully yet retain in their souls secrets and ingenuous torments: Elinor Dashwood and Anne Elliot. There is the girl who lives on the point of blossoming yet never seems to achieve it: Fanny Price. There is the most sincere emanation of romance in Marianne Dashwood. There is a woman whose brightness is so intense that she can be presumptuous—Emma Woodhouse—and a woman of irresistible but unencumbered malice, Mary Crawford. Catherine Morland embodies naïveté, while Elizabeth Bennet is a feminine kaleidoscope, with a ready attitude and benevolent yet witty smile. So Austen spoke of her: "I must confess that I think [Elizabeth] as delightful a creature as ever appeared in print, and now I shall be able to tolerate those who do not like her I do not know."

Jane Austen's literature is also a study of women's relationships with the costars of their daily realities. In each of the novels, there are balancing and opposing forces to the protagonist. *Pride*'s Bingley is surely one of Jane Austen's simplest men. Hearty, always cheerful, out of touch—he's the right half for Jane Bennet, who's also lovable and incapable of conceiving evil. Edward Ferrars in *Sense and Sensibility* matches Elinor's goodness of heart with some ingenuity. George Knightley (*Emma*) is the most just and wise man in the world, and Captain Wentworth (*Persuasion*), with his frown of disappointment and hints of sentiment, has a great narrative charm. Figures such as Sir Walter Elliot (*Persuasion*), the Reverend Collins (*Pride and Prejudice*), Mr. Elton (*Emma*), and Henry Crawford (*Mansfield Park*) are totally negative figures, distinguished by vanity, selfishness,

opportunism, or lust. Yet other male characters are very complex. Mr. Darcy, though crippled by prejudices (his for others and others' for him) that sometimes makes him unpleasant, reveals himself to possess remarkable dignity and unrivaled generosity.

Reading and Overcoming

In the six novels of the Jane Austen canon, a reader can find not only principal motifs—such as dances and finances—but also an infinite number of smaller recurring elements. The importance of reading and studying is another subject very dear to Austen. *Northanger Abbey*, for example, presents reading as an activity that can profoundly affect an individual's outlook. *Persuasion* refers to contemporary poetry and literature from the point of view of its creation and its reception. In *Mansfield Park*, books are the only company that Fanny enjoys. Readers densely populate Jane Austen's works because she was a frenzied reader herself. From childhood onward, she liked to spend time in the volumes of her father's library, encountering the works of Geoffrey Chaucer, William Shakespeare, John Milton, Johann Wolfgang von Goethe, Samuel Johnson, and novelists such as Charlotte Smith, Maria Edgeworth, Ann Radcliffe, and Fanny Burney.

Surely, though, the most crucial aspect common to all of Austen's novels is the portrait that she offers of women who grow and change. Her protagonists affirm themselves within their social contexts, showing true persistence. They pursue not economic advancement but self-expression. The stories' basic plots—in which a girl overcomes adversity and the story ends in a long-awaited wedding—have often misled some readers, who find in these novels nothing more than the trivial or the simplistic. On the contrary, Jane Austen's heroines have gained a prominent role in the history of literature because—in spaces dominated by patriarchal power—their strenuous willpower protects their bodies and their personal dignity.

—MARA BARBUNI

Mara Barbuni has a PhD in English literature and works as a language teacher and translator. She deals mainly with women's writing of the early nineteenth and twentieth centuries. She translated the novels *Sylvia's Lovers* and *Wives and Daughters* by English writer Elizabeth Gaskell and is the author of monographs about Gaskell, the poet Anna Laetitia Barbauld, and Jane Austen. She is also the director of *Due pollici d'avorio* (*Two Inches of Ivory*), the literary magazine of the Jane Austen Society of Italy.

A Jane Austen Timeline

December 16, 1775: Jane Austen is born in Steventon, a village in the English county of Hampshire

1787: Austen begins to write the stories, poems, and plays that later become known as her *Juvenilia*

1795: Austen writes *Elinor and Marianne*, a draft of the story that later becomes her novel *Sense and Sensibility*.

Austen meets Thomas Langlois Lefroy during Lefroy's time in Steventon.

1796: Thomas Lefroy returns to London.

Austen begins to write *First Impressions*, a novel that later becomes known as *Pride and Prejudice*.

1797: Austen completes *First Impressions* and begins to revise *Elinor and Marianne*.

1798–1799: Austen writes *Susan*, a story that later becomes known as her novel *Northanger Abbey*

1803: London publisher Benjamin Crosby purchases the publishing rights to Austen's manuscript for *Susan*.

Austen begins work on the novel *The Watsons*.

1805: Austen's father, George Austen, passes away. His death leaves Jane and her sisters with a more limited income and a reduced class status.

Austen abandons work on *The Watsons*.

1811: Austen begins work on the novel *Mansfield Park*. Austen resumes work on *First Impressions*.

Publisher Thomas Egerton releases *Sense and Sensibility*. The original edition does not identify Austen as its author, with Austen remaining anonymous in this and other novels published during her lifetime.

1813: Thomas Egerton releases *Pride and Prejudice*.

1814: Austen begins work on the novel *Emma*. Thomas Egerton releases *Mansfield Park*.

1815: Austen begins work on the novel *Persuasion*. Publisher John Murray releases *Emma*.

1816: Austen continues work on *Persuasion*.

Austen begins to experience signs of illness that will persist until the time of her death.

Austen's brother, Henry Austen, purchases back the publishing rights to *Susan*, following Benjamin Crosby's refusal to publish it.

July 18, 1817: Austen passes away from chronic illness in the Hampshire town of Winchester.

1817: John Murray releases *Northanger Abbey* (previously *Susan*) and *Persuasion* together in a single edition. This book includes a "Biographical Notice of the Author" by her brother Henry Austen, crediting Austen as the author of these and her previous works.

A portrait of Jane Austen by her sister, Cassandra Austen, drawn c. 1810.

About the Author

Manuela Santoni is an illustrator and a cartoonist from Rome, Italy. Born in 1988, she studied art at Rome's Liceo Artistico (High School of the Arts). In 2012 she received a degree in contemporary art history from Sapienza Università di Roma (Sapienza University of Rome). She also attended Scuola Romana dei Fumetti (the Roman School of Comics), and in 2013 she received a master's degree in illustration at Ars in Fabula in Macerata, Italy. Passionate about graphic novels and comics, Santoni works as a freelancer, creates books for children, and publishes her online comic *Nowhere Fast* at Verticomics. She has also illustrated the young adult stories *Girl R-Evolution* by Alberto Pellai (De Agostini, 2016) and *Storie proprio buffe* by Paul Jennings (Il Castoro, 2016). She lives in Fonte Nuova, a community in the countryside of Rome.

Acknowledgments

Thanks to those who helped me to realize this graphic novel. To Mara Barbuni, who assisted me on the historical facts of Jane's life. To Veronica He, who was my official photographer. To Eleonora Delprato and Claudio Lodi. To the friends who supported me. And above all, to BeccoGiallo.

—M.S.

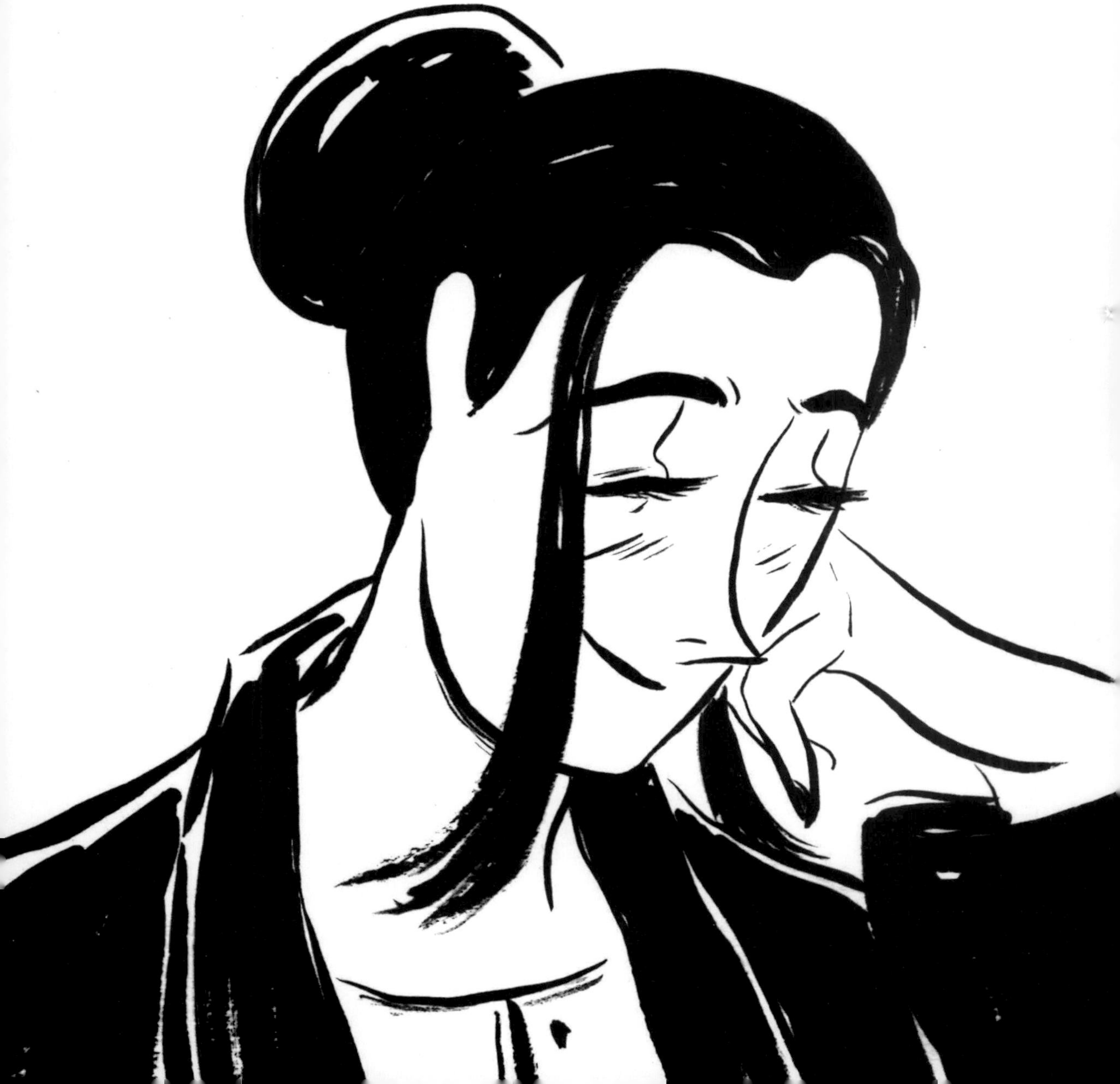